P9-CJZ-755

GU

DATE DUE 1/79

~~OL 50 W~~			
~~NY 9 '03~~			
~~JY 14 05~~			
~~AP 21 09~~			
MY 12 09			

DEMCO 38-296

PENGUIN BOOKS

LIFE IS ELSEWHERE

Milan Kundera was born in Brno, Czechoslovakia, in 1929. Since 1975 he has been living in France. Kundera is the author of the novels *The Joke, Life Is Elsewhere, The Farewell Party, The Book of Laughter and Forgetting,* and *The Unbearable Lightness of Being,* and a collection of short stories, *Laughable Loves.*

Peter Kussi is a translator and writer who has helped to introduce the work of contemporary Czech authors to American readers. In addition to two novels by Milan Kundera, he has translated the fiction of Jiří Gruša, Joseph Škvorecký, and Ivan Klíma, as well as works of classical Czech literature. He teaches at Columbia University in New York.

MILAN KUNDERA

Life Is Elsewhere

Translated from the Czech by Peter Kussi

Penguin Books

York 10010, U.S.A.
England
ia

Penguin Books Canada Ltd, 2801 John Street,
Markham, Ontario, Canada L3R 1B4
Penguin Books (N.Z.) Ltd, 182–190 Wairau Road,
Auckland 10, New Zealand

Penguin Books Ltd, Registered Offices:
Harmondsworth, Middlesex, England

English translation by Peter Kussi of *Život je jinde* by Milan Kundera originally
published in the United States of America by Alfred A. Knopf, Inc.
English translation copyright © Alfred A. Knopf, Inc., 1974

There was no Czech edition of this book but there was a French translation.
© Editions Gallimard, 1973. © Milan Kundera, 1973.

This edition with a new preface by the author first published in
Penguin Books 1986
Published simultaneously in Canada

10 9 8 7

Preface, original Czech version, copyright © Milan Kundera, 1986
Preface, English translation by Peter Kussi,
copyright © Viking Penguin, Inc., 1986
All rights reserved

LIBRARY OF CONGRESS CATALOGING IN PUBLICATION DATA
Kundera, Milan.
   Life is elsewhere.
   Translation of: Život je jinde.
   Definitive ed. with a new preface by the author.
   I. Title.   II. Series.
PG5039.21.U6Z3513   1985   891.8′635   85-12387
ISBN 0 14 00.6470 2

Printed in the United States of America by
R. R. Donnelley & Sons Company, Harrisonburg, Virginia
Set in Electra

PREFACE

"Life Is Elsewhere" is a celebrated sentence of Rimbaud. It is cited by André Breton at the conclusion of his Surrealist Manifesto. In May 1968, Paris students scribbled it on the walls of the Sorbonne as their slogan. But the original title of my novel was "The Lyric Age." I changed it at the last moment when I saw anxiety on the faces of my publishers, who doubted anyone would buy a book with such an abstruse title.

The lyric age is youth. My novel is an epos of youth, and an analysis of what I call "the lyric attitude." The lyric attitude is a potential stance of every human being; it is one of the basic categories of human existence. Lyric poetry as a literary genre has existed for ages, because for ages man has been capable of the lyric attitude. The poet is its personification.

Starting with Dante, the poet is also a great figure striding through European history. He is a symbol of national identity (Camões, Goethe, Mickiewicz, Pushkin), he is a spokesman of revolutions (Béranger, Petőfi, Mayakovsky, Lorca), he is the voice of history (Hugo, Breton), he is a mythological being and the subject of a virtually religious cult (Petrarch, Byron, Rimbaud, Rilke), but he is above all the representative of an inviolable value which we are ready to write with a capital letter: Poetry.

But what has happened to the European poet in the past half century? Today his voice is barely audible. Without our being quite aware of it, the poet has passed from the great, noisy world scene. (His disappearance is apparently one of the symptoms of that dangerous time of transition in which Europe finds itself and which we have not yet learned to name.) Through a kind of satanic irony of history, the last brief European period when the poet still played his great public role was the period of post-1945 communist revolutions in Central Europe.

It is important to stress that these peculiar pseudo-revolutions, imported from Russia and carried out under the protection of the army and the police, were full of authentic revolutionary psychology and their adherents experienced them with grand pathos, enthusiasm, and eschatologic faith in an absolutely new world. Poets found themselves on the proscenium for the last time. They thought they were playing their customary part in the glorious European drama and had no inkling that the theatre manager had changed the program at the last moment and substituted a trivial farce.

I witnessed this era "ruled hand in hand by the hangman and the poet" (p. 270) from up close. I heard my admired French poet Paul Éluard publicly and ceremonially renounce his Prague friend whom Stalinist justice was sending to the gallows. This episode (I wrote about it in *The Book of Laughter and Forgetting*) hit me like a trauma: when an executioner kills, that is after all normal; but when a poet (and a great poet) sings in accompaniment, the whole system of values we considered sacrosanct has suddenly been shaken apart. Nothing is certain any longer. Everything turns problematic, questionable, subject of analysis and doubt: Progress and Revolution. Youth. Motherhood. Even Man. And also Poetry. I saw before me a world of shaken values and gradually, over many years, the figure of Jaromil, his mother and his loves took shape in my mind.

Don't say that Jaromil is a bad poet! That would be too cheap an explanation of his life's story! Jaromil is a talented poet, with great imagination and feeling. And he is a sensitive young man. Of course, he is also a monster. But his monstrosity is potentially contained in us all. It is in me. It is in you. It is in Rimbaud. It is in Shelley, in Hugo. In all young men, of all periods and regimes. Jaromil is not a product of communism. Communism only illuminated an otherwise hidden side, it released something which under different circumstances would merely have slumbered in peace.

Even though the story of Jaromil and his mother takes place in a specific historic period which is portrayed truthfully (without the slightest satiric intent), it was not my aim to describe a period. "We did not choose that epoch because we were interested in it for its own sake, but because it seemed to offer an excellent trap for snaring Rimbaud and Lermontov, lyricism and youth." (p. 271) In other words: for a novelist, a given historic situation is an *anthropologic laboratory* in which he explores his basic question: *What is human existence?* In the case of this novel, several related questions also presented themselves: What is the lyric attitude? What is youth? What mysterious role does a mother play in forming the lyric world of a young man? And if youth is the time of inexperience, what is the connection between inexperience and a longing for the absolute? Or between a longing for the absolute and revolutionary fervor? And how does the lyric attitude reveal itself in love? Are there "lyric forms" of love? And so on, and so on.

The novel, of course, does not answer any of these questions. The questions are already an answer in themselves, for as Heidegger put it: the essence of man has the form of a question.

The first idea for this novel arose long ago, in the middle of the nineteen-fifties. I wanted to solve an esthetic problem: how to write a novel which would be a "critique of poetry" and yet at the same time would itself be poetry (transmit poetic intensity and imagination). I finished the novel in 1969. It never came out in Bohemia. It was first published in France, in 1973, and a year later in America in Peter Kussi's excellent translation which won him a National Book Award nomination. Kussi is by far the best American translator from the Czech. The fact that he returned to this novel after many years in order to revise it and make it even more faithful to the original shows that he is possessed by a longing for perfection; in other words, that he is a true artist among translators. I thank him from my heart for his beautiful piece of work and clasp his hand as a friend.

Milan Kundera

NOTE ON THE TEXT

This edition, prepared in close collaboration between author and translator, contains the definitive English text of *Life Is Elsewhere*.

CONTENTS

Part 1:
The Poet
Is Born

1

Exactly when and where was the poet conceived?

When his mother pondered this question, only three possibilities seemed worthy of serious consideration: either a certain evening on a park bench, or a certain afternoon in the apartment of a colleague of the poet's father, or a certain morning in the romantic countryside near Prague.

When the poet's father asked himself the same question, he came to the conclusion that the poet had been conceived in the apartment of his friend, on a certain day that had been especially unlucky. The poet's mother had been reluctant to go there, they had had two quarrels about it and two reconciliations, and when they finally got around to making love somebody noisily turned the key in the adjoining flat, the poet's mother took fright, they broke off their embrace, and finished the love act in nervous haste. It was this interval of flustered haste on which he blamed the poet's conception.

The poet's mother, however, refused to admit the possibility that the poet had been conceived in the borrowed flat (it was a typically untidy bachelor's place, she was repelled by the disheveled bed and rumpled pajamas), and Maman also rejected the second alternative: that conception had taken place on a park bench, where she had engaged in love-making quite reluctantly, disgusted by the thought that such benches were a common place for harlots and streetwalkers. She was therefore quite certain that the poet could have been conceived only on a particular sunny summer morning behind a huge boulder picturesquely silhouetted against a green valley traditionally favored by the citizens of Prague for Sunday outings.

For a number of reasons, this scenery was an appropriate setting for the poet's conception: Under the wide gaze of the noonday sun it was a scene of light rather than darkness, day rather than night; it was surrounded by open nature, suggesting wings and free flight; finally, although not far from the apartment houses on the outskirts of the city, it was a romantic landscape full of crevices and rocks and convoluted ground. It seemed like an eloquent symbol of her experience at the time. After all, had her great love for the poet's father not been a romantic revolt against the prosaic orderliness of her parents? And was there not an inner parallel between the wild, untrammeled landscape and the sweeping courage that made her—the daughter of a rich merchant—choose a penniless young engineer?

The poet's mother had been living a great love, and nothing could alter that, not even the disappointment that came only a few weeks after the beautiful afternoon among the boulders. She announced to her lover that the intimate indisposition which monthly perturbs her life had not made its expected appearance. She broke the news to him full of joyous excitement—only to be rebuffed with infuriating indifference (as it now seems to us in retrospect, this indifference had been superficial and largely feigned). He dismissed the matter as an unimportant disturbance of the physiologic cycle, of a purely temporary and insignificant nature. Maman sensed that her lover did not wish to share her joyous hopes, was offended, and stopped talking to him until the doctor officially told her that she was pregnant. The poet's father said that one of his chums was a gynecologist who would discreetly rid her of her problems, and Maman broke into tears.

The pathetic end of revolts! First she rebelled against her parents for the sake of the young engineer, and then she sought her parents' assistance against him. Her parents did not fail; they had a heart-to-heart talk with the engineer, who realized there was no way out and agreed to a showy wedding. He readily accepted the large dowry which later enabled him to establish his own construction firm; he packed all his belongings into a pair of suitcases and moved into the villa where his new wife had been born and raised.

The engineer's ready capitulation, however, did not hide from the poet's mother the sad realization that the adventure into which she had plunged so impulsively—and which had seemed so intoxicatingly beautiful—had not turned out to be the great, mutually fulfilling love she was convinced she had a full right to expect. Her father was the owner of two prosperous Prague pharmacies, and her morality was based on strict give-and-take; for her part, she had invested everything in love (she had even been willing to sacrifice her parents and their peaceful existence); in turn, she had expected her partner to invest an equal capital of feelings in the common account. To redress the imbalance, she gradually withdrew her emotional deposit and after the wedding presented a proud, severe face to her husband.

The sister of the poet's mother had moved out of the house shortly before (she had married and moved into an apartment in the center of the city), so the old couple continued to live downstairs and their daughter settled on the top floor with the engineer. This floor consisted of three rooms, two quite large, furnished precisely the way they had been twenty years before when the old pharmacist had built the villa. The engineer thus inherited a completely furnished apartment. On the whole, this was a satisfactory arrangement for him, because he had no property except what fitted into the two aforementioned suitcases. Nevertheless, he did suggest certain minor changes in the apartment; but his wife had no intention of permitting a man who had been ready to sacrifice her to the abortionist's knife to manhandle a world which expressed the spirit of her parents as well as two decades of sweet habit and safety.

On this occasion, too, the young engineer capitulated without a struggle, allowing himself only a small protest which we duly note: In the bedroom was a small table topped by a heavy disk of gray marble on which stood a figurine of a nude male; in his left hand the figure was holding a lyre, propped against his hip. The right arm was flung out in a pathetic gesture as if the fingers had just struck the strings. The right leg was extended, the head slightly tilted back so that the gaze was directed upward. Let us add that the face was extremely beautiful, the hair wavy, and the whiteness of the alabaster from which it was made gave the statuette a gentle, girlish, or perhaps virginally divine air; as a matter of fact, we have not used the word "divine" in vain: According to the inscription chiseled into the base, the figure with the lyre represented the Greek god Apollo.

It was difficult for the poet's mother to look at the figurine without getting angry. Most of the time either the god was turned so that his rear end faced the room, or else he was converted into a rack for the engineer's hat or his musing head became a stand for the engineer's shoe. Occasionally, a smelly sock was stretched over the statuette—an especially heinous desecration of the Muses and their lord.

The poet's mother reacted with great irritation. This was not due simply to a lack of a sense of humor. Rather, she quite correctly perceived that by draping Apollo in a sock her husband was flashing a message which he was too polite to express directly: In the guise of a joke, he was letting her know that he was rejecting her world and that his submission was only temporary.

The alabaster statuette had thus become a true antique divinity: an otherworldly being who now and then intervenes in human affairs, tangles the course of human lives, launches intrigues, and reveals mysteries. Our young heroine regarded him as her ally and her wistful feminine imagination turned him into a living being whose pupils seemed to glitter with animation and whose lips trembled with the very breath of life. She fell in love with that naked youth who was being humiliated for her sake. As she gazed into his comely face she conceived the wish that the child growing in her abdomen would resemble this graceful rival of her husband's. She hoped for a resemblance so strong that she could look at her child and imagine this Greek youth to be his real father. She begged the god to use his powers and change the past, to change the story of her son's conception, to repaint it as the great Titian once painted a masterpiece over a bungler's ruined canvas.

In the Virgin Mary she unwittingly found her model of motherhood free of the need for human fructification, and she thus created an ideal of mother love in which the father does not interfere. She felt an intoxicating longing for the child to be called Apollo, a name that to her meant the same as *"he who has no human father."* She knew, of course, that her son would have a difficult time bearing such an exalted name, and that people would ridicule both him and her. She therefore searched for a Czech name that would be worthy of a youthful Olympian, and she decided on Jaromil—*"he who loves the spring"* as well as *"he who is beloved by the spring."* This choice met with general approval.

And in fact spring was in full glory, with lilacs in bloom, when they drove her to the hospital; after a few hours of pain the young poet slipped out unto the soiled sheet of this world.

2

They put the poet into a tiny crib next to her bed and she listened to the sweet howling; her aching body was full of pride. Let us not begrudge Maman's body its satisfaction. Until then it had not known much pleasure, even though it was fairly attractive: true, it had a rather shapeless rear and the legs were somewhat short, but the breasts were unusually full and firm, and under the fine-textured head of hair (so fine that it was difficult to set) there was a face that was not dazzling but inconspicuously attractive.

Maman had always been more aware of looking inconspicuous than of looking attractive. This was largely the result of having been brought up in the proximity of an older sister who was a superb dancer, worked in the salon of Prague's foremost couturiere, and—jauntily sporting a tennis racket—moved easily in the world of elegant men. Her sister's success in the social swing helped to strengthen Maman's defiant modesty; out of sheer protest she had learned to love the sentimental gravity of music and books.

It is true that before her acquaintance with the engineer she used to go out with a certain young medical student, the son of friends of her parents, but this relationship had not been capable of awakening her body to self-confidence. It was with him, one night in a summer cottage, that she had had her first experience of physical love. She broke up with him the next morning, with the melancholy conviction that neither her emotions nor her senses were destined ever to partake of a great love. As she was just about to complete her final examinations, the experience was perfectly timed for her to announce that she came to see life's goal in intellectual labor and that she had decided to enroll in the faculty of philosophy (her practical-minded father notwithstanding).

Her disappointed body, after sitting for some five months on the hard benches of the university auditorium, was met on the street one day by a fresh young engineer who insolently addressed it and several meetings later possessed it. Because on that occasion the body was deeply (and surprisingly) gratified, the soul quickly forgot its ambition of a scholarly career and hastened to the body's assistance (as a true soul always should). It readily agreed with the engineer's opinions, praised his gay carelessness, and admired his charming irresponsibility. Although Maman realized that these traits were foreign to the atmosphere in which she had been brought up, she was prepared to identify herself with the engineer's qualities, for in their presence her somberly chaste body acquired confidence and to its own astonishment began to enjoy itself.

Then was Maman happy at last? Not quite; she writhed between faith and doubt. When she undressed before the mirror, she tried to examine herself through his eyes: sometimes she seemed enchanting, at other times uninteresting. She surrendered her body to the judgment of someone else's eyes—and that was a source of anxious uncertainty.

But no matter how she wavered between hope and disbelief, she was completely cured of her premature resignation. She was no longer depressed by her sister's tennis racket, her body was alive at last and Maman learned to savor the pleasures of physical existence; she longed for the assurance that this new life would prove to be a permanent reality rather than a mere deceptive promise; she yearned for the engineer to take her away from the university lecture-hall and from her parental home, and to convert a love story into a real life story. That is why she enthusiastically welcomed her pregnancy. She contemplated herself, the engineer, and her child, and the trio of figures seemed to reach the stars and to fill the universe.

We have already touched on this in the previous chapter: Maman soon learned that the man who had been so avid for a love adventure was afraid of a life adventure, and had no wish to join her in a journey to the stars. But we already know that on this occasion, too, her self-regard withstood her lover's chilly response. A very important change had taken place: Maman's body, long at the mercy of a lover's gaze, entered upon a new phase of its history; it ceased to be a mere object of someone else's eyes, and became a living body devoted to someone who as yet had no eyes. Its outer surface lost its importance; it was touching another body along an interior, invisible surface. The eyes of the outer world could thus grasp only its unimportant external envelope. The engineer's judgment no longer had any significance, for it could in no way influence the body's great destiny. At last it had become fully independent and self-sufficient; the belly, which kept growing bigger and uglier, became a swelling reservoir of pride.

After delivery, Maman's body entered upon still another phase. When she first felt her son's groping mouth attach itself to her breast, a wave of sweet vibration thrilled deep inside and radiated to all parts of her body; it was similar to love, but it went beyond a lover's caress, it brought a great calm happiness, a great happy calm. She had never experienced that feeling before; when her lover had kissed her breast, it had been a brief moment that was supposed to have made up for hours of doubt and mistrust; but now she knew that a mouth was attached to her breast with unending devotion, a devotion of which she could be perfectly certain.

Something else was different now, too. In the past, whenever her lover touched her naked body, she had felt ashamed. Mutual drawing together was always an overcoming of strangeness, and the moment of closeness was intoxicating precisely because it was only a moment. Shame never slept, it made love-making more exciting but it also watched over the body to prevent its plunging into full surrender. But now shame had disappeared; it was gone. The two bodies opened to each other with full abandon, and there was nothing to hide.

She had never given herself to another body in this way, and no body had ever so given itself to her. Her lover had used her belly but he had never lived there, he had touched her breast but he had never drunk from it. Ah, the joy of suckling! She lovingly watched the fishlike motions of the toothless mouth and she imagined that with her milk there flowed into her little son her deepest thoughts, concepts, and dreams.

It was a *paradisiac* state: the body was allowed to be a body, and had no need to cover itself with a figleaf; mother and son were submerged in infinite tranquillity; they lived together like Adam and Eve before they had tasted of the fruit of knowledge; they lived in their bodies beyond good and evil. And more, in paradise there is no distinction between beauty and ugliness, so that the body's components were neither ugly nor beautiful but pleasurable. The toothless gums were delightful, the breast was delightful, and so were the belly button and the tiny rear end. Delightful was the intestine, the workings of which were carefully followed, delightful were the tiny hairs budding on the comical skull. She zealously watched over her son's burping, peeing, and kakamaking, and this was not just a matter of conscientious concern for the infant's health—no, she occupied herself in all the processes of his body with *passion*.

This was an entirely new attitude, because ever since her childhood Maman had felt an intense aversion toward all physicality, including her own; she abhorred herself whenever she sat down on the toilet (she tried to make sure that nobody saw her going to the bathroom) and at one time she had been ashamed to eat in public because the processes of chewing and swallowing had seemed disgusting to her. Now, the elevation of her son's physicality beyond any taint of ugliness had a peculiarly cleansing effect on her, and served to legitimize her own body as well. The dribble of milk which occasionally appeared on the wrinkled skin of the nipple seemed as poetic as a droplet of dew. She would often reach for her breast and squeeze it slightly in order to produce the magic droplet. She wet the tip of her little finger with the white liquid and tasted it: she told herself that she was doing so in order to learn more about the fluid that nourished her son, but actually she was curious about the taste of her own body, and the sweet taste of the milk reconciled her to all the body's other juices and excretions. She began to think of herself as tasty; her body had become

as agreeable and legitimate as any other object of nature—
a tree, a bush, a lake.

Unfortunately, with all the happiness that her body
was giving her, Maman was not paying sufficient attention
to its needs. By the time she realized her neglect it was
already too late: the skin on her belly had become coarse
and wrinkled, with the underlying ligaments showing through
in whitish streaks; the skin did not look like a real part of
the body, but rather resembled a loose sheet. Surprisingly,
Maman was not unduly upset by this discovery. Wrinkled
or not, her body was a happy one, because it existed for
eyes which had perceived the world only in vague outline
and which had not yet become aware (these were *paradisiac*
eyes) that in the fallen, cruel world bodies were divided into
the beautiful and the ugly.

But though unseen by the eyes of the infant, the changes
were of course noticed by the eyes of the husband, who
after the birth of Jaromil attempted a reconciliation with
Maman. After a prolonged interval they were again making
love. But it was no longer the same; they set aside certain
definite periods for physical intimacy, they made love in the
dark, hesitantly. Maman did not mind: she was aware of
her disfigured body and she feared that passionate, open
love-making might make her lose the inner peace bestowed
on her by her son.

No, no, she would never forget that the excitement
her husband made her feel was full of risk and uncertainty;
whereas her son gave her a tranquillity full of happiness;
that is why she continued to cleave to him for consolation
(he was already toddling, walking, talking). At one point
the child became gravely ill, and for fourteen days Maman
hardly closed her eyes; she ministered to his little body
which was hot and writhing in pain. This period, too, was
one of ecstasy; when the illness faded, it seemed to her
that she had walked through the realm of the dead carrying her son's body in her arms, and that after this expe-

rience nothing could ever separate the two of them again.

Her husband's body, robed in a suit or in pajamas, discretely self-enclosed, was moving away from her, day by day losing more of its intimacy, while her son's body continued to depend on her; she was no longer suckling but she was teaching her son to use the toilet, she dressed and undressed him, fixed his hair and chose his clothes, and was in daily touch with his insides through the food which she lovingly prepared for him. At four years of age, when he began to show signs of a lack of appetite, she became strict with him, forced him to eat, and for the first time felt that she was not only his body's friend but its *ruler* as well. The body resisted, did not wish to swallow, but it had to yield; with a peculiar pleasure she watched this vain rebellion, this submission, this fragile neck through which she could trace the passage of the unwanted morsel.

Ah—her son's body, her paradise and home, her kingdom...

3

And what about her son's soul? Was that not part of her kingdom too? Oh yes, yes! When Jaromil uttered his first word and that word was "mama," she was deliriously happy. She told herself that her son's mind—now still consisting of only a single concept—was completely filled by her, and that even later on when his mind would begin to grow, branch out, and flower, she would continue to remain its root. Pleasantly stimulated, she carefully followed her son's future attempts at words, and because she sensed that life is long and memory short, she bought a notebook bound in dark red and proceeded to write down everything that issued from her son's mouth.

If we were to consult Maman's notebook we would see

that after "mama" there soon followed a number of further words, "dada" taking seventh place after "baba," "yaya," "toot," "huf," "hum," and "lulu." After those simple expressions (Maman's notebook always included a brief commentary and date), we find the first attempts at sentences. We learn that before his second birthday he declared, *Mama nice*. Several months later he said, *Mama is kaka*. For this statement, made when Maman refused to give him raspberry juice before lunch, he received a whack on the behind. In tears, he shouted, *I find another mama!* But not long afterward he made his mother very happy by saying, *my mama is beautiful*. On another occasion he said, *Mama, I lick you a kiss*, which meant that he stuck out his tongue and licked Maman's entire face.

If we skip a few pages we come to a statement which is striking in its rhythmic effect. The maid Anna once promised Jaromil that she would give him a banana but then she forgot and ate the fruit herself. Jaromil felt cheated, got extremely angry, and vehemently repeated, *ugly Anna stole banana*. In a certain sense this utterance is similar to the previously cited thought that *Mama is kaka*. However, this time Jaromil was not whacked on the behind, but everybody including Anna laughed and the statement was subsequently often quoted to everyone's merriment (which of course was not lost on Jaromil). At that time, Jaromil could hardly have grasped the underlying reason for his success, but we know perfectly well that what saved him from a spanking was rhyme. This was Jaromil's first encounter with the magic power of poetry.

The next pages of Maman's notebook are filled with a number of rhymed statements, and from her comments it is obvious that they caused joy and amusement for the entire household. For example, this was the concise portrait that Jaromil created of the maid's appearance: *our maid's coat is like a goat*. A little further we read: *we play in the wood and our heart feels so good*. Maman was under the impression that, in addition to Jaromil's powerful and original talent, his poetic activity stemmed from the influence of rhymed children's books. She was in the habit of reading these to him with such zeal and persistence that the child might well have assumed his entire native language consisted of nothing but trochees. But here we must enter a correction: the real source of Jaromil's poetic output was neither talent nor emulation of literary models, but Grandpa. A sober, practical man and a sworn foe of poetry, Grandpa thought up the stupidest possible couplets and secretly taught them to his grandson.

Jaromil soon became aware of the interest which his words produced, and began to act accordingly. At first, he had used speech merely to make himself understood, but now he spoke in order to elicit approval, admiration, or laughter. He looked forward to the effect which his words would produce, and because it happened quite frequently that the expected response failed to materialize, he tried to call attention to himself with all sorts of nonsense and improprieties. Once he paid for this; he told Mother and Dad, *all of you are pricks* (he had heard the word used by a boy in a neighboring yard and he remembered that all the other boys broke into loud laughter), but Dad was not amused and gave him a box on the ear.

From that time he paid careful notice to the way adults used words—what they prized about them, what they found agreeable or disagreeable, what shocked them. Such observation made it possible for him one day, while standing in the garden with Maman, to utter a melancholy sentence that echoed Grandma's frequent lamentations: *Mom, life is really just like those weeds*.

It is hard to say precisely what he had in mind. It is clear that he was not thinking of that energetic uselessness and useless energy which constitute the property of weeds. Probably he only wanted to express the rather vague notion of the sadness and vanity of life. But even though he said something different from what he intended, the effect of his words was imposing: Maman became still, then she stroked his hair and looked into his face with moist eyes. Jaromil was so intoxicated by that gaze full of rapturous praise that he yearned to be rewarded by it again. While taking a walk with Maman, he kicked a stone and said, *Mom, I just kicked a stone and now I'm feeling sorry for it*—and he bent down and gently caressed the stone.

Maman was convinced that her son was not only talented (he had learned to read when he was only five), but that he was extraordinarily sensitive and quite different from other children. She often confided this opinion to Grandpa and Grandma, while Jaromil—pretending to be playing with his soldiers or hobbyhorse—was all ears. He stared into the eyes of guests imagining that the adult visitors saw him as a singular, gifted child, or perhaps as a special being who was not a child at all.

As his sixth birthday approached and he was about to enter school, the family insisted that he be given his own room and sleep by himself. Maman sighed over the cruel passage of time, but she agreed. She and her husband decided to give their son a small room on the top floor as a birthday present, and to equip it with a couch and other appropriate furniture: a book-case, a mirror to encourage cleanliness and neatness, and a small writing-desk.

Dad offered to decorate the room with Jaromil's own drawings, and set about pasting the walls with childish scrawls of apples and houses. Maman walked up to him and said, "There is something I want you to give me." He looked at her, and her voice—shy and determined at the same time—continued: "I want you to give me a few sheets of paper and some paints." She sat down at the dressing-table in her room, spread out the sheets, and for quite a while practiced drawing large capital letters; at last she dipped the brush in red paint and began drawing the first letter, a large L. The letter I followed, and soon the whole line was done: *Life is like weeds.* She examined her work with satisfaction; the letters were all about the same height and evenly spaced. All the same, she took up a new sheet and lettered the line again, this time in a dark blue color which seemed to express more appropriately the profound melancholy of her son's thought.

Then she recalled that Jaromil had also said *ugly Anna stole banana* and with a happy smile on her lips she began to write (this time in bright red), *our dear Anna loves a banana.* With an inner smile she remembered, *all of you are pricks,* but she did not copy this expression. Instead, she lettered (in green), *we play in the wood and our heart feels good.* She also added (in purple), *our Annie's coat is as soft as a goat* (Jaromil had actually said "our maid's coat," but Maman thought that the word "maid" was too coarse). Then she remembered the time Jaromil petted a stone, and after a moment's deliberation she traced out (in light blue), *I would not even hurt a stone.* With slight embarrassment, she added (in orange), *Mama, I lick you a kiss,* and finally, in gold, *my mama is beautiful.*

On the eve of his birthday the parents sent the excited Jaromil downstairs to sleep with his grandma, and set out to move furniture and to decorate the walls of his room. In the morning, when they called the child into the transmuted room, Maman was overwrought and Jaromil's reaction perplexed her. He was clearly taken aback, and stood in the middle of the room silent and abashed. He showed signs of interest only in the desk, and even this interest was uncertain and shy. It was an odd piece of furniture resembling a school-desk: the hinged, diagonally-set top served as a writing surface and doubled as a cover for a small storage compartment, forming a single unit with the seat.

Maman could not contain herself any longer: "Well, what do you say? You like your room?"

"Yes, I do," answered the child.

"And what do you like best of all? Come on, tell us!"

prompted Grandad, watching with Grandma from behind a half-ajar door.

"This," said the boy. He sat down at the desk and started moving the hinged top up and down.

"And how do you like the pictures?" Dad pointed at the framed drawings.

The child lifted his head and smiled. "I know them."

"But how do you like them hanging on the wall?"

The boy continued sitting at the desk and nodded, to indicate he liked the drawings on the wall.

Maman's heart was aching and she felt like vanishing from sight. But she had to go through with it. She could not ignore the brightly-colored inscriptions because her silence might imply censure. She therefore said, "And look at these!"

The child, with lowered head, stared into the desk drawer.

"You know, I wanted . . . ," continued Maman in great confusion, "I just wanted you to have something to remember, something to remind you how you grew up, from your cradle all the way to your school-desk, because you were such a clever little boy and you made us all so happy . . ." She was talking apologetically, and in her embarrassment she repeated the same thing several times until she no longer knew what to say and turned silent.

But she was wrong if she thought that Jaromil had not appreciated the gift. He, too, did not know what to say, but he was not dissatisfied. He had always been proud of his words and he did not wish them to vanish in the air. Seeing them carefully traced on paper and turned into pictures, he had a sense of success—indeed, a success so great and unexpected that he did not know how to respond and it made him uneasy. He understood that he was *a child uttering significant words*, and he felt that such a child was expected to say something significant at the present moment, but nothing occurred to him and that's why he mutely hung his head. But when out of the corner of his eye he glimpsed his own words spread across the room, solid, more permanent, bigger than himself, he was enraptured; it seemed to him that he was surrounded by his own self, that there was so much of him—he filled a room, he filled a whole house.

4

Jaromil knew how to read and write even before he started school. Maman therefore decided that he could go straight into the second grade; she managed to obtain special permission from the Ministry of Education, and after having been examined by a commission Jaromil was allowed to take his seat among pupils a year older than he. Everyone in school admired him, so the classroom seemed to him to be merely a mirror reflection of home. On Mother's Day, during school festivities, when the pupils performed before an audience of parents, he appeared last on the podium and recited a moving poem about mothers, for which he was rewarded by prolonged applause.

One day he learned, however, that behind the public which applauds there lies in wait another and quite different public, treacherous and hostile. While visiting the dentist for an appointment, he happened to meet one of his schoolmates. They stood near the window of the crowded waiting room, chatting, when Jaromil noticed that a certain older man was listening to their conversation with a friendly smile. That stimulated Jaromil to raise his voice and to ask his fellow pupil what he would do if he were Minister of Education. The boy didn't know what to say, whereupon Jaromil began to expound ideas which he had frequently heard on this subject from his grandfather. Well then: if Jaromil were Minister of Education, school would last only two months and vacations would last ten, the teacher would have to obey the children and fetch them cakes from the bakery; all sorts of other remarkable changes would take place, which Jaromil proceeded to describe with great zest and at great volume.

The doors of the treatment room opened and out walked a patient accompanied by the nurse. A lady who was holding a book in her lap, her finger marking the spot where she had stopped reading, turned to the nurse with an angry quaver in her voice: "Please, miss, try to do something about this child over there. It's terrible the way he is carrying on and showing off."

Right after Christmas the teacher had each child come to the front of the class and give a little speech about the holidays. When Jaromil's turn came, he launched into a description of the marvelous Christmas presents he had received—building sets, skis, skates, books; but after a while he noticed that the children were not sharing his enthusiasm, that some of them were looking at him with indifference or even with hostility. He stopped short without enumerating the rest of his other presents.

No, no, have no fear—we are not about to repeat the hackneyed old story about the rich boy and his poor schoolmates. After all, Jaromil's class included several boys from families far more well-to-do than his, and yet these children got along well with the rest of the class and nobody envied them their comfortable background. What was it then about Jaromil that irritated his classmates?

We are almost embarrassed to say it: it was not wealth, it was mother love. That love left its traces everywhere; it clung to his shirt, to his hair, to the briefcase in which he carried his school books, to the very books he read for amusement. Everything was specially chosen and lovingly prepared for him. The shirts sewn for him by his thrifty grandmother somehow resembled girls' blouses more than boys' shirts. His long hair was held back by Maman's hairpins, to keep it from falling in his eyes. When it rained, Maman waited for him in front of the school with a big umbrella, while his schoolmates waded through puddles with their shoes slung over their shoulders.

Mother love stamps the forehead of boys with a stigma that repels the friendship of buddies. With time, Jaromil became skilled in concealing this sign, but his glorious debut at school was followed by a bitter year or two when his schoolmates were eager to ridicule and humiliate him, and on several occasions they even thrashed him. But even in his darkest days Jaromil had several trusty friends and throughout his life he remained grateful to them for their loyalty. Let us say a few words about them:

Friend number one was his dad. Sometimes he and Jaromil would go out into the yard with a soccer ball (Dad had been a fair soccer player in his youth) and Jaromil would stand between two trees. Dad kicked the ball at him, and Jaromil pretended that he was the goalkeeper for the Czechoslovak national team.

Grandpa was friend number two: he used to take Jaromil to visit his two shops; one was a big pharmacy, which was already being run by Grandpa's son-in-law; the other enterprise was a perfume shop, with an attractive lady in charge; she would smile politely at the little boy and let him sniff all the perfumes, so that Jaromil learned to distinguish the various brands by smell. He would close his eyes and urge Grandpa to test his ability to identify the scent from tiny bottles that Grandpa stuck under his nose. "You're an olfactory genius," Grandpa would praise him, and Jaromil dreamed about becoming an inventor of new perfumes.

Friend number three was Alik, a nervous little dog that had been living in the house for some time; even though it was untrained and disobedient, Jaromil daydreamed about the animal as a faithful companion who waited for him outside the classroom and who accompanied him from school with a devotion envied by all his schoolmates.

Canine reveries became the passion of Jaromil's solitude, and led him to a curious Manichaeanism: dogs became the symbol of animal *goodness*, the incarnation of all natural virtues. He imagined great wars of dogs against cats (wars featuring generals, officers, and all the paraphernalia and military cunning which he had practiced in his games with tin soldiers) and was always on the side of the dogs, as a man should always be on the side of justice.

He spent a lot of time in Dad's room with pencil and paper, and dogs became the main subject of his drawings: they were an endless variety of epic scenes in which dogs were presented as generals, soldiers, football heroes, and knights. As their four-legged posture interfered with proper performance of human roles, Jaromil began drawing the animals with human bodies. That was a great discovery! Whenever Jaromil had tried to draw human beings, he always ran up against a serious difficulty: he did not know how to portray a human face. On the other hand, Jaromil had a real knack for drawing the elongated head of a dog, ending in a black ink-spot of a snout. And so out of dreams and awkwardness there arose a peculiar world of dog-headed people, a world of figures which could be quickly rendered and readily linked to represent wars, football contests, and exotic adventures.

A schoolmate was relegated to serve as friend number four; his father was the school janitor, a jaundiced little man who often complained to the principal about certain pupils. These boys revenged themselves on his son, who therefore led something of a dog's life at school. After Jaromil was gradually abandoned by the students as a body, the janitor's son remained his sole faithful admirer, and so it happened that he was invited to spend a day at the villa. He was given lunch and supper, the two boys played with a construction set, and later Jaromil helped his friend with homework. The following Sunday Jaromil's dad took them to a football game. It was an exciting match, and Dad made a grand impression;

he knew the names of all the players, he spoke about the game like a real insider so that the janitor's son hung on his words and Jaromil was proud.

On the surface, the two friends made an odd pair: Jaromil always immaculately dressed, the janitor's boy in a frayed, tattered coat; Jaromil's homework always scrupulously prepared, his comrade a slow student. All the same, Jaromil felt at ease with his devoted friend, because the janitor's son was exceptionally strong physically. One winter afternoon the two were attacked by a large group of boys, and managed to hold them at bay; Jaromil was pleased that they had given such a good account of themselves; still the glory of successful defense is not the same as the glory of attack.

Once, as they were sauntering through vacant lots on the outskirts of the city, they encountered a boy who was so well-scrubbed and neatly dressed that he might have come from a children's ball. "Mama's little darling," said the janitor's son, barring the boy's way. They jeered at him, asked derisive questions, delighted at his frightened response. At last the boy gathered courage and tried to push them aside. "How dare you! You'll pay for that!" shouted Jaromil, as if the boy's gesture had been a mortal insult; the janitor's son took that as a signal and hit the boy in the face.

Intellect and physical force can strike an admirable partnership. Did not Byron feel warm affection for the boxer Jackson, who diligently trained the frail lord in all kinds of sports? "Don't hit him, just hold him!" Jaromil shouted to his friend. He pulled up a bunch of stinging nettles growing in the rubbish; they forced the boy to undress and lashed him all over his body. "Your mama will be pleased to see such a nice red little boy!" mocked Jaromil. He was swept by a wave of warm, comradely affection for his schoolmate, and by comradely hatred against all sissified mama's darlings.

5

But why did Jaromil continue to remain an only child? Was his mother not interested in having a larger family?

The very opposite was true: she longed to relive the blissful time of her first maternal experience, but her husband always found reasons for postponement. After a while she stopped pleading with him, because she was afraid of further rebuffs and the humiliation they entailed.

But the more she resisted the impulse to talk about her maternal yearning, the more it occupied her mind; she thought of her longing as something unacceptable, secret, illicit even; the idea that her husband could produce a child inside her began to take on provocatively indecent coloring; *come here and make me a little daughter,* she would mentally tease her husband, and it sounded quite lascivious.

Late one night the couple came home from a party in a gay mood. Jaromil's father lay down next to his wife, put out the light (it should be noted that since the wedding he had always taken possession of her blindly, letting touch rather than sight guide his desire), pulled back the cover and mated with her. Perhaps it was the rarity of their amorous contacts, or the influence of wine, but that night she gave herself to him with a rapture which she had not experienced for a long, long time.

The thought that *they were making a baby* filled her whole mind; as she felt that her husband was nearing his climax she could no longer control herself and she began to shout at him ecstatically to throw caution to the winds, to stay with her, to make her a child, to make her a little baby girl, and she was holding him in such a firm spasmodic grip that he had to exert his utmost strength to free himself and to make sure that her wish would not be fulfilled.

Afterward, as they lay exhausted next to one another, Maman nestled close to him and again whispered in his ear that she longed to have one more child with him; she did not mean to harass him, no, she was only trying to explain why a while ago she had acted so violently and impulsively (and perhaps improperly, too, she was ready to admit). She mumbled that this time they would surely have a girl, a little daughter who would become the apple of his eye just as Jaromil had become the apple of hers.

The engineer retorted by reminding her (for the first time since the wedding) that he himself had never wanted a child at all; he had been forced to compromise then, and it was her turn to compromise now; and if she really wanted him to see his own image in another child, he could assure her that he would see himself best in that child which would never be born at all.

They lay silently for a while, then Maman began to cry and she sobbed the whole night through; her husband did not touch her, he only murmured a few soothing words which hardly succeeded in penetrating even the outer shell of her sorrow. It seemed to her that she understood everything at last: the man by whose side she was living never loved her at all.

The grief into which she was plunged was the deepest she had ever known. Fortunately, while her husband did not offer any consolation, someone else did: History. About three weeks after the night just described, her husband received a military mobilization order. He packed his suitcase and left for the frontier. The atmosphere was charged with war, people bought gas masks and built underground shelters. Maman clutched her country's tragic fate to her bosom as if it were her salvation; she submerged herself in the national pathos, and spent many long hours in educating her son to what was happening to the country.

The big powers met in Munich and came to an agreement. German troops occupied the border fortifications, and Jaromil's father came home. After that they would all sit downstairs in Grandfather's room night after night to discuss the various steps taken by History. It seemed to them that History had been asleep until recently (or at least had pretended to be asleep), and now suddenly it stretched, stood up, and overshadowed everything by its huge figure. Oh, how welcome was this huge shadow to Maman! Throngs of Czechs fled the border regions, Bohemia was as bare and defenseless in the midst of Europe as a peeled orange; six months later German tanks suddenly appeared in the streets of Prague and Maman was wedded to a soldier who had been cheated of his chance to fight for his country; she completely forgot that this was also the man who had never loved her.

But even during epochs when the storms of history rage, sooner or later the banal, the every-day emerges out of the shadows and the conjugal bed looms huge in its monumental triviality and staggering persistence. One night, when Jaromil's father placed his hand on Maman's breast, she became aware that the man who was touching her was the same individual who had humiliated her. She pushed his hand away and gently reminded him of the cruel words which he had said to her.

She had no intention of being vindictive. She only wanted to suggest that the humble histories of hearts cannot be brushed aside forever by the great events of nations; she wanted to give her husband an opportunity to make amends for his unkind words and to heal the injury. She believed that the national tragedy had made him more sensitive and she was ready to accept any tender gesture as a token of a new start in the story of their love. Alas, the husband whose advancing hand had been rebuffed simply turned over and soon fell asleep.

After the great student demonstration in Prague the Germans closed Czech universities and Maman waited in vain for her husband to reach under the covers for her breast.

Grandfather found out that the attractive lady in the perfume shop had been robbing him blind for years, became extremely agitated and died of a stroke. Czech students were shipped in cattle cars to concentration camps and Maman visited a physician who deplored the bad state of her nerves and recommended a prolonged rest. He told her about a rooming house near a small spa close to several lakes and a river, where throngs of nature-lovers congregated every summer for fishing, swimming, and sailing. It was now early spring and Maman was charmed by the idea of quiet walks along the lake-shore. But then she was troubled by the thought of gay dance music, which always seems to hang in the air of outdoor summer restaurants as a nostalgic reminder of summers past, her own sadness made her anxious, and she decided she could not possibly go on a vacation alone.

But of course—she realized at once whom to take along! Lately, she had almost forgotten about him, what with all the marital troubles and the longing for a second child. How silly of her, how self-destructive to forget about her darling! She bent over him penitently: "Jaromil, you're my first child and my second one, too!" She hugged him close, babbling the crazy sentence: "You're my first and my second and my third and my fourth, fifth, sixth, tenth child . . . ," and she kissed him all over his face.

6

They were met at the station by a tall, gray-haired lady of haughty bearing; a strapping porter picked up the two suitcases and carried them out to the sidewalk, where a black buggy was already waiting; the porter climbed up on the driver's box, while Jaromil, his mother, and the tall lady sat down facing one another on the upholstered seats; the clip-clopping horse trotted them through the streets of the small town, past the square bordered on one side by a renaissance arcade and on the other by the green-fenced garden of an old, ivy-covered chateau. Then they made their way down to the river; Jaromil saw a row of yellow cabins, a diving board, white tables and chairs; in the background he glimpsed a line of poplars along the shore, and then the buggy was already speeding them toward the isolated villas dotting the river-front.

In front of one of them, the horse came to a halt, the driver dismounted and picked up the luggage. Jaromil and his mother followed him through a garden, a hallway, up a flight of stairs and into a room with twin beds, placed side by side in the arrangement customary for married couples. There were two large French windows, one of which swung open onto a balcony facing the garden and the river. Maman grasped the balcony railing and took a few deep breaths. "Ah, what heavenly quiet!" she said and again breathed deeply in and out, gazing toward the landing, where a red rowboat was gently bobbing.

At supper that evening Maman made friends with an elderly couple who occupied the pension's other guest room; thereafter, night after night, quiet conversation rustled through the small dining room; Jaromil was liked by everyone, and Maman enjoyed listening to his stories, ideas, and discreet boasting; yes, *discreet*: Jaromil would never forget his humiliating experience with the lady in the dentist's waiting room, and he would always look for a shield to protect himself from her mocking gaze; of course, he was still avid for admiration, but he had learned to gain it by means of succinct phrases expressed with naiveté and modesty.

Jaromil had entered an enchanted world: the villa set in the midst of a tranquil garden; the dark river with the moored boat launching dreams of long voyages; the black carriage pulling up in the driveway from time to time to whisk away the tall lady who looked like a fairy-tale countess; the deserted bathhouse to which one could go by buggy like shuttling from century to century, from dream to dream; the renaissance square with its narrow arcade in the shadows of which once duelled gallant knights.

This beautiful fairy-tale world also included the man with the dog. When they first saw him, he was standing motionless at the riverbank, gazing at the waves; he was wearing a leather coat, and at his side sat a black Alsatian dog; in their petrified posture both looked like figures from some other world. The next time they met him it was in the same place; the man (again in a leather coat) was throwing sticks and the dog was retrieving them. When they encountered him the third time (the scenery was the same: river and poplars), the man made a slight bow toward Maman, and after they had passed he turned his head several times, as the inquisitive Jaromil ascertained. The following day, as they were returning from a walk, they saw the black Alsatian sitting in front of the entrance to the villa. When they entered the hall they heard the sound of conversation and they entertained no doubt that the masculine voice belonged to the dog's owner; they were so overcome by curiosity that they lingered in the hall, idly milling about and chatting, until finally their hostess came out.

Maman pointed at the dog: "Who is the gentleman he belongs to? We always seem to run into him on our walks."

"He's the art teacher at our high school." Maman declared that she would be greatly interested in talking to an art teacher, for Jaromil loved to draw and she was eager to hear an expert's opinion. The lady introduced the man to Maman, and Jaromil was sent running upstairs to his room to fetch his sketchbook.

Then the four of them sat down in the small salon— the lady, Jaromil, the owner of the dog, who was examining the drawings, and Maman, who provided a running commentary; she explained that Jaromil always showed a preference for scenes of action rather than landscapes of still-lifes; and it really seemed to her, she said, that his drawings did have remarkable life and movement, even though she was puzzled as to why all the characters were dog-headed people; perhaps if Jaromil drew real human figures his work might have some value; this way she was not quite sure whether there was any sense to the boy's attempts at all.

The owner of the dog inspected the drawings with pleasure; then he observed that it was precisely the combination of animal head and human body which he found so bewitching. For that fantastic union of two worlds was obviously no accident; the profusion of drawings on this subject clearly showed that the concept was a compelling one for the boy, something rooted in the mysterious depths of childhood. It would be a mistake to judge the child's talents merely by his ability to reproduce the outer world; anybody can learn to do that. What fascinated him as an artist (thus indicating that teaching was merely a necessary evil to earn a living) was the highly original inner world which the lad was projecting upon paper.

Maman was pleased to hear Jaromil praised, the lady stroked the boy's hair and pronounced that he had a great future ahead of him, while Jaromil stared at the floor, engraving every word on his memory. The artist said that next year he would be transferred to a school in Prague, and that he hoped Maman would bring further examples of Jaromil's work to show him.

Inner world! Those were big words, and Jaromil heard them with enormous satisfaction. He had never forgotten that as a five-year-old he had already been proclaimed an unusual child, different from others; the behavior of his schoolmates, the ridicule they heaped on his briefcase or his shirt served as constant reminders of his uniqueness (albeit bitter ones). Until now, however, his differentness had been something empty, vague, an incomprehensible hope or an incomprehensible rejection; but now it had received a clear designation at last: original inner world. At the same time the designation was given definite, clear content: images of a dog-headed world. Of course, Jaromil knew perfectly well that he owed his lauded discovery of dog-people to sheer accident, that it derived purely and simply from his inability to draw a human face; this gave him the impression that the uniqueness of his inner world did not emanate from any active endeavor but consisted of everything that passed willy-nilly through his head. It was bestowed upon him as a gift.

From that time on he began to pay careful attention to all his thoughts and ideas, and to admire them. For example, it occurred to him that if he were to die the world in which he had been living would cease to exist. At first, this thought just flashed through his mind, but aware now of his inner originality, he did not let the thought escape as so many other ideas had done earlier. He grasped it, observed it, examined it from all sides. He was walking along the river; now and again he would close his eyes and ask himself whether the river existed even when his eyes were closed. Of course, every time he opened his eyes the river continued to flow before him, but the remarkable thing was that this in no way proved it was there when Jaromil was not looking at it. This seemed extremely interesting to him, he spent the better part of a day on this experiment and then told Maman all about it.

The nearer their vacation came to its end, the greater the joy they found in their conversations. After dark, they would go out, sit on the crumbling wooden bench, hold hands, and gaze at the waves on which a huge moon rocked to and fro. "Isn't that beautiful!" sighed Maman, and her son watched the circle of water lit up by moonbeams and dreamt of the river's long journey. Then Maman thought of the barren days which were destined to resume so soon and said, "Darling, there is a terrible sorrow inside me. But you can't possibly know what I mean." And then she saw her son's eyes and they seemed to be full of love and the longing to understand. This frightened her: confiding a woman's problems to a child! All the same, those under-standing eyes attracted her like a secret vice. They were stretched out next to each other on the twin beds and Maman recalled how they had lain this way until Jaromil was six years old, and how happy they had been in those days; then it occurred to her that her son was really the only male with whom she had been happy in bed. She had to laugh at the thought, but after taking a second look at his gentle eyes she told herself that this child was not only able to distract her from sorrowful matters (thus giving her the *consolation of forgetting*), but he was also capable of listening to her attentively (thus giving her the *consolation of understanding*). "Let me tell you a big secret: there is very little love in my life," she said to him. And on another occasion she even told him: "As a mama I am happy, but a mama is also a woman."

Yes, these half-confided intimacies held the fascina-tion of a sin, and she knew it. Once, when he answered her unexpectedly: "Mommy, I am not so little as you think, I understand you," she became frightened. Of course, the boy did not have anything concrete in mind, he only wanted to indicate to his mother that he was eager to share all her sorrows. Nonetheless, his words had several possible mean-ings. They opened a sudden vision of dangerous depths, depths of forbidden intimacy and illicit understanding.

7

And how did Jaromil fare with his unique inner world?

Not too well; the schoolwork which had been easy child's play for Jaromil during his public school years became much more difficult in high school, and in the gray routine of lessons and homework the glory of his inner world began to fade. The teacher talked derisively about pessimistic books which deal only with the world's aches and pains, and Jaromil's idea about life as weeds seemed insultingly banal to him now. He was no longer quite sure whether anything he had ever thought or felt was truly his own property, or whether his thoughts were merely a common part of the world's store of ideas which had always existed ready-made and which people only borrowed, like books from a library. Who was he, then? What was his inner self really like? He tried to lean over his inner being to take a searching look, but all he ever glimpsed was the mirror reflection of his spying gaze.

And so he began to yearn for the man who two years ago had first talked of his inner world. His marks in art were consistently mediocre (when using watercolors, the paints always spilled beyond the penciled outlines). Maman therefore decided there was good reason for her to accede to her son's wishes, seek out the artist, and arrange for private tutoring to help Jaromil catch up in class and improve his art grades.

And so it was that one day Jaromil found himself in the artist's studio. It was on the top floor of an apartment building and consisted of two rooms; the first was full of bookshelves; the second was windowless and had a skylight made of large panes of milky glass set into the slanting roof. In this atelier were several easels holding unfinished paintings and a long table scattered with papers and small bottles of colored inks; the wall was covered by strange black faces the artist described as tracings of African masks; a dog which was quite familiar to Jaromil sat on the couch in the corner, silently observing the visitor.

The artist sat Jaromil down at the long table and thumbed through his sketchbook. "These drawings are all the same," he said at last. "This won't get you anywhere."

Jaromil felt like reminding the artist that these were the very dog-people he had liked so much before, and that he had drawn them specially for his sake, but he was so full of disappointment and self-pity that he could not say a word. The artist put a fresh sheet of paper in front of Jaromil, opened a bottle of ink, and put a brush in his hand. "Start drawing anything that comes to mind, don't think too much about it and just let yourself go..." But Jaromil was so frightened that he could not think of anything, and when the artist prodded him again, in his anxiety he fell back on the old tried-and-true dog's head growing out of a skinny body. The artist was dissatisfied and, flustered, Jaromil said he would like to learn how to use watercolors properly, because in school he never managed to stay neatly inside the penciled outline.

"So your mother told me," replied the artist. "But now forget all about watercolors and about dogs, too." Then he placed a thick book in front of the boy, and opened it to a page showing a playfully childish line wiggling across a colored background. It reminded Jaromil of centipedes, starfish, bugs, stars, and moons. The artist wanted the boy to use his imagination and draw something similar. "But *what* should I draw?" asked Jaromil, and the artist told him, "Draw a line. Draw the kind of line that pleases you. Remember, it's not the artist's job to copy anything, but to create a world of his own lines on paper." And so Jaromil drew lines which he did not like at all, covering sheet after sheet, and finally, according to Mother's instructions, he handed the artist a banknote and went home.

The visit had thus turned out quite different from what he had expected. It had not led to a rediscovery of his lost inner world. Quite the contrary, the only productions that Jaromil could truly call his own, football players and soldiers with dogs' heads, were taken away. Nevertheless, when his mother asked him how he liked the lesson, he gave her an enthusiastic report; and he was not being hypocritical: his visit may not have returned his inner world to him, but at least it provided him with a unique outer world which was not open to everyone and which had already rewarded him with some privileged glimpses: for example, he had seen remarkable pictures which had confused him but which conveyed the clear distinction (he realized at once what a distinction it was) of being totally different from the land-scapes and still-lifes hanging at home; he had also heard several noteworthy statements which he appropiated at once: he understood, for example, that the word "bourgeois" was an insult; the bourgeois is the person who wants pictures to look like real life; but we can laugh at such people because (and Jaromil loved this part) because they were dead and did not know it.

And so Jaromil eagerly continued to visit the artist, longing for a repetition of the success he had once achieved with his drawings of dog-people; but in vain: the scrawls and scribbles that were supposed to be variations of Miró's paintings were mechanical imitations and possessed none of the charm of childlike fantasy; drawings of African masks remained clumsy copies and failed to awaken the boy's own imagination as the artist had hoped. Jaromil was finding it unbearable that he had already visited his tutor so many times without having received a single word of praise, and so he decided on a daring action: he brought in his secret sketchbook, containing his drawings of nude female bodies.

They were modeled mainly on photographs which Jaromil had seen in a magazine taken from Grandpa's library. The drawings on the first few pages of the sketchbook were therefore mature, statuesque women in noble attitudes typical of allegoric figures of the nineteenth century. The next section, however, had something far more interesting: one page showed a drawing of a headless woman; at the place representing the woman's neck the paper had been cut, so that it looked as if the head had been chopped off, leaving the traces of an imaginary axe. The slit in the paper had been made by Jaromil's penknife; Jaromil found one of the girls in his class extremely attractive. He often stared at her clothed body, longing to see it naked. It so happened that he had a photograph of the girl, and by cutting out the head and sticking it into an incision in the sketchbook he accomplished his wish. All the nudes on the following pages were headless and equipped with an incision. Some of the figures were in rather odd situations: in a squat suggesting urination, atop a flaming pyre like Joan of Arc, or subjected to other scenes of torture. For instance, one headless woman was impaled on a pole, another had her leg cut off, a third was missing an arm. Others were part of certain scenes which we had better pass over.

Naturally, Jaromil had no idea what the artist's reaction to these drawings would be; they were certainly far removed from the canvases in his studio and from the pictures in his thick books. All the same, Jaromil felt that the drawings in his secret sketchbook had something in common with the artist's work: they were illegitimate; they were different from the paintings at home; like the artist's paintings, they would be condemned and misunderstood by any committee made up of Jaromil's family or their usual household guests.

The artist flipped through the sketchbook. Without saying anything, he handed the boy a big volume, then sat down and busied himself with sheets of paper on the table. Jaromil started to examine the book. He saw a naked man with his rear end sticking out so far that it had to be supported by a crutch; an egg giving birth to a flower; a face full of crawling ants; a man whose hand was turning into a rock.

The artist drew near to Jaromil. "Notice," he said, "what a marvelous draftsman Dali is!" Then he placed a small plaster statue of a nude in front of Jaromil. "We've been neglecting the craft of drawing, and that was a mistake. Before we can make radical changes in the world we've got to learn to see it the way it is." And Jaromil's sketchbook began to fill up with female bodies, with corrected outlines and proportions where the artist had gone over Jaromil's sketches.

8

If a woman fails to live sufficiently through her body, she comes to regard her body as an enemy. Maman had not been too happy with the strange scrawls Jaromil was bringing home from his lessons and when he started to show her drawings of nude women her uneasiness turned to vehement distaste. A few days later she watched from the window the servant-girl, Magda, picking cherries. Jaromil was holding the ladder for her, and his eyes kept straying under the girl's skirt. It seemed to Maman that lately she had been besieged by armies of female bosoms and rear ends, and she decided to launch a counteroffensive. That afternoon, Jaromil was supposed to have his usual art lesson; she dressed quickly and reached the artist's studio ahead of her son.

"I am no puritan," she said, sinking into an armchair, "but you know that Jaromil is now entering upon a dangerous age."

She had carefully gone over in her mind what she would say to the artist, but now she found herself at a loss for words. Of course, she had rehearsed her sentences in the familiar atmosphere of her home, against a backdrop of garden greenery which always silently applauded her thoughts. But here there was no trace of green nature. Here she was surrounded by strange paintings on easels and a dog with his head between his paws staring at her from the couch like a skeptical sphinx.

The artist curtly rejected Maman's criticism, and went on to say that he had no interest whatever in Jaromil's school grades, for art taught in schools only kills any talent a child might possess. No, what fascinated him about her son's drawing was his peculiar, almost morbidly sensitive imagination.

"Notice the strange pattern. The pictures of his which you showed me a few years ago—all had people with dogs' heads. Lately he's been drawing nude women—but all of them headless. Don't you find it significant that he refuses to acknowledge the human face, that he refuses to give people their humanity?"

Maman remarked she found it hard to believe that her son had already turned into such a pessimist as to deprive people of humanity.

"Naturally, he didn't come to his drawings through any pessimistic cogitations," retorted the artist. "Art doesn't have its sources in reason. Jaromil's impulse to draw people with dogs' heads or to draw headless women came to him spontaneously. I'm sure he had no idea how these things dawned upon him. His subconscious whispered these shapes to him—forms which are strange, yet far from senseless. Don't you think there is a kind of mysterious link between Jaromil's visions and the War? The War which shakes us and makes us tremble every hour of the day and night? Didn't the War rob man of his face and his head? Aren't we living in a world full of headless men longing for torsos of headless women? Isn't a so-called realistic view of the world the greatest illusion of all? I ask you—isn't there more truth and reality in your son's drawings?"

She had come to chide the artist, and now she was

flustered like a timid girl afraid of chastisement. She did not know how to answer.

The artist rose from his chair and walked over to the corner of the studio, where a number of unframed canvases were propped against the wall. He pulled one out, turned it so that the painted side faced the room, took a few steps backward, and squatted on his haunches. "Come over here," he said to Maman, and when she obediently came near he put his hand on her waist and drew her closer, so that now they were squatting side by side and Maman was looking at a strange grouping of red and brown shapes which could be taken for smoldering flames in a bare, burnt-out landscape, or perhaps streaks of blood. A figure was scratched into this landscape (with a palette knife), a peculiar figure that seemed to be made of white ropes (this effect was produced by bare canvas). It seemed to be floating rather than walking, shimmering at a distance rather than actually present.

Once again, Maman did not know what to say, but the artist resumed his discourse; he talked about the phantasmagoria of war which surpasses by far the fantasy of modern painters, he spoke of the terrifying image of a tree with human flesh intertwined in its branches, a tree with fingers and a trunk from which stares a human eye. Then he said that nothing interested him any longer in such a time of devastation except war and love. A love that shines behind the bloody reality of war like the figure Maman sees in that painting. (For the first time during the conversation, Maman felt that she understood the artist, for she too had perceived the picture as some sort of battleground and she too had recognized the white shape as a human figure.) The artist spoke about the riverbank where they first saw one another. He said that she had appeared out of the mist and fog like the shy white body of love.

Then he turned the squatting Maman toward himself and kissed her. He kissed her before she had any inkling of what was happening. This was actually in keeping with everything that had happened between them; events struck Maman out of the blue, they always seemed to run ahead of her ideas and expectations; the kiss was here, before she could think about it, and subsequent reflection could not change what had happened but only establish the fact that something wrong had taken place; but Maman could not be sure even about that, and so she postponed solving this problem until some future time and concentrated on the present moment.

She felt his tongue in her mouth and in an instant realized that her own tongue was lifelessly limp and that it must feel to the artist like a damp washcloth. She became ashamed and the angry thought flashed through her mind that it was no wonder her tongue had changed into a wash-cloth—after all those loveless weeks and months! She quickly replied to the artist's tongue with the pointed tip of her own, and he lifted her up, carried her to the couch (the dog, whose eyes had been fixed on them all along, jumped off and lay down near the door), eased her gently onto her back, and caressed her breasts. She felt a sense of satisfaction and pride; the artist's face looked young and passionate. She was afraid she no longer knew how to respond in kind, and for that very reason she ordered herself to try to act young and passionate, and before she realized it (again, the event happened faster than she had time to think) he had become the third man to have entered deep inside her body and her life.

Suddenly she was aware that she really had no idea whether she wanted him or not. It occurred to her that she was still behaving like a silly, inexperienced little girl and that if she had given the least thought to what she was doing the present situation could never have developed. This idea calmed her, for it meant that her breach of marital fidelity was caused not by lust but by innocence. The thought of innocence, in turn, evoked increased anger toward the man who had left her in a state of immature naiveté, and this anger covered her mind like a curtain so that she stopped thinking altogether and was aware only of her own rapid heartbeat.

When their breathing eased her mind awoke, and to hide from her own thoughts she buried her head on the artist's chest, let him stroke her hair, inhaled the soothing smell of oil paints, and waited to see who would be first to speak.

But the first sound came neither from him nor from her—it was the doorbell. The artist rose, quickly pulled on his trousers and said, "Jaromil."

She was terrified.

"It's all right, don't worry." He caressed her hair and stepped out of the studio.

He greeted the boy and sat him down at a desk in the front room. "I have a visitor in the studio, so we'll stay here. Show me what you brought with you." Jaromil handed the artist his sketchbook. The artist looked over Jaromil's homework, put paints in front of him, handed him paper and brushes, suggested a subject, and asked him to start painting.

He returned to the studio, where he found Maman fully dressed and ready to leave. "Why did you let him stay? Why didn't you send him away?"

"Are you in such a hurry to leave me?"

"This is madness," she said, and the artist embraced her again. This time she neither resisted his touch nor reciprocated. She stood in his arms like a body without a soul. The artist whispered into this inert body's ear, "Yes, it is mad. Love is either madness or nothing at all." And he sat her down on the couch, kissed her and caressed her breasts.

Then he went out again to see what Jaromil had achieved. This time, the theme which he had assigned was not intended to develop the boy's manual dexterity. Rather, he had asked him to paint a scene from some recent dream which had made an impression on him. The artist took a glance at Jaromil's work and launched into a discourse on fantasy. The most beautiful thing about dreams is that fantastic meetings can take place, encounters between people and objects that could never happen in ordinary life. In a dream a boat could sail into a room through an open window, a woman dead for twenty years could rise from a bed, get into the boat and the boat could suddenly change into a coffin and the coffin could float by flower-strewn banks of a river. He cited the famous dictum of Lautréamont about beauty—the beauty to be found *in the random meeting of an umbrella and a sewing machine on an operating-room table*. Then the artist said, "Such a meeting is no more beautiful than the meeting of a woman and a boy in an artist's apartment."

Jaromil noticed that his teacher seemed to be more animated than usual. He was aware of a peculiar warmth in the artist's voice when he talked about dreams and poetry. Jaromil liked it, he was pleased that he himself had been the stimulus for such impassioned talk, and he understood the artist's last remark, about the meeting of a woman and a boy. When the artist had first told him that they would stay in the front room, Jaromil surmised at once there probably was a woman in the studio; and not just any woman, but somebody special, if Jaromil was not allowed to get even a glimpse of her. But he was still too far removed from the adult world to try solving this mystery; he was more interested in the way the artist had, in his last words, linked his—Jaromil's—name with that mysterious lady. It seemed to Jaromil that his very presence had somehow made the lady more significant to the artist. Jaromil was pleased by the idea that the artist liked him, that he probably saw him as somebody with influence on his own life, that there was some sort of deep, secret affinity between the two of them, an affinity which the young and inexperienced Jaromil could not quite grasp but which his wise, adult tutor clearly perceived. These thoughts made Jaromil happy and when the artist gave him the next assignment, he eagerly dipped his brush in paint and bent over his sketchpad.

In the studio, the artist found Maman in tears: "Be so good as to let me go home at once!"

"Go ahead, you can both leave together. Jaromil is just finishing his assignment."

"You are a devil," she said through her tears, and the artist kissed her. Then once again he shuttled to the adjoining room, praised Jaromil's work (ah, how happy the boy had been that day!), and sent him home. He returned to the studio, settled the weeping Maman on the old paint-spattered couch, kissed her soft mouth and wet cheeks, and made love to her.

9

Maman's love affair with the artist never lost the character preordained for it from the very first: it was not a love to which she had dreamily looked forward or carefully examined beforehand; it was an unexpected love, one which seized her unawares.

This love continually reminded her of her *unpreparedness* in matters of the heart. She was inexperienced, she did not know how to act, how to talk; before the artist's distinctive, eager face she felt ashamed of every one of her words and gestures. Nor was her body any better prepared; for the first time, she began to regret the way she had neglected it after the birth of Jaromil and was terrified by the image of her belly in the mirror, the wrinkled, sad, pendulous folds of skin.

Ah, how she had always yearned for a love in which body and soul would harmoniously grow old together. (Yes, *that* kind of love she did anticipate in advance, she did look straight in the eye.) But in this demanding relationship into which she had so abruptly entered, her soul seemed painfully young and her body painfully old, such that she moved through her adventure as if her trembling feet were walking a tightrope, and immaturity of soul or senescence of body equally could bring about her downfall.

The artist lavished attention on her and tried to draw her into the world of his paintings and thoughts. Maman liked that. It proved to her that their union was not merely a conspiracy of bodies exploiting a favorable situation. But if love comes to occupy not only the body but the soul as well, it requires more time; to justify her increasing absence from home (especially to Grandma and Jaromil) Maman had to keep inventing new friends.

She would sit by the artist's side as he worked, but that did not satisfy him; he explained to her that art, as he understood it, was only one method of mining life's miraculous gifts; such gifts could be discovered even by a child at play or by an ordinary person recalling a dream. Maman was given paper and colored inks; she was asked to make ink-blots on the paper and to blow on them; colored rays ran unevenly across the paper and covered it with an intricate network; the artist mounted Maman's products behind the glass panels of his book-case and proudly showed them off to his guests.

During one of her very first visits, as she was leaving, he put several books in her arms for Maman to read at home. She had to read them clandestinely because she was afraid that Jaromil might get curious and ask her where the books came from, or that someone else in the family might ask a similar question. It would be difficult to come up with a good answer, because even the covers of the books looked quite distinctive and unlike any books on the shelves belonging to her relatives and friends. She therefore hid them in the clothes-hamper under her bras and nightshirts and read them during intervals when she was alone. Perhaps the sense of doing something illicit and the fear of discovery kept her from concentrating. We suspect she did not get much out of her reading, and in fact there were many pages she did not understand even though she went over them two or three times.

When she returned them to the artist she was as nervous as a schoolgirl who hadn't done her homework, because he would immediately ask her how she had liked a particular book and Maman knew that he was not interested in hearing a vague positive answer but that he wanted to share with her a mutually discovered truth. Maman knew all that, but this did not help her understand what the book was all about, nor what the artist considered so significant. So like a sly schoolgirl, she reached for an excuse: she complained that she had to read the books in secret to keep from being discovered, and that she consequently could not concentrate on them properly.

The artist acknowledged the validity of the excuse, and found an ingenious solution. When Jaromil arrived for his next lesson, the artist gave him a lecture on the currents of modern art and then lent him several books on the subject which the boy eagerly accepted. When Maman first saw these volumes on Jaromil's desk and realized that this contraband was covertly intended for her she was frightened. Up till then the entire weight of her adventure had been borne only by herself, whereas now her son (that image of purity!) became an unwitting courier of adulterous love. But there was nothing to be done. The books were lying on his desk and Maman had no choice but to look them over under the cloak of justified maternal solicitude.

On one occasion she gathered enough courage to tell the artist that the poems which he had lent her seemed unnecessarily vague and unclear. She was sorry the moment she said it for the artist considered the slightest disagreement with his own opinion as treason. Maman hastened to undo the damage. As the artist turned his frowning face toward the canvas, she quickly took off her blouse and bra. She had beautiful breasts and knew it. Now she proudly (yet somewhat uncertainly) carried them across the studio and stopped in front of the artist, half-hidden by the canvas on the easel. The artist morosely dabbled his brush over the canvas, now and then darting angry looks at Maman peeking out from behind the picture. She pulled the brush from his hand, stuck it between her teeth, and mumbled a word which she had never before said to anyone—a vulgar, suggestive word. She repeated it several times, until she saw that the artist's anger was turning into amorous desire.

No, she had never acted this way before, and was doing so now with effort and clenched muscles. But she understood from the beginning of their affair that he yearned to have her express her feelings with playfulness and abandon, that he wanted her to be completely free, unfettered by convention, shame, inhibition. He was fond of saying, "I don't want anything from you except your freedom. I want you to give me your own complete free-ness as a gift!" And he demanded constant proof of this gift. Gradually, Maman became more or less convinced that such uninhibited behavior must be something very beautiful, but at the same time she was afraid that she would never learn how to achieve it. The harder she tried to learn how to be free, the more difficult a task her freedom became. It turned into a duty, into something for which she had to prepare at home (to ponder what word, what wish, what act would best surprise the artist and convince him of her spontaneity), such that she began to groan under the imperative of freedom as if under a heavy burden.

"The worst thing is not that the world is unfree, but that people have unlearned their liberty," he would say to her and she realized how aptly this applied to her, how much she belonged to that old world which the artist believed had to be fully and totally rejected. "If we cannot change the world, let's at least change our lives and live them freely," he would say. "If every life is unique, let's live uniquely. Let's reject everything that is not fresh and new. It is necessary to be absolutely modern," he cited Rimbaud, and she listened religiously, full of faith in his words and full of doubt in herself.

It occurred to her that the artist's love might be based on a complete misunderstanding and she would ask him why he really loved her. He would answer that he loved her the way a boxer loves a butterfly, the way a singer loves silence, the way an outlaw loves a village maiden. He would say that he loved her as a butcher loves the timid eyes of a calf or as lightning loves the quietly idyllic roof. He told her he adored her because she was an exciting woman rescued from a dull world.

She listened to him with rapture, and went to see him whenever she managed to steal a moment. She felt like a tourist who gazes at the most beautiful landscapes but is too hurried and breathless to enjoy the scenery. She could not really enjoy her love affair, but she knew that it was something big and beautiful and that she must not let it go.

And Jaromil? He was proud that the artist was lending him books from his own library (the artist let the youngster know on several occasions that he normally never let his books out of the house but that he was making a special exception in Jaromil's case), and having lots of time on his hands he dreamily pored over the pages. In those days, modern art had not yet become the shopworn property of the bourgeois masses and retained the fascinating aura of a sect, a magical exclusivity fascinating to childhood—an age always daydreaming about the romanticism of secret societies, fraternities, and tribes. Jaromil basked in the magic atmosphere of these books with a receptivity quite different from that of his mother, who diligently read the books from A to Z like textbooks on which she would be examined. Jaromil, who had no examination to fear, did not actually read a single one of the volumes thoroughly. He dawdled

LIFE IS ELSEWHERE

over them, leafed through them, paused over a page now and then, mused over a few lines of verse, unconcerned that the rest of the poem seemed rather meaningless. A single line of poetry or a single paragraph of prose was sufficient to make him happy, not only because they were beautiful but because they were magic doors opening into the realm of the elect, those whose souls are sensitive to things hidden from others.

Maman knew that her son was not content to be a mere courier and that the books which were supposed to be only passed on were read by him with real interest. She therefore began to talk to him about their mutual reading matter and asked him questions which she dared not pose to her lover. She was startled to find that her son championed the borrowed books with an even greater warmth than did the artist. She noticed that in a collection of Éluard's poems he had underlined certain verses in pencil. *Asleep, the moon in one eye the sun in the other.* "What do you see in that? Why should I sleep with the moon in one eye? *Legs of stone, with stockings of sand.* How can stockings be made of sand?" Jaromil suspected that his mother was making fun not only of the poems but of him, too, thinking that he was too young to understand. So he sulked and answered grumpily.

My God, she failed even before a thirteen-year-old child! That day she went to see the artist, feeling like a spy in enemy uniform. Her behavior lost any remnants of spontaneity and everything she did and said resembled the performance of an amateur actress gripped by stage fright, declaiming her lines with the fear of being booed off the stage.

In those days the artist had just discovered the magic of the camera. He showed Maman his first photographs, a tranquil world of oddly assembled objects, a bizarre view of abandoned and forgotten things. Then he made her pose under the skylight and began to take pictures. At first, Maman was relieved, for she did not have to say anything. She was only expected to stand or to sit, to smile, to listen to the artist's directions and to the praise which he now and then accorded her figure or her face.

But all of a sudden his eyes took on a bright luster; he picked up the brush, dipped it in black paint, gently tilted Maman's head backward and made two thick lines across her face. "I crossed you out! I canceled God's creation!" he laughed and photographed Maman on whose nose two heavy lines crossed one another. Then he led her to the bathroom, washed her face, and wiped it with a towel.

"I crossed you out just now so that I can create you all over," he said. He picked up the brush once more and again started to draw on her face. He was making circles and lines resembling ancient hieroglyphics. "Face— message, face—letter," he said, again placed Maman in the light streaming from the slanted skylight and kept on pressing the shutter.

After a while he posed her lying on the floor. He placed a plaster of paris cast of an antique head next to hers, and painted on it the same lines he had painted on Maman's face. He photographed both heads—the real one and the statue—then washed off the markings on Maman, painted some new ones, and took more pictures. Then he put her on the couch and began to undress her. Maman was afraid that he was about to paint markings on her breasts and legs, and she even attempted a smiling objection (that took quite a bit of courage, because she had always been afraid that her attempts at humor would miscarry and be considered in bad taste), but the artist had no further interest in painting her. He made love to her instead, fondling her head as if he found it especially exciting to make love to a woman who was his own creation, a product of his own fantasy, his own image—as if he were God lying with a woman whom He had created for Himself.

Actually, at that moment Maman really was little

more than his image and his invention. She knew it, and she tried with all the self-control at her command to keep him from knowing it too, to keep him from realizing that she was not his partner, not a magical counterpart worthy of love, but only a lifeless reflection, an obedient looking glass, a passive surface on which he was projecting the images of his longing. She succeeded. The artist reached the climax of his joy and happily slid off her body. When she returned home, she felt as if she had undergone a great ordeal, and before going to sleep that night she wept.

On her next visit to the studio, the painting and picture-taking resumed. This time the artist uncovered her breasts and painted over their beautifully arched surfaces. But when he tried to undress her completely, Maman rebelled against her lover for the first time.

It is hard to appreciate the skill, the cleverness whereby she succeeded—in all her various amorous games with the artist—to hide her belly. Even when undressed, she would keep on her garter-belt, suggesting that this made her nudity even more exciting; she would plead for semidarkness; she would gently draw her lover's caressing hands from her belly and place them on her breasts. And when she had exhausted all other ruses, she would appeal to her shyness, which the painter recognized and which he adored (he told her many times that she was the incarnation of whiteness and that his first conception of her inspired a white shape scratched into the canvas with a palette knife).

But now she was supposed to stand naked in the middle of the studio like a living stature, offering herself to his eyes and his brush. She resisted, and when she told him—as she had done during her first visit—that what he wanted was mad, he answered the same way he had then, *yes, love is mad*, and pulled off her clothes.

And so she stood in the middle of the room and could

think of nothing except her belly. She was afraid to look down but she saw it before her eyes as she knew it from a thousand desperate glances into the mirror. It seemed to her that she was nothing but a huge belly, a bag of ugly wrinkled skin. She felt like a woman on an operating table, someone whose mind is supposed to be completely blank, someone expected to submit in the faith that everything would be all right in the end, that the surgery and the pain would finally be over and in the meantime there was nothing to be done but endure.

The artist picked up his brush, dipped it in paint, touched her shoulder, her navel, her legs, stepped back and picked up the camera; then he led her into the bathroom, where she had to lie down in an empty tub. He placed the snaky metallic shower-hose across the body, with the perforated head at one end, and told her that this metal snake did not spit out water but deadly gas and that it was weighing upon her like the hand of war on the throat of love and then he led her back into the room and took more photographs and she went obediently, no longer trying to cover up her abdomen, but she still saw it before her in her imagination, she saw his eyes and her belly, her belly and his eyes...

When at last he laid her down on the rug, all covered with paint, and made love to her beside the cool, beautiful antique head, Maman could not stand it any longer and began sobbing in his arms. He probably failed to comprehend the significance of her weeping, for he was convinced that his own passionate absorption, transformed into beautiful, persistent, pulsating movement, could evoke no response other than rapture and happiness.

Maman realized that the artist did not grasp what was happening, so she pulled herself together and stopped crying. But when she reached the stairs of her home she was overcome by dizziness and she fell and scraped her knee.

Grandma, frightened, led her to her room, felt her forehead, and stuck a thermometer under her arm.

Maman had a fever. Maman had a nervous breakdown.

10

A few days later, Czech parachutists sent from London killed the German overlord of Bohemia, martial law was declared, and on street corners appeared posters with long lists of executed persons. Maman lay in bed and the doctor came every day to stick a needle into her posterior. Her husband would come to sit on her bed, grasp her hand, and gaze into her eyes; Maman knew that he ascribed her breakdown to the horrors of contemporary events, and she realized with shame that she was deceiving him, while he was being kind and gentle and wanted to help her through her difficult time as a true friend.

The servant Magda, who had been living in the villa for several years and about whom Grandma was fond of saying—in the spirit of good old democratic traditions—that she regarded her not as a servant but as a member of the family, came home weeping one day, having learned that her fiancé had been arrested by the Gestapo. And indeed, several days later his name appeared in black letters on a dark red poster among the names of executed hostages and Magda got a few days off so she could visit the parents of her young man.

When Magda came back, she said that the family of her fiancé had not even gotten an urn with his ashes and that they would probably never learn the whereabouts of their son's remains. She broke into sobs, and continued to weep almost every day. She generally cried in her own tiny room, so that her sobs were muffled by the wall, but sometimes she would break into tears right during dinner; from the time of her misfortune the family let her eat at the family table (before that she had eaten by herself in the kitchen), and the extraordinary nature of this kindness reminded her every day anew that she was in mourning and that she was an object of pity, so that her eyes would redden and a tear would roll down her cheek and fall on the plate of dumplings. Magda tried to hide her tears and her bloodshot eyes; she lowered her head and she longed for her grief to pass unnoticed, but this only made them all the more solicitous; somebody was bound to say a few cheerful words, to which she would reply with a loud outburst of sobs.

Jaromil observed all this as an exciting theatrical performance; he looked forward to glimpsing a tear in the girl's eyes, then to seeing the girl's shyness as she tried to cover up her sorrow, then watching as the sorrow would triumph and the tear would drop. He gazed avidly into her face (secretly, for he had the sense of doing something forbidden), and was suffused with excitement and the longing to cover that face with gentleness, to caress and solace it. At night, when he was alone in bed, he imagined himself caressing it, saying *don't cry, don't cry, don't cry*, for he could think of nothing else to say.

Maman's attack of nerves subsided (she had fallen back on the time-tested home cure of a good long rest in bed), and she began again going around the house, marketing, and looking after the household, even though she continued to complain of headaches and palpitations. One day she sat down at the desk and started writing a letter. She had hardly written the first sentence before realizing that the artist would think her stupid and sentimental, and she was afraid of his verdict. But then she calmed down and told herself that these were words to which she neither demanded nor expected an answer, the last words she would ever address to him, and this gave her the courage to continue. With a sense of relief (and an odd feeling of defiance) she formed sentences in which she once more recognized her own self—her true, familiar self of the good old days before she had met him. She wrote that she loved him and that she would never forget the magic moments they had lived together, but that the time had come to tell him the truth: she was different, quite different from what he imagined; in reality she was just an ordinary, old-fashioned woman, afraid that some day she would not be able to look her innocent son in the eye.

Was she thus telling him the real truth at last? Alas, not at all. She did not even hint to him that what she had called the happiness of love was actually only a strenuous effort; she wrote him nothing about her ugly belly nor about her breakdown, her skinned knee or her week's bed-rest. She did not write about those things because such sincerity would have been foreign to her. She finally wanted to be herself and she could be herself only in being insincere. After all, if she had poured out everything with complete candor, it would have been just like lying down in front of him with her wrinkled belly showing. No, she was through exposing herself to him, inside or out; she wanted to conceal herself safely in her modesty, and therefore she had to be untruthful and write about nothing except her child and her holy duties as a mother. By the time she finished the letter she was quite convinced that it was neither her belly nor the exhausting pursuit of the artist's ideas that had brought on her nervous crisis, but only her maternal feelings which revolted against a great but sinful love.

At that point, she saw herself not only as infinitely sad but also noble, tragic, and firm; the sorrow which a few days ago had merely hurt was now couched in dignified words and gave her a certain consoling pleasure. It was a beautiful sorrow, and she saw herself, illumined by its melancholy glow, mournfully beautiful.

What a remarkable coincidence! Jaromil, who had been enraptured by Magda's weeping eyes, knew all about

the beauty of sorrow and fully immersed himself in its enjoyment. He continued to leaf through the artist's book,
endlessly reciting the poems of Éluard, letting himself be
carried away by the enchanted lines: *in the stillness of her
body a tiny snowball the color of an eye*, or *the far-away
sea that washes your eyes*, or *sadness inscribed in eyes that
I love*. Éluard had become the poet of Magda's calm body
and of her eyes bathed by a sea of tears. He saw his entire
life locked in the spell of a single line: *sorrow-lovely face*.
Yes, that was Magda: sorrow-lovely face.

One evening the family went out to the theater and
he remained alone with her in the house. He had already
committed to memory all her domestic habits, and he knew
that it was Saturday night and Magda would take her bath.
Because his parents and Grandma had planned their visit
to the theater a week in advance, he had had time to make
everything ready. Several days before he had lifted the keyhole cover on the bathroom door and had fixed it in place
by means of a kneaded chunk of bread. To make a larger
viewing area, he had pulled the key out of the door and
hidden it. Nobody noticed its disappearance because members of the family were not in the habit of locking themselves
in the bathroom. The door was locked only by Magda.

The house was quiet and empty, and Jaromil's heart
pounded in his chest. He was upstairs in his room and had
propped open a book just in case anybody asked what he
was doing; but he was not reading, only listening. At last
he heard the sound of water rushing through the pipes and
the stream hitting the bottom of the tub. He put out the
light in the hall and tiptoed down the stairs; he was lucky;
the keyhole remained uncovered and when he pressed his
eye against it he saw Magda bent over the bathtub, undressed, her breasts bare, with nothing on except her panties.
His heart pounded terribly, for he was seeing what he had
never seen before, and he knew that soon he would see
even more and that nobody could prevent it. Magda straight-

ened up, stepped over to the mirror (he saw her profile), looked at herself for a while, then turned again (now he saw the front of her) and walked to the tub. She stopped, took off her panties, threw them aside (he still saw her front), then climbed into the tub.

Jaromil could still see her even in the bathtub, but because the surface of the water reached all the way to her shoulders she had turned once again into nothing but a face, the same well-known, sad face with an eye washed by a sea of tears—and yet at the same time it was a different face. In his mind, he had to add to it (now, the next time, forever) a pair of bare breasts, a belly, thighs, a rear end. It was a *face illumined by the body's nakedness*. It still elicited tenderness in him, but even the tenderness was different, because it was accompanied by the rapid beating of his heart.

And then he suddenly noticed that Magda was looking him straight in the eye. He was afraid that he had been discovered. She was gazing at the keyhole and was smiling (a little shyly, a little kindly). He jumped away from the door. Had she seen him or not? He had tested the keyhole many times and was sure that a spying eye could not be observed from the inside. But how to explain Magda's expression and smile? Or did she happen to look in his direction quite accidentally, and perhaps smiled only at the *possibility* that Jaromil was peeping in? Be that as it may, his encounter with Magda's gaze threw him into such a state of bewilderment that he did not dare go near the door again.

But after a while he calmed down, and an extraordinary idea flashed through his mind: the bathroom was not locked, and Magda had not told him that she was going to take a bath. Suppose he pretended complete ignorance and simply ambled into the bathroom? His heart began to pound once more. He imagined the scene: he stops, startled, in the open door, then remarks quite casually, *I just want to get my toothbrush*, walks nonchalantly past the naked, speechless Magda; her beautiful face looks abashed, just the way it looked when sudden tears gushed at the dinner-table, he walks by the bathtub to the washstand, picks up the toothbrush, stops at the tub and bends over Magda, over her nude body shimmering under the greenish screen of water; he gazes into her face, her bashful face, he strokes and caresses it . . . Ah, when he reached this point in his imagination, he was swept by a wave of excitement which blotted out everything and which kept him from thinking any further.

To make his entrance look quite natural, he climbed silently back up the stairs and then came down, loudly exaggerating every step; he became aware of his trembling and was seized by the fear that he would be quite unable to say in a calm and indifferent tone of voice *I just want to get my toothbrush*; he proceeded anyway, and when he had almost reached the bathroom and his heart was thumping so hard that he could barely breathe, he heard, "Jaromil, I'm taking a bath! Don't come in!" He answered, "Oh, no, I'm on my way to the kitchen," and he really crossed the foyer to the other side, to the kitchen, opened and closed the kitchen door, and then returned to his room.

Only then did he realize that the unexpected words were no reason for his cowardly capitulation, that he easily could have answered *It's all right, Magda, I'm just coming to get my toothbrush* and walked right in, for Magda surely would not snitch on him; she liked him because he had always been nice to her. And he imagined once more how he might have marched straight into the bathroom with Magda lying in the tub right in front of his nose, shouting *What are you doing, go away!* But there would have been nothing she could do. She had no way of defending herself, she was as helpless as she had been against the death of her fiancé, because she was lying imprisoned in the tub with him leaning over her face, over her big eyes . . .

But this fantasy had vanished irretrievably, and Jaromil

heard the muffled sound of water draining from the tub into distant pipes; the marvelous opportunity had been lost forever, and this infuriated him, for he knew that it might be a long time before he would again find himself alone with Magda, and that even if it were to happen, the key to the bathroom door would long since have been replaced and Magda would be securely locked in. He was propped up on his couch in utter dejection. But even more than the lost opportunity his lack of courage began to torment him— his weakness, his stupidly pounding heart which had deprived him of his presence of mind and spoiled everything. He was seized by violent distaste for himself.

What was to be done about such distaste? The feeling was quite different from sorrow; in fact, it was the very opposite of sorrow. When people were nasty to Jaromil he often locked himself in his room and cried, but those were happy, almost delightful tears, almost *loving* tears, whereby Jaromil pitied and consoled Jaromil. In contrast, this sudden distaste which showed Jaromil the failings of Jaromil repelled him from his very soul. This distaste was as clear-cut and blunt as an insult, as unmistakable as a slap in the face. The only salvation was flight.

But if we suddenly come face to face with our own pettiness, where can we run? From *debasement* the only escape is to move *upwards!* He therefore sat down and opened a book (that precious book which the artist claimed never to have lent to anyone but Jaromil) and tried hard to concentrate on his favorite poems. And once more he read about *the far-away sea that washes your eyes* and saw Magda before him. The snowball in the stillness of her body was there and the splashing of the waves echoed in the poem like the sound of a river through a window. Jaromil was overcome by sadness and closed the book. He picked up a pencil and started to write. Just as he imagined it done by Éluard, Nezval, and other poets, he wrote short lines one under another, without rhythm or rhyme. They were a series of variations on poems he had just read, but the variations also contained his own life experience. They contained the *sorrow*, which *melts and turns into water,* they contained *green waters*, whose surface rises *higher and higher till it reaches my eyes,* and they contained the body, the *mournful body,* the body in the water, after which *I stride, I stride through endless realms of water.*

He read his poem aloud several times, with a chanting, pathetic voice and he was elated. At the heart of the poem was the bathing Magda, and his face pressed to the door. He thus did not find himself *outside the bounds* of his experience, he was soaring *above* it; his distaste for himself remained below. Down below, his palms sweated nervously and he breathed heavily but here above, in the realm of the poem, he had risen far above his clumsiness. The episode with the keyhole and his own cowardice had turned into a mere trampoline above which he was now soaring. He was no longer mastered by his experience; his experience was mastered by what he had written.

The next day, he asked Grandma for permission to use the typewriter; he copied the poem on special paper and it was even more beautiful than when he had recited it aloud, for it had ceased to be a mere group of words and had become an *object*; its independence was beyond doubt; ordinary words exist only to perish as soon as they are uttered, for they serve only the moment of communication; they are subordinate to objects; they are only their signs. By means of the poem, words had been transmuted into objects themselves and were no longer subordinate to anything. They were not destined for ephemeral signaling and quick extinction, but for permanence.

What Jaromil had experienced the day before was now embodied in the poem, but at the same time it was slowly fading just like a seed dying inside a fruit. *I am submerged in water and the beating of my heart makes circles on the surface.* This verse described a boy who had been trembling in front of the bathroom door, but at the same time this boy was swallowed up by the verse; it surmounted and survived him. *Alas, my aquatic love*, said another line, and Jaromil knew that the aquatic love was Magda; but he also knew that nobody else could find her in that line, that she was lost, extinguished, buried in the verse; the poem he had written was as independent and unintelligible as reality itself. Reality does not discuss, it simply *is*. The independence of the poem provided Jaromil with a marvelous world of concealment, the possibility of a *second* existence. He liked it so much that the next day he tried writing some more poems, and he gradually succumbed to this activity.

11

Even though she had left her sickbed and moved about the house like a convalescent, she was by no means happy. She had discarded the love of the artist, but she had not received her husband's love to replace it. Jaromil's daddy was so seldom at home! They got used to his returning late at night, they even got used to his three- and four-day absences, for they knew that his work involved numerous business trips, but this time he had said nothing at all, he simply failed to come home in the evening and Maman had no idea where he was.

Jaromil saw his father so seldom that he was not even aware of his absences. He was in his room, thinking about poetry: if a poem is to be a true poem, it must be read by somebody else besides the author; only then can it prove that it is not merely a disguised diary and that it is capable of living its own life, independent of the person who had written it. At first he thought that he would show his poems to the artist, but they were far too important for him to dare submit them to such a severe critic. He longed to find someone who would feel as he did about the poems and he soon realized who this foreordained reader was; he saw his potential reader moving about the house with sad eyes and pained voice and it seemed to Jaromil that she was walking straight toward his verses. Excitedly, he gave Maman several carefully typed poems and ran off to his room to wait for her to go through them and to call him.

She read and she cried. Perhaps she herself was not aware why she was crying, but it is not difficult for us to guess. Four kinds of tears flowed from her eyes.

First, she was struck by the similarity between Jaromil's poems and the poems which the artist had lent her, and her eyes filled with tears of lament for her lost love;

then she sensed a certain general sadness emanating from her son's lines, and she recalled that this was the second day her husband had been absent from the house without telling her anything, and she wept tears of insult and hurt;

but almost at once, she felt tears of consolation, for her son—who had brought her his poems with such shy devotion—was a source of balm for all wounds;

and after reading the poems over several times she finally shed tears of poignant admiration, for the verses seemed incomprehensible to her and she therefore had the impression that they contained more than she was able to grasp and that, consequently, she was the mother of a marvelously gifted child.

She called him in, but once he was standing in front of her she felt the same way she had when the artist would question her about the books he lent her; she did not know what to say about the poems; she saw his eagerly expectant face and could think of nothing but to hug and kiss him. Jaromil was nervous and he was relieved to be able to bury his face on Maman's shoulder. She, in turn, feeling his little body in her arms, freed herself of the artist's oppressive shadow, gathered courage, and began to speak. But she was unable to mask the huskiness of her voice or the dampness of her eyes, and these were more significant to Jaromil than the words she was uttering. The signs of emotion in his mother's voice and eyes were a sacred guarantee that his verses had power—real, physical power.

It was turning dark, Dad was not coming home, and it occurred to Maman that Jaromil's face was full of a gentle beauty which no artist or husband could match; this improper thought was so insistent that she could not free herself of it; she started to tell him about the time of her pregnancy, how she used to gaze imploringly at the statuette of Apollo. "And you see, you really are as beautiful as that Apollo, you look just like him. They say a child picks up something of the mother's thoughts when she's pregnant, and I'm beginning to think it's more than a superstition. You even inherited his lyre."

Then she told him that literature had always been her greatest love. She had even gone to the university mainly to study literature and it was only marriage (she did not say pregnancy) that prevented her from devoting herself to this deepest inclination. If she now saw Jaromil as a poet (yes, she was the first to pin this great title on him), it is a wonderful surprise, and yet it is also something she had long expected.

They found consolation in one another, these two unsuccessful lovers, mother and son, and talked long into the night.

Part 2: Xavier

1

His ears were still full of the din of recess, which was almost over. Soon the old math prof would enter the class and start tormenting his schoolmates with a blackboard full of numbers. The buzz of a stray fly would fill the endless space between the professor's question and the student's answer . . . But by then he would be far away!

It was springtime a year after the great war, and the sun was shining. He made his way to the Moldau and sauntered along the quay. The universe of the classroom was far away, and he was connected to it only by a small brown briefcase in which he carried a few notebooks and a textbook.

He reached the Charles Bridge. The row of statues leaning out over the water beckoned to him to cross. Almost every time he played hooky from school (and he played hooky so often and so eagerly!) the Charles Bridge exerted a great pull on him and he was drawn. He knew that today, too, he would cross the bridge and stop at its foot, where the bridge came to dry land alongside an old yellow house whose third-floor window was level with the bridge's stone ledge, just a skip and a jump away. He liked to gaze at that window (it was always closed) and to wonder who lived there.

This time, though (perhaps because it was such a nice sunny day), the shutters were open. A cage with a bird was hanging on the wall. He stopped, watched the rococo cage of intricately wrought white wire, and then he noticed that a figure was outlined against the darkness of the room. Even though he saw it from the back, he recognized that it was a woman, and longed for her to turn around so that he could see her face.

The figure did move, but in the opposite direction; it disappeared in the darkness. But the window was open and he was convinced that it was an invitation, a silent intimate hint.

He could not resist. He jumped up on the ledge. The window was separated from the bridge by a moat, the bottom of which was paved with stone. The briefcase was in his way. He tossed it through the open window into the dusky room and then jumped in after it, landing on the window sill.

2

___

The dimensions of the high rectangular window in which Xavier was framed were such that his outstretched arms touched its sides while his figure totally filled its height. He examined the room from back to front (in the manner of people who are lured by distance), and so the first thing that met his eyes was a door in the rear, then a big-bellied wardrobe along the left wall, on the right-hand side a wooden bed with carved head- and foot-boards, and in the middle of the room a round table with a knitted cover on which stood a vase of flowers. Only then did he notice his briefcase, which was lying under his feet, on the tasseled edge of a cheap carpet.

Just as he saw it and prepared to lower himself into the room to retrieve it, the door in the dim back of the room opened and a woman appeared. She noticed him at once; the room was dark and the rectangle of the window shone as if it was night on one side and day on the other. From the woman's side, the man appearing in the window seemed like a black silhouette on a golden ground; a man poised between day and night.

If the woman dazzled by the light was unable to see

the intruder's facial features, Xavier fared somewhat better. His eyes had already become accustomed to the semidarkness and he was able to make out the softness of the woman's outlines and the melancholy of her face, the pallor of which would have been apparent even in deepest dusk. She stood in the door and gazed at Xavier; she was neither so uninhibited as to express her fear with a gasp, nor so quickwitted as to address him.

Only after a few long seconds of examining each other's indistinct faces did Xavier break the silence: "My briefcase is here."

"Briefcase?" she asked, and as if the sound of Xavier's voice had reassured her she closed the door behind her.

Xavier hunched down on the windowsill and pointed to the leather case lying on the floor. "It's full of important things. A math notebook, a science text, and a Czech composition book. I've just written an exercise, on the theme *How Spring Arrived This Year*. It took me a lot of work and I'd hate to have to rack my brains all over again."

The woman took a few steps into the room, so that Xavier was able to see her in better light. His first impression had been accurate: softness and melancholy. He saw two large eyes afloat in the nebulous face, and another word occurred to him: fright. Not fright over his unexpected arrival, but something that had happened long ago, something that remained in her large staring eyes, in her pallor, in her gestures which seemed to be asking forgiveness.

Yes, the woman was really asking forgiveness! "Excuse me," she said, "but I really have no idea how your briefcase could have gotten into our room. I was just cleaning the room a while ago and I didn't see anything that didn't belong here."

"All the same," said Xavier, still squatting on the window sill. He pointed to the floor: "I'm glad to see it's still here!"

"I'm glad you found it," she said and smiled.

They were facing each other and all that separated them was the table with its knitted cover and glass vase filled with wax-paper flowers.

"Yes, it would have been a nuisance to lose it!" said Xavier. "The language prof hates me anyway, and he'd be sure to flunk me if I lost my homework."

Sympathy appeared in the woman's face. Her eyes became so big that Xavier was aware of nothing else, as if the rest of her face and body were mere appendages to the eyes. He had no clear idea what the features of the woman's face or the outlines of her body looked like—all that was on the periphery of his attention. The dominant impression of the woman was actually limited to her huge eyes, which were bathing everything with a brownish glow.

It was toward those eyes that Xavier now moved, walking around the table. "I'm an old repeater," he said, putting his hand on her shoulder (ah, that shoulder was as soft as a breast!). "Believe me," he continued, "there is nothing sadder than coming back to the same class a year later, to sit down once more at the same old desk..."

Then he saw those brown eyes rising toward him, and a wave of happiness engulfed him. Xavier knew that he could now move his hand lower and touch her breast or her belly or anything else, and that she was ruled by fright. But he did not move his hand; he was cupping her shoulder in his palm, a beautiful round knoll, and that seemed sufficiently beautiful and satisfying; he wanted nothing more.

For a few moments, they stood motionless. The woman seemed to be listening attentively, then she whispered: "You have to leave, quickly. My husband is coming back!"

Nothing could have been simpler for Xavier than to pick up his briefcase, jump through the window and onto the ledge of the bridge, but he did not do it. He was filled with the blissful feeling that the woman was in danger and that he had to stay with her: "I can't desert you!"

"My husband! Go away!" she pleaded.

"No, I'll stay with you! I'm no coward!" declared Xavier, while the sound of steps was already clearly audible from the stairway.

The woman tried to push Xavier toward the window, but he knew that he must not abandon a woman in danger. From the depths of the apartment he could already hear the opening of doors. At the last moment, Xavier threw himself on the floor and crawled under the bed.

3

The space between the floor and the bed, five boards supporting a torn mattress, was no bigger than a coffin. But, unlike a coffin, the space smelled pleasant (the straw smell of the mattress), it was acoustically perfect (the sound of steps reverberated loudly), and full of visions (projected against the gray mattress cover appeared the face of the woman whom he knew he must never abandon, a face punctured by three wisps of straw sticking out of the mattress ticking).

The steps which he heard were heavy, and when he turned his head he saw a pair of boots tramping through the room. Then he heard a female voice and a sense of poignant sorrow swept over him: that voice sounded just as melancholy, frightened, and enticing as it had when it had spoken to him a few moments before. But Xavier was reasonable and overcame his sudden pang of jealousy; he understood that the woman was in danger and that she was protecting herself with the weapons at her disposal: her face and her melancholy.

He heard a man's voice, and it seemed to match perfectly the black boots he had seen striding across the floor. Then he heard the woman saying no, no, no. The steps staggered toward his hiding place, and the low roof under which he was lying sank even further, almost touching his face.

He again heard the woman saying no, no, not now, please, and Xavier beheld her face against the coarse ticking, and that face seemed to be communicating its humiliation to him.

He felt like rising up in his coffin, he longed to save the woman, but he knew that he mustn't. Her face seemed so near, it bent over him, begged him, and three wisps of straw stuck out of it like three arrows. The boards above Xavier began to sway rhythmically and the straw piercing the woman's face like three arrows were rhythmically tickling Xavier's nose, so that he suddenly sneezed.

All motion above Xavier's head ceased; the bed became still. Not a sound could be heard, and Xavier, too, held his breath. Then, "What was that?" "I didn't hear anything," answered the woman's voice. There was a moment of silence, and then the man said, "Whose bag is that?" Xavier heard loud steps and saw the boots striding toward the window.

"That fellow was making love with his boots on!" Xavier thought indignantly. He was angry, and he felt that his moment had come. He leaned on his elbow and slid out from under the bed far enough to see what was going on in the room.

"Who's there? Where did you hide him?" shouted the male voice and Xavier saw that the black boots were topped by a pair of dark blue breeches and the dark blue jacket of a policeman's uniform. The man scanned the room intently and then leaped toward the pot-bellied wardrobe, the shape of which hinted that a lover was hiding inside.

At that moment, Xavier jumped up from his hiding place, quiet as a cat and agile as a panther. The uniformed man had opened the wardrobe full of clothes and reached inside. But by then Xavier was already standing behind him, and as the man was again about to poke in his hand to seize a hidden lover, Xavier grabbed him from behind by the collar and shoved him inside the wardrobe. He closed the door, locked it, put the key in his pocket, and turned to the woman.

4

He was facing the wide-open brown eyes and hearing the pounding within the wardrobe, the noise and the shouting so muffled by the profusion of clothing that the words were unintelligible.

He sat down under the gaze of the huge eyes, touched the woman's shoulder, and only then, when he felt her bare skin under his palm, did he realize that she was dressed only in a wispy slip, under which her soft nude bosom was heaving enticingly.

The banging from the wardrobe continued and Xavier was holding the woman in a firm embrace, trying to drink in her shape, but her outlines seemed to dissolve until only her large limpid eyes remained. He told her not to be afraid, he showed her the key as proof that the wardrobe was safely locked, he reminded her that her husband's prison was made of solid oak and that the captive could neither unlock it nor break it open. He then proceeded to kiss her (his hands were still cupped over her naked shoulders, so delightfully lovely that he was afraid to move his hands lower and touch her breasts, afraid to risk their dizzying allure), and as his lips touched her cheek it seemed to him that he was drowning in immense bodies of water.

"What are we going to do?" he heard her asking.

He caressed her shoulder and answered that there was no need to worry, that everything was all right, that he was happier than he'd ever been before, and that the din in the wardrobe interested him as little as the sound of a storm coming from a record-player or the barking of a dog coming from the other end of town.

To demonstrate his mastery of the situation, he got up and calmly surveyed the room. Then he laughed, because he saw a blackjack lying on the table. He picked it up, stepped toward the wardrobe, and answered the pounding coming from within by a few smart blows on the wardrobe's side.

"What are we going to do?" the woman asked again and Xavier replied, "We'll go away."

"And what about him?" she asked. "A person can go without food for two to three weeks," said Xavier. "When we come back after a year we'll find a skeleton dressed in a uniform and boots." He stepped once more to the noisy piece of furniture, hit it with the blackjack, laughed, and looked at the woman in the hope that she would laugh with him.

But she remained serious, and repeated, "Where will we go?" Xavier tried to explain, but she interjected that this was her home while the place Xavier was trying to take her to had neither her wardrobe nor her bird. Xavier answered that home meant neither wardrobe nor bird in a cage, but the presence of a person we love. And then he added that he himself had no home, or rather that his home consisted of motion, of journey. He said that he could live only by crossing from one dream into another, from one landscape into another, and that if he remained in one place too long he would perish just as surely as would her husband if he stayed in the wardrobe more than a few weeks.

In the middle of this conversation they both became aware that the wardrobe had become quiet. That stillness was so striking that it roused them like the bracing interlude after a storm; the canary began to sing, and the window was full of the yellow glow of the setting sun. It was as beautiful as an invitation to a journey. It was as beautiful as the Lord's mercy, as beautiful as the death of a policeman.

The woman caressed Xavier's face and it was the first time she had touched him of her own free will. It was also the first time that Xavier had seen her clearly, in her true, firm contours. She said, "Yes, we will go. We'll go wherever you wish. Just wait a moment, I'll take a few things with me."

She caressed him once more, smiled, and walked to the door. He watched her with eyes full of sudden peace; he saw her step, supple and flowing like the step of an aquatic being.

Then he lay down on the bed. He felt wonderful. The wardrobe was quiet, as if the man inside had fallen asleep or hanged himself. The stillness whispered of wide spaces, of the murmuring of the Moldau and the muffled hum of the city, a sound so distant that it resembled the rustling of a forest.

Xavier felt that he was once again open to journeys. And there is nothing more beautiful than the moment before a voyage, the moment when tomorrow's horizon comes to visit us, to announce its promises. Xavier was lying on crumpled blankets and everything melted into a marvelous unity: the soft bed resembled a woman, the woman resembled water, the water seemed like a supple, resilient berth.

The door opened, and the woman came back in. She was dressed in blue. Blue like water, blue like the eternally beckoning horizon, blue like the sleep into which he was slowly but helplessly drifting.

Yes. Xavier fell asleep.

5

Xavier does not sleep in order to recharge himself for waking life. No, that monotonous pendulum—sleep, wakefulness—which swings back and forth three hundred and sixty-five times a year, is unknown to him.

For him, sleep is not the opposite of life—sleep is life, and life is a dream. He crosses from dream to dream as if he were crossing from one life to another.

It is dark, pitch-dark except for the lanterns. In the cones of light they cut through the night, large snowflakes are swirling.

He ran through the station gate, quickly crossed the waiting room, and reached the platform, where a train with brightly lit windows was hissing steam. An old man swinging a lantern went by him closing the doors of the cars. Xavier quickly jumped aboard, the old man swung his lantern in a high arc, the calm tone of the signal-trumpet answered from the other end of the platform, and the train was on its way.

6

Once inside the car, he halted, trying to catch his breath. Once more, he had made it at the last moment, and arriving in the nick of time was his special pride. Others always came on time according to a well-arranged schedule, so they lived their whole lives without surprise, as if they were copying a test assigned by their teacher. He imagined them sitting in the train compartments, in their prearranged seats, conducting conversations well-known in advance—

about the cottage in the mountains where they are about to spend a week, about the daily order of life which they had already learned by heart in school so that they could always live blindly, automatically, without a single mistake.

Xavier, on the other hand, arrived quite unexpectedly, at the eleventh hour, thanks to a sudden impulse. He was now standing in the passageway of the train-car, wondering what possessed him to take part in a school excursion with boring schoolmates and bald-pated professors with fleas in their beards.

He began strolling through the car: boys were standing in the passageway breathing on frost-covered windows and peering out through the melted peepholes; others were lazily lounging on the compartment seats, their crossed skis propped against suitcases in the overhead racks. Somewhere in the back they were playing cards, in another compartment they were bellowing an endless song made up of a simple melody and seven words repeated over and over: *my canary bird is dead and gone, my canary bird is dead and gone, my canary bird* . . .

He stopped at that compartment and looked in. Inside were three older boys and a blonde girl who was from his class. When she saw him she blushed but tried to hide it by continuing to sing, her big eyes fixed on Xavier: *my canary bird is dead and gone, my canary bird* . . .

Xavier pulled himself away and passed other compartments, from which resounded student songs and merriment. He saw a man in a conductor's uniform walking toward him, stopping at each compartment door and asking for tickets. Xavier did not let the uniform fool him—under the conductor's cap he recognized the unmistakable face of the Latin prof and he knew that he must avoid him at all cost, not only because he didn't have a ticket but also because it had been ages (he could not even remember how long) since he had attended Latin class.

He made use of the moment when the Latin teacher

leaned forward into a compartment to squeeze quickly past him to the front of the car, where a pair of doors led to two small cubicles: the washroom and the toilet. He opened the door to the washroom and saw a strange couple locked in embrace: the teacher of Czech, a strict, severe woman in her fifties, and one of his classmates, who always sat in the first row and to whom Xavier during his rare appearances in class never paid much attention. When they saw him, the two startled lovers quickly parted and bent over the washstand, diligently rubbing their hands under a thin stream of water trickling from the faucet.

Xavier had no wish to disturb them, and he went back to the car platform; there stood the blonde classmate, looking at him with her large blue eyes; her lips were no longer moving, she was no longer singing about the canary, a song which Xavier had thought might go on forever. Ah, what madness, he thought, to believe in a song lasting forever, as if everything in this world had not been doomed from the very beginning.

With this thought in mind, he gazed into the blonde's eyes and knew that he must not assent to the false game in which the ephemeral passes for the eternal and small pretends to be big, that he must not say yes to that false game called love. That is why he turned around and once again entered the washroom in which the tall Czech teacher had resumed nestling against the short schoolboy, holding him around the waist.

"Please, I beg you, don't start washing your hands again!" Xavier said to them. "I'll wash up myself." He squeezed discreetly past them, turned on the water, and leaned over the washstand, seeking thus to gain some solitude for himself and some privacy for the two lovers standing embarrassed behind him. "Let's go next door," said the teacher in a resolute whisper. Then Xavier heard the click of the door and the sound of four feet on their way to the adjoining toilet. He was alone. Satisfied, he leaned against the wall and gave himself over to thoughts about the vanity of love, sweet thoughts illumined by a pair of big, imploring blue eyes.

7

The train stopped, there was the sound of a bugle, hilarity, banging, stamping; Xavier left his hideaway and joined the gang rushing to the platform. He could see hills, a huge moon, shining snow; they tramped through the night which was as clear as day. It was a long procession and the skis pointed upward like sacred symbols, like pairs of fingers swearing a holy vow.

It was a long procession and Xavier was marching with his hands in his pockets because he was the only one without skis, the votive symbols. He marched and he listened to the talk of his flagging companions. He turned around and saw that the blonde girl, fragile, small, was all the way in the rear, stumbling under her heavy skis and sinking into the snow. After a while he turned again and saw that the old math teacher was putting her skis on his shoulders, on top of his own, and with his free arm was supporting the girl. It was a bittersweet picture, unhappy old age solacing unhappy youth; Xavier watched and felt fine.

Then they heard the faint sounds of dance music, which gradually became louder as they reached a restaurant surrounded by wooden pavilions where Xavier's colleagues began to make themselves at home. But Xavier had no room reserved and no skis to put away or clothes to change into. He therefore went straight to the main hall. There was a dance floor, a jazz band, and several guests sitting at tables. He immediately noticed a woman in a dark red sweater and tight slacks surrounded by several men who were drinking beer. But Xavier recognized at once that the woman was elegant and proud, and that she was bored. He walked up to her and asked for a dance.

They danced in the middle of the floor, all alone. Xavier observed that the woman's neck was beautifully wilted, the skin around her eyes was beautifully wrinkled and there were deep furrows in her face. And he was happy that he had so many years of life in his arms, that he—a mere schoolboy—was holding in his arms an almost completed life. He was proud to be dancing with her, and he was hoping that the blonde girl would come and witness his exalted superiority, as if the age of his partner was a lofty mountain and the young girl a mere blade of grass lifting itself imploringly at its foot.

And that's just what happened: the boys began to swarm into the hall, accompanied by girls who had changed their ski-pants for skirts; they took up all the free tables, so that Xavier was dancing with the dark red woman in the middle of a sizable audience. He saw the blonde at one of the tables and was satisfied. She had on a beautiful dress, much too good for the dingy hall, a white delicate dress that made her seem even more fragile and vulnerable. Xavier knew that she was wearing it for his sake and he was firmly determined that he must not let her go, that he should live this evening entirely for her sake.

8

He told the woman in the dark red sweater that he did not feel like dancing anymore: he couldn't stand the stupid faces staring at them over beer mugs. The woman agreed, laughing. Even though the band was in the middle of a number and they were all alone on the platform they stopped dancing (in plain sight of everybody) and left the dance floor hand-in-hand, past the tables and into the white outdoors.

They were met by icy air and Xavier was thinking about the fragile, sickly girl in the white dress who would soon follow them out into the cold. He took the dark red woman by the arm and led her farther out onto the plain. It seemed to him that he was a pied piper and his woman companion a flute on which he was playing.

Soon, the doors of the restaurant opened and the blonde girl emerged. She seemed even frailer than before, her white dress merging with the snow so that she seemed to be snow moving through snow. Xavier pressed the woman in the sweater to him—a warmly dressed, superbly old woman—he kissed her, felt her body under the sweater, and out of the corner of his eye watched the little snowmaiden gazing sadly at them.

Then he laid the old woman down in the snow and tumbled on top of her. He knew that it was getting later and later, that the girl's dress was thin, and that the frost was caressing her calves, her knees, that it was reaching her thighs, stroking her higher and higher until it touched her lap and her belly. Then they got up and the old woman led him to one of the cottages, where she had a room.

The room was on the ground floor and the window was almost level with the snowy plain. Xavier saw that the blonde girl was only a few steps away, watching him. He did not want to lose sight of that maiden whose image was filling his whole being, so he turned on the light (the old woman laughed lasciviously at his need for light), took her by the hand, stepped to the window, and framed in the window he embraced her and lifted up her thick, shaggy sweater (a warm sweater for an old body) and thought about the girl, who was probably freezing, so cold that she no longer felt her own body, a thin fluttering spark in frozen, insensitive flesh which had lost all sense of touch and was nothing but a dead envelope for a soul which Xavier loved—ah, which he adored with such enormous love.

Who could bear such an enormous love? Xavier felt his arms getting weak. They were not able even to lift the heavy sweater high enough to uncover the old woman's breasts. He felt a heaviness in his whole body and sank down on the bed. It is difficult to describe his sense of blissful satisfaction. When a person is extremely happy, sleep comes as a reward. Xavier smiled and fell into a deep slumber. He sank into a beautiful sweet night lit up by two frozen eyes, two icy moons...

9

Xavier does not live just one single life that runs from birth to death like a long gray thread. No, he does not live his life—he sleeps it, and in that sleep-life skips from dream to dream. He dreams and in the middle of the dream falls asleep and dreams another dream, so that his sleep is like a series of boxes, one inside another.

Look! At this very moment he is sleeping at the same time in a house by the Charles Bridge and in a mountain cottage. Those two sleeps linger like two long-lasting organ tones. These two tones are now being joined by a third:

He is standing and looking around. The street seems empty; shadows flit by now and then, quickly vanish around a corner or inside a doorway. He, too, does not want to be seen. He is stalking through suburban side-streets, while the sound of gunfire resounds from the other end of town.

At last he enters a house and descends the stairs. Several doors open off the basement passage. For a moment he searches for the right one, then knocks. Three times—pause—then three times more.

10

The door opened and a young man in overalls asked him in. They passed through several rooms filled with odds and ends, clothes on hangers, but also guns stacked in corners. Then they went down a long passage (they must have gone far beyond the limits of the house proper) into a small, subterranean hall, where about twenty-five men were seated.

He sat down on an empty chair and examined those assembled, of whom he knew only a few. At the head of the hall three men were sitting behind a table. One of them, wearing a peaked cap, was just speaking—about a secret, rapidly approaching date when everything would be decided. Everything would go according to plan: leaflets, newspapers, radio, post office, telegraph, weapons. Then he questioned individual men on their assigned tasks. At last he turned to Xavier and asked him whether he had brought the list.

That was a terrible moment. In order to make sure it was in a safe place, Xavier had long ago copied the list on the last page of his Czech notebook. This notebook was with his other schoolbooks in his briefcase. But where was the case? He did not have it with him!

The man in the cap repeated the question.

My God, where was that briefcase? Xavier thought feverishly and then from the depths of his mind a vague, insistent memory floated to the surface, accompanied by a wave of sweet bliss. He wanted to grasp that memory but there was no time because all faces were turned on him, waiting. He had to admit that he didn't have the list.

The expressions of all these men—his trusted comrades—turned grim, and the man in the cap said in an icy voice that if the enemy were to get hold of the list, the event on which they had pinned all their hopes would be ruined and would remain like other dates: empty and dead.

But before Xavier was able to reply, a door opened behind the chairman's table, a man stuck in his head and whistled sharply. Everybody knew that this was the alarm signal. Before the man in the cap could give any order, Xavier shouted, "Let me be the first to go!" He said that because he realized that the journey waiting for them would be a dangerous one and that the man in the vanguard would be risking his life.

Xavier knew that because he had forgotten to bring the list he must wipe out his guilt. But it was not only a sense of guilt that drove him to meet danger. He was repelled by the pettiness that reduced life to mere existence and that turned men into half-men. He wanted to lay his life on a balance, the other side of which was weighted with death. He wanted to make his every action, every day, yes, every hour and minute worthy of being measured against the ultimate, which is death. That was why he wanted to lead the file, to walk the tightrope over the abyss, his head illumined by a halo of bullets, to grow in everyone's eyes until he had become as immense as death itself...

The man with the cap looked at him with cool, severe eyes in which a spark of understanding flashed. "All right," he said. "You lead the way."

11

He squeezed through a metal door and found himself in a narrow courtyard. It was dark, the sound of gunfire could be heard from afar, and when he looked up he saw the beams of searchlights wandering over the rooftops. A narrow iron ladder led from the ground all the way to the top of a five-story building. He began to climb. The others followed into the courtyard and huddled against the walls. They waited for him to reach the roof and give them a signal that the way was clear.

Then they crept over the rooftops, quietly and carefully, with Xavier leading the way. He moved like a cat, his eyes piercing the darkness. At one point Xavier stopped and motioned to the man with the cap, pointing to tiny scurrying figures far, far below, peering all around, holding short-barreled weapons in their hands. "Lead us on," the man said to Xavier.

And Xavier resumed the trek, jumping from roof to roof, climbing short metal ladders, hiding behind chimneys, and dodging the annoying searchlights which were continually probing the houses, the edges of roofs, and the canyons of the streets.

It was a beautiful journey of quiet men turned into a swarm of birds, to fly by the enemy waiting below and alight on roofs on the other side of town, where there was no danger. It was a beautiful, long journey, but it was becoming too long, and Xavier began to feel fatigue, the kind of fatigue that blunts the senses and fills the mind with hallucinations. He thought he was hearing a funeral march, the well-known Marche Funèbre of Chopin commonly played by brass bands at country funerals.

He did not slow down, but tried with all his might to

gather his wits and surmount the ominous hallucination. In vain; the music pulsed insistently in his ears, as if foretelling his impending doom, as if trying to pin the black veil of impending death over this moment of battle.

Why did he resist this hallucination with such vehemence? Did he not wish for a noble death that would make his rooftop odyssey a memorable, magnificent exploit? Was not the funeral dirge that foretold his death a triumphal paean to his courage? Was it not marvelous that his battle was a funeral rite, and his final rite a battle—that life and death merged in such an exquisite union?

No, Xavier was not terrified because death was calling, but because at this moment he could no longer rely on his own senses, he was no longer able (he, who had pledged the safety of his comrades!) to hear the enemy laying his treacherous snares because his ears were drugged by the melancholy sounds of a funeral march.

But was it really possible for a hallucination to bear such close resemblance to reality? Was it possible that an imaginary Chopin march could be so full of sloppy rhythm and flat trombone notes?

12

When he opened his eyes he saw a room with one shabby wardrobe and one bed, on which he happened to be lying. He noted with satisfaction that he had been sleeping with his clothes on, so there was no need to get dressed, only to slip on his shoes, which were lying under the bed.

But where was that sad funeral music coming from, the brass band that sounded so real?

He stepped to the window. Against a landscape which was almost barren of snow, a small group of people was standing motionless. They were dressed in black, their backs toward him, mournful and orphaned like the surrounding countryside. All that remained of the white snow was dirty strips and tatters on the moist ground.

He opened the window and leaned out. Now he understood. The somberly-dressed people were gathered around a coffin resting by the side of a deep hole. Another group in black, on the other side of the hole, had brass instruments with small music pads clipped on. They were looking intently at the notes while playing the Chopin march.

The window was almost flush with the ground. He jumped out and joined the mourning throng. At that moment, two strapping fellows put ropes under the coffin, swung it over the hole, and slowly eased it down. An old couple standing among the mourners began to sob, and the others took them by the arms and tried to comfort them.

The coffin touched bottom and the people in black, one after another, walked up and threw handfuls of soil on top of it. Xavier, too, the last one in line, picked up some soil mixed with chunks of snow and dropped it into the hole.

He was the only one present who was a total stranger to everybody else, and he was the only one who knew everything that had occurred. He was the only one who knew how and why the blonde girl died. Only he knew about the icy hand that had touched her calves, her abdomen, and her breasts. No one but he knew who had caused her death. Only he knew why she had wished to be buried in this spot where she suffered and where she had longed to die rather than see her love betrayed and abandoned.

He was the only one who knew. The others were present only as an uncomprehending public, or as uncomprehending victims. He saw them against the background of a great mountainous landscape and it seemed to him that they were lost in immense distances just as the dead girl was lost in an immensity of earth. It seemed to him that he himself (who knew all) was even more immense than the damp countryside, so that everything—the mourners, the dead girl, the grave diggers with their shovels, the meadows and the hills—entered into him and vanished in his vastness.

He was filled by the landscape, by the sorrow of the survivors and the death of the girl, and he felt a stretching inside his body as if a tree were growing there. He felt himself getting big and he now perceived his own body only as a cloak, a mask, a mask for his modesty. In this disguise of his own self he now approached the parents of the dead girl (the father's face reminded him of her features, although it was red with weeping) and he expressed his sympathy. Lifelessly they gave him their hands and he felt how fragile and insignificant they were in his palm.

For a long time he remained at the wooden pavilion where he had last seen the blonde girl and where he had fallen asleep, leaning against the wall and watching the funeral guests separate into small groups and lose themselves in the misty distance. Suddenly, he felt a caress on his face. Yes, he clearly felt the touch of a hand. He felt certain that he understood that gesture and he accepted it gratefully. He knew it was the hand of forgiveness. The blonde girl was letting him know that she had not stopped loving him and that love continued to live beyond the grave.

13

He floated through his dreams.

The most beautiful moments were those when one dream was still vivid while another into which he was waking was already beginning to dawn.

The hands that caressed him as he stood on the mountain plain already belonged to the woman in the next dream, but Xavier did not know this as yet, so the hands existed by themselves; disembodied, unattached, miraculous hands in empty space, hands between two adventures, between two lives, hands not burdened by a body and a head.

Oh, let that caress of magic hands last and last!

14

Then he felt not only hands but a large soft bosom pressing against his chest and he saw the face of a dark-haired woman and heard her voice. "Wake up! For heaven's sake, wake up!"

He was lying on a rumpled bed, in a little gray room with a huge wardrobe. Xavier remembered that he was in the house by the bridge.

"I know you'd like to sleep some more," she said, as if to excuse herself, "but I had to wake you because I'm afraid."

"What are you afraid of?"

"My God, you don't know anything!" she said. "Listen!"

Xavier tried to listen carefully. Firing could be heard from the distance.

He jumped out of bed and ran to the window. Groups of men in blue denim, carrying automatics, were patrolling the bridge.

It was like a memory echoing through several walls. Xavier knew that armed workers were guarding the streets, but he still had the feeling that he had forgotten something, something that could explain his own relation to what he was seeing. He knew that he actually belonged in that scene and that through some error he had fallen out of it, like an actor who forgets to make his entrance on the stage at the proper time, such that the crippled play continues without him. And then suddenly he remembered.

At the instant of recollection he scanned the room and sighed with relief: the briefcase was still there, propped against the wall, nobody had taken it. He leaped for it and opened it. Everything was there: the math notebook, the Czech exercise book, the science text. He pulled out the Czech notebook, opened it from the back and sighed again. The list which the dark-haired man had demanded of him was there—written in a careful, tiny but legible hand. Xavier was pleased anew by his clever idea of concealing this important document in a school notebook, the front of which contained a composition on the theme *How Spring Arrived This Year.*

"What in the world are you looking at?"

"Nothing," answered Xavier.

"I need you, I need your help. You see what's going on! They're moving from house to house, dragging people out and executing them."

"Don't worry," he laughed. "There'll be no executions!"

"How do you know?" she protested.

How did he know? The list of all the enemies of the people, who were to be executed on the first day of the revolution, was in his notebook: therefore, no executions could take place. Anyway, he was not the least bit interested in the anxiety of the beautiful woman. He heard gunfire, he saw the men guarding the bridge, and he could think of nothing except that the event which he had been so enthusiastically planning with his comrades had suddenly come, and he had slept right through it. He had been elsewhere in another room, in another dream.

He wanted to run out, to present himself to the comrades in denim, to deliver the list which nobody else had and without which the revolution was blind, ignorant of whom to arrest and whom to execute. But then he realized that this was impossible: he did not know the password for the day, he had long been regarded as a traitor, and nobody would believe him. He was in a different life, in a different story, and there was no longer any way of saving that other life, the one he had left behind.

"What's the matter with you?" the woman asked anxiously.

And it occurred to Xavier that if he could no longer save the life he had lost, he could at least ennoble the one he was living at that moment. He gazed at the beautiful, supple woman and knew he must leave her, for life was outside, far beyond the windows through which the soft sounds of shooting drifted like the cooing of a bird.

"Where are you going?" she shouted.

Xavier smiled and pointed out the window.

"But you promised to take me with you!"

"That was long ago."

"Do you mean to betray me?"

"Yes. I'll betray you."

She fell on her knees before him and embraced his legs.

He looked down at her and realized how lovely she was and how difficult it would be to tear himself away. But the world beyond the window was even more beautiful. And if he was leaving a beloved woman for its sake, then that world would be even more enhanced by the price of a betrayed love.

"You are beautiful," he said. "But I must betray you."

Then he tore himself from her arms and strode toward the window.

Part 3:
The Poet
Masturbates

1

The day that Jaromil brought his poems to Maman, she waited in vain for Dad's return. He didn't come home in the succeeding days, either.

Instead, Maman received an official notification from the Gestapo that her husband had been arrested. Toward the end of the war, another official notification arrived, to the effect that her husband had died in a concentration camp.

Her marriage may have been a sorry affair, but her widowhood was grand and noble. She had a large photograph of her husband dating from the days of their courtship which she put in a gold frame and hung on the wall.

Then the war ended, to the great jubilation of the citizens of Prague, the Germans pulled out of Bohemia, and Maman began a life illumined by the austere beauty of renunciation; the money which she had inherited from her father was gone, so that she was forced to dismiss the maid. After the death of Alik she refused to buy a new dog, and she had to look for a job.

Further changes took place: her sister decided to donate her apartment in the center of town to her newly married son, and to move with her husband and younger son to the ground floor of the parental villa. Grandma, in turn, moved up to the second floor with the widowed Maman.

Maman had nothing but contempt for her brother-in-law, ever since she had heard him declare that Voltaire was a physicist who invented volts. His family was a noisy bunch preoccupied with crude entertainments. The merry life on the ground floor was worlds apart from the melancholy realm of the upper story.

And yet Maman walked with a prouder posture than in the days of prosperity, as if she carried on her head (like Balkan women carrying baskets of grapes) the invisible urn of her husband.

2

The bathroom shelf was full of little perfume bottles and tubes of ointments and creams, but Maman hardly ever used them any longer. Still, she often paused to look at them with a sigh, for they reminded her of her deceased father, his pharmacy (now the property of the detested brother-in-law), and the vanished, carefree years of her former life.

Her past life with parents and husband seemed enveloped in mournful half-light, and this sense of dusk oppressed her. She realized she was able to appreciate the beauty of those years only now, after they had vanished forever, and she reproached herself for her marital infidelity. Her husband had no doubt been exposing himself to mortal dangers and his mind must have been heavy with cares, but to preserve her tranquillity he never breathed a word to her about his underground life. She still had no idea why he had been arrested, which resistance group he had belonged to, and what his actual mission had been. She knew nothing about all that, and she regarded her ignorance as humiliating punishment for her feminine small-mindedness, her inability to conceive of her husband's behavior as anything but coldness of heart. When she considered that her infidelity had coincided precisely with the period of his greatest peril, she felt utter contempt for herself.

She examined herself in the mirror and noted with surprise that her face was still young—needlessly young, in fact, as if time had blundered and passed it by. Recently she had learned that someone who saw her walking down the street with Jaromil was under the impression they were brother and sister. That seemed quite comical to her. All the same, she was flattered, and from that time on she took even greater pleasure in taking Jaromil to the theater and to concerts.

Anyway, what else was left to her except Jaromil?

Grandma was gradually losing her memory and her health. She sat at home darning Jaromil's socks and ironing her daughter's dresses. She was full of regrets, memories, and solicitous care. She exuded a loving, melancholy atmosphere. Jaromil thus lived in a house of women, a twice-widowed house.

3

His childhood bon mots no longer graced the walls of his room (Maman regretfully stored them away in a drawer); they were replaced by some twenty small cubist and surrealist reproductions which Jaromil had cut out of magazines and pasted on cardboard. A telephone receiver with a piece of wire dangling from it was also hanging on the wall (the legacy of a telephone repairman; in the severed receiver Jaromil perceived the kind of object which gains magic power by being torn out of its ordinary context, and which may rightfully be called a *surrealistic object*). However, the image which he gazed on most frequently was the reflection in the mirror hanging on the same wall. He studied nothing with greater care than his own face, nothing tormented him more than his face, and there was nothing in which he had greater faith (even though that faith was won at the cost of enormous effort):

This face resembled his mother's, but because he was a man the delicacy of its features was more striking: he had a beautiful, fine, tiny nose and a small, mildly receding chin. It was the chin that pained him so. He had read in Schopenhauer's famous essay that a receding chin was especially repulsive since it was the shape of the chin that differentiated man from the ape. But later Jaromil happened to come across a photograph of Rilke and found that he, too, had a receding chin and this gave him solace and encouragement. He would spend long periods of time gazing into the mirror, desperately oscillating in that enormous realm bounded by an ape at one end and Rilke at the other.

Actually, the retraction of Jaromil's chin was extremely slight, and Maman quite rightly considered her son's face to be that of an attractive child. But this was precisely what tormented Jaromil even more than the chin itself: the fineness of his features made him look several years younger, and, because his classmates were a year older than he, the childishness of his looks was striking, inescapable, continually alluded to, and Jaromil could not forget it for an instant.

What a burden it was, to carry such a face! What a heavy burden, those fragile, delicate features!

(Jaromil sometimes had terrible nightmares: he dreamt that he had to lift some extremely light object—a teacup, a spoon, a feather—and he couldn't do it. The lighter the object, the weaker he became, *he sank under its lightness*. He would wake up trembling, his face drenched. We believe that these dreams concerned his delicate face, as airy as a spider's web—a web which he vainly tried to brush off.)

4

Lyric poets generally come from homes run by women: the sisters of Esenin and Mayakovsky, the aunts of Blok, the grandmothers of Hölderlin and Lermontov, the nurse of Pushkin and, above all, of course, the mothers—the mothers that loom so large over the fathers. Lady Wilde and Frau Rilke dressed their sons like little girls. Is it a wonder that the boy kept gazing anxiously into mirrors? *It is time to become a man*, Orten wrote in his diary. The lyric poet spends a lifetime searching for signs of manhood in his face.

Jaromil kept staring at himself in the mirror until he saw what he longed to see: a hard expression in the eye, a cruel line of the mouth. To accomplish that, he of course had to put on a certain special smile, or, rather, sneer, in which his upper lip was convulsively drawn back. He also tried to change his face by changing the way he wore his hair. He tried to bunch it over his forehead to form thick, unruly locks. Alas! His hair, which Maman loved so much that she wore a lock of it in a medallion, was the worst possible kind for Jaromil's purposes: as yellow as the down of a newly hatched chicken, as delicate as dandelion fluff. There was no way to give it shape. His mother often stroked it and said it was the hair of an angel, but Jaromil hated angels and loved devils. He yearned to dye his hair black, but he didn't dare do it because tinting one's hair was even more effeminate than being blond. All he could do was let it grow as long as possible and keep it away from brush and comb.

He examined and adjusted his appearance at every opportunity. He never passed a single shopwindow without casting a quick look at himself. The closer he followed his own visage, the more familiar it became, but at the same time it also became more troubling and painful. Look:

He is coming home from school. The street is empty, except for a young woman walking toward him from afar. They are inevitably drawing closer and closer. Jaromil sees that the woman is beautiful and he thinks of his own face. He tries to put on his practiced cruel smile, but he fears that he won't succeed. He can think only of his silly face, the girlish childishness of which is making him ridiculous in the eyes of women. He is completely incarnated in that foolish little visage which is now stiffening and—horrors!—blushing. He speeds up his steps to cut down the chances of the woman looking at him, for if a beautiful woman were ever to catch him red-faced—he'd never live down the shame!

5

The hours spent in front of the mirror always plunged him to the very bottom of despair. Fortunately, however, there was another mirror which raised him to the stars. That heavenly mirror was his poetry; he thirsted for the verse he had not yet written and for that already created, he recollected his poems with the pleasure men get from remembering beautiful women; he was not only their author, but their theoretician and historian; he wrote essays about his poetry, he classified his works into individual stages, he designated these epochs with names, so that in the course of two or three years he learned to regard his poetry as a process of development worthy of a literary historian's loving attention.

This gave him solace: down *below*, he existed in a realm of everyday existence, where he went to school, lunched with Mother and Grandma, and faced a flat monotonous emptiness. But *up above* was another region, full of brightly lit guideposts where time was segmented into a brilliant spectrum. He enthusiastically leaped from one segment to another, confident each time that he was about to land in a new era, an era of immense creativity.

Another source of confidence was Jaromil's conviction that he was heir to a unique treasure, that in spite of the insignificance of his features (and of his life) he was one of the *elect*.

Let us clarify this word:

Jaromil continued to see the artist, but not too often, because Maman discouraged these visits; he had stopped sketching long ago, but on one occasion he had brought the artist some verse and from that time on he gradually showed him his whole stock of poems. The artist read them with keen interest and sometimes kept them to show his friends. That made Jaromil soar with joy, for the artist—who had once been so skeptical about his drawings—remained for Jaromil an unshakable authority. Jaromil believed there was an objective standard for measuring artistic value (enshrined in the minds of initiates like the platinum meter-bar preserved in a French museum), and that the artist was privy to it.

But one thing puzzled Jaromil: he could never guess beforehand which of his poems the artist would single out for approval. One day he would praise some little composition which Jaromil had dashed off with his left hand, and another time he would yawn over a poem which its author regarded as one of his masterpieces. What did that mean?

If Jaromil was unable to recognize the value of his own work, didn't that imply that he was creating poetry unwittingly, willy-nilly, automatically, without true comprehension, and therefore without true merit (just as he had charmed the artist with a world of dog-people created quite by accident)?

"Look here," the artist once said when the conversation touched on this topic, "the conception which you put into the poem wasn't the result of your conscious mind, was it? No, not at all: it just occurred, it happened, it came to you out of the blue, suddenly, unexpectedly. The real author of that idea is not you but somebody inside you, a poet inside your head. That poet is the mighty unconscious stream that flows through every human being. It's no accomplishment of yours that this stream—which plays no favorites—happened to pick you as its violin string."

The artist intended these words as a homily on modesty, but Jaromil at once discovered in them a glittering jewel to adorn his self-esteem. All right, suppose it wasn't he who created poetic images. All the same, some mysterious power had chosen him as its instrument. He could thus pride himself on something far greater than *merit*; he could pride himself on *election*.

Moreover, he had never forgotten the prediction of the lady at the spa resort: *that child has a great future ahead of him*. He believed in such statements as if they were prophecies. In Jaromil's mind, the future was the unknown realm beyond the horizon in which a hazy idea of revolution (the artist often spoke of its inevitability) merged with an equally vague idea of the bohemian freedom of poets. He knew that this realm of the future would be filled with his glory, and this awareness gave him a sense of security which coexisted (disconnected and independent) alongside all his painful doubts.

6

Ah, the long emptiness of afternoons, when Jaromil is locked in his room and gazes into his mirrors, now into one, now into the other!

How was it possible? After all, people were always saying that youth was the richest period of life! Why then did he feel such a lack of vital sap? Such emptiness?

That word was as unpleasant as the word "defeat." And there were other words which nobody dared say in his presence (at least at home, in that citadel of emptiness). For example, the word "love" or the word "girls." How he hated that trio of relatives occupying the ground floor! They often had parties lasting until the middle of the night, one could hear boisterous talk and laughter, the shrill voices of women which tore at the very soul of Jaromil huddled in a cocoon of blankets, unable to sleep. His cousin was only two years older, but those two years made all the difference. His cousin, a university student, brought attractive young ladies to his room (with the understanding approval of his parents) and treated Jaromil with benevolent unconcern. Jaromil's uncle was seldom home (he was preoccupied with the inherited business), but his aunt's voice continually resounded through the house. Whenever she met Jaromil, she asked him the same stereotyped question: *How are you doing with the girls?* Jaromil longed to spit in her face, because her condescendingly jovial question touched on the whole crux of his misery. Not that he didn't have any contact with girls, but his dates were rare events, as isolated as the stars in the sky. The word "girls" was depressing, like the word "loneliness" and the word "failure."

Though the actual time he spent with girls was so small, he spent hours in expectation before each date. Not in mere daydreaming, but in hard preparation. Jaromil was convinced that the success of a date depended first of all upon his ability to speak well, to avoid painful interludes of silence. A rendezvous was thus mainly an exercise in the art of conversation. He prepared a special notebook in which he wrote down suitable stories to recount. These were not anecdotes about other people, but stories about his own life. Because he had experienced so few adventures himself, he invented them. He used good taste: the stories which he made up (or read or heard) and in which he inserted himself as the main protagonist did not turn him into a hero. They were meant only to propel him inconspicuously across the boundary from a region of dreary immobility into a region of action and adventure.

He also copied out lines from various poems (we may note that these were not poems he himself especially admired) in which feminine beauty was extolled and which could be passed off as his own observations. For example, he jotted down the line: "A proud tricolor is your face: your lips, your eyes, your hair..." Such lines, with all rhythmic elements removed, would be told to a girl as a sudden original thought, like a witty compliment: "You know, I just realized that your face makes a lovely tricolor! Your eyes, mouth, hair. From now on I will serve under no other flag!"

Look: Jaromil is out on a date. He can think of nothing but his prepared lines, he worries that his voice seems unnatural, that his words sound as if he is reciting them by heart, like a bad amateur actor. At the last moment he decides not to use them, but because he's been concentrating on nothing else he has nothing to say. The evening turns out to be painful and awkward, Jaromil senses that the girl is secretly laughing at him, and he says good night with a feeling of utter defeat.

When he gets home he sits down at his desk and starts scribbling in hasty fury: *The glance of your eyes feels like lukewarm piss, I fire my flintlock at the flimsy sparrows of your stupid thoughts, fat frogs plop into a puddling pond between your thighs...*

He writes on and on, then reads his lines with great satisfaction, pleased with his ferocious, uninhibited fantasy.

I am a poet, I am a great poet, he tells himself, and writes it down in his diary: *I am a great poet, I have great sensitivity, I have diabolic fantasy, I dare to feel...*

Maman comes home and goes off to her room.

Jaromil stands in front of the mirror, examining his hateful childish face. He gazes at it so long until at last he discerns a glimmer of something extraordinary, something elect.

In the next room, Maman stretches on tiptoe to take her husband's gold-framed picture off the wall.

7

She had learned earlier that day that her husband had been having a prolonged love affair with a Jewish girl, even before the war. When the Germans occupied Bohemia and Jews had to wear the humiliating yellow stars on their sleeves he did not reject her, continued to see her, and helped her as much as he could.

Then they dragged her off to the Terezin ghetto and he decided on a mad scheme: with the help of a few Czech guards, he succeeded in smuggling himself into the closely guarded compound and in seeing his beloved for a few moments. Deceived by his success, he tried to repeat the exploit, was caught, and neither he nor the girl ever returned.

The invisible urn which Maman carried on her head was discarded, along with her husband's picture. There was no longer any reason for her to walk proudly erect, there was nothing left to make her carry her head high. All the moral pathos was now the legacy of others:

The voice of an old Jewish woman rang in her ears. She had been a relative of her husband's beloved, and had told her the whole story: "He was the bravest man I've ever known." And: "Now I'm all alone in the world. My whole family was wiped out in the concentration camp."

The Jewish woman sitting facing her was in the full majesty of her pain, whereas the suffering Maman was feeling had no glory at all. It was a mean pain, hunched miserably inside her.

8

You haystacks smoking in the mist
Burning the incense of her heart

he wrote, imagining a girl's body buried in the fields.

Death appeared very frequently in his poems. But Maman (who was still the first reader of all his compositions) was wrong in explaining this preoccupation as a premature ripening of her son's sensibility, brought on by untimely exposure to the tragedy of life.

The death which Jaromil wrote about had little to do with real death. Death takes on reality only when it begins to penetrate through the crevices of old age. For Jaromil it was infinitely far away; it was abstract; it was not reality, but a dream.

What was he seeking in that dream?

He was searching for immensity. His life was hopelessly small, everything around him was flat, gray. Death is absolute. It cannot be divided or diluted.

His real experience with girls was negligible (a few caresses and many meaningless words), but their absolute absence was majestic. When he imagined a girl buried in the fields, he suddenly discovered the nobility of sorrow and the grandeur of love.

Yet in his dreams of death he searched not only for the absolute, but for happiness as well.

He dreamed about a body slowly dissolving in the soil, and it seemed to him that this was a beautiful act of love, a sweet transformation of body into earth.

The world was continually wounding him. He blushed before women, he was ashamed, and he saw ridicule everywhere. In his fantasy of death, everything was still, and one could live uninterruptedly, silently, happily. Yes, Jaromil's death was *lived*. It bore a remarkable resemblance to that period when there is no need to enter the world because one is a world unto oneself, under the sweet arch of mother's belly.

He longed to be united with a woman in such a death, a death akin to eternal happiness. In one of his poems the lovers remained locked in an embrace until they grew into one another, until they became a single being incapable of movement, slowly transforming themselves into a solid mineral which would live for ages beyond time.

At other times he imagined that the lovers remain together for so immensely long a time that they are overgrown by moss and ultimately turn into moss themselves. Then someone accidentally steps on them and (because moss happens to be in bloom just then) they soar like pollen through space, as indescribably happy as only a pair of soaring lovers can be.

9

You think that just because it's already happened, the past is finished and unchangeable? Oh no, the past is cloaked in multicolored taffeta and every time we look at it we see a different hue. Just a short while ago Maman was reproaching herself for having betrayed her husband with the artist—and now she's in despair that out of a sense of loyalty to her husband she had betrayed her only true love.

What a coward she'd been! Her engineer-husband had been living a great romantic adventure, while she had had to content herself with dull leftovers, like a household servant. And to think that all the time she had been so tormented by anxiety and pangs of conscience that she had barely grasped the significance of her adventure with the artist before it rolled over her. Now she saw it all clearly: she had thrown away the only great opportunity which life had offered her heart.

The artist began to occupy her thoughts with feverish persistence. It should be noted that her memories were not projected upon the background of his city studio where she had known moments of sensual love, but upon the background of an idyllic landscape with river, boat, and the renaissance arcade of a small vacation spa. She set the scene of her paradise of the heart in those tranquil, relaxed days when love had not yet been born but only conceived. She longed to see the artist again, to beg him to return with her to that pastel-colored landscape of their first meetings so that they could relive their love story anew, freely, gaily, and without hindrance.

One day she climbed the stairs to his top-floor studio, but didn't ring the bell because she heard a talkative female voice behind the door.

During the next few days she walked back and forth in front of his house until she saw him. As usual, he was wearing his leather coat; he was taking a young girl to the tram station, leading her by the arm. When he started back she contrived to cross his path. He recognized her and greeted her with surprise. She pretended that she, too, was surprised by the unexpected encounter. He asked her up to his studio. Her heart started pounding, for she knew that at the first casual touch she would melt in his arms.

He offered her some wine, showed her his new paintings and smiled at her in a comradely fashion—the way we smile at the past. He never touched her at all, and escorted her back to the station.

10

One day when class was over and his schoolmates were clustered at the front of the room, Jaromil thought his moment had come; unnoticed, he made his way to the girl sitting alone at her desk; he had liked her for a long time, and they often exchanged long looks; now he sat down next to her. When their boisterous classmates saw them huddling together, they decided to play a practical joke; whispering and giggling, they crept out of the classroom and locked the door behind them.

As long as he had been surrounded by his classmates, Jaromil had felt inconspicuous and free, but as soon as he found himself all alone with the girl in the deserted classroom it was as if he were sitting on a brightly lit stage. He tried to conceal his uneasiness with witty conversation (by now he had learned to talk without relying entirely on prepared anecdotes). He said that the action of their classmates was a perfect example of a plan that had misfired: it was disadvantageous for the perpetrators (they were locked out and unable to satisfy their curiosity) and advantageous for the supposed victims (they were together just as they had wished). The girl agreed and said they should make full use of the situation. A kiss hung in the air. All he had to do was to lean closer. And yet he seemed to find the route to her lips long and difficult. He talked on and on, without a kiss.

Then the bell rang which meant that the teacher was about to return and to order the gang clustered outside to open the door. That roused the pair inside. Jaromil said that the best way to revenge themselves on the class was to make them envious. With his fingertip he touched the girl's lips (where did he get the courage?) and said with a smile

that a kiss by lips so beautifully painted would surely leave
an indelible mark on his face. She agreed it was a pity they
hadn't kissed each other. The teacher's angry voice could
already be heard in the hall.

Jaromil said that it was too bad neither the teacher nor
their fellow students would see the sign of a kiss on his face.
Once more he yearned to lean closer, and once more her
lips seemed as far away as Mount Everest.

"Come on, let's really make them jealous," said the
girl. She pulled a lipstick and a handkerchief out of her bag
and smeared Jaromil's face a bright red.

The door swung open and the class burst in, led
by the fuming teacher. Jaromil and the girl sprang to their
feet the way well-behaved students are supposed to stand
up when the teacher enters. They stood alone amid rows
of empty desks, facing a throng of spectators whose eyes
were glued to the beautiful red splotches on Jaromil's face.
He was happy and proud.

11

A colleague from Maman's office was courting her.
He was married and tried to persuade her to invite him to
her house.

She was anxious to find out what kind of attitude
Jaromil might take about her erotic freedom. She spoke to
him carefully and indirectly about widows of men who had
been killed in the war, and about the difficulties they were
having in starting a new life.

"What do you mean, 'a new life'?" he reacted angrily.
"You mean life with a new man?"

"Well, certainly, that's part of it, too. Life has to go
on, Jaromil, life has its needs..."

A woman's loyalty to a fallen hero belonged among

Jaromil's most sacred myths. It was a guarantee that the absolute power of love was not merely a poetic fiction, but a real value worth living for.

"How can women who have known a great love go on to wallow in bed with somebody else?" he berated faithless widows. "How can they bear to touch another man when they still remember a husband who had been tortured and killed? How can they torment him beyond the grave, to kill him a second time?"

The past is cloaked in multicolored taffeta. Maman rejected the pleasant colleague and her whole past once more took on an entirely different cast:

It wasn't true that she had betrayed the artist for her husband's sake—it had been for Jaromil's sake. She had wanted to safeguard a proper home for her son! If her own nakedness made her anxious to this day, it was because Jaromil had marred her belly forever. She had even lost her husband's love because of Jaromil, having stubbornly insisted on bringing him into the world.

From the very first, he had taken from her all she had!

12

Once (he had already known many kisses by then) he was strolling along the deserted paths of the Stromovka Park with a girl he met at dancing class. The pauses in their conversation kept getting longer and longer until at last the only sound they heard was that of their own footsteps, their common steps, which made them realize something they had not dared to face before: they were going on dates together. And if they were dating they must like one another. The sound of their footsteps confirmed this idea, their pace became slower and slower, until the girl suddenly put her head on Jaromil's shoulder.

It was an extremely beautiful moment, but before Jaromil could fully savor its magic he felt he was getting excited, and in a manner readily apparent to anyone. He tried to command his body to put an immediate end to this shameful display, but the more he tried the less he succeeded. He was terror-stricken by the thought that the girl's glance might move down his torso and come upon the compromising gesture of his body. He tried to turn her gaze upward by talking about clouds and birds in the treetops.

That walk was filled with bliss (no woman had ever rested her head on his shoulder before, a gesture which he regarded as a pledge of devotion reaching to the very end of his life), but at the same time the outing had covered him with shame. He was afraid that his body might repeat the painful indiscretion. After long deliberation, he took a long wide ribbon out of Maman's linen closet and before his next rendezvous made the proper arrangements under his trousers to make sure that the semaphore of his excitement would remain securely tied to his leg.

13

We selected this episode out of dozens in order to show that the pinnacle of happiness Jaromil had experienced up to this point in his life was having a girl's head on his shoulder.

A girl's head meant more to him than a girl's body. He didn't know much about the female body (What do beautiful legs look like, anyway? How do you judge a derrière?), whereas he felt confident in judging a face and in his eyes the face alone decided whether a woman was lovely or not.

We don't wish to imply that Jaromil was not interested in bodily beauty. The mere idea of a girl's nudity made him dizzy. But let us mark this fine distinction:

He didn't long for the nudity of a girlish body; he longed for a girlish face illumined by the nudity of her body.

He didn't long to possess a girl's body; he longed to possess the face of a girl who would yield her body to him as proof of her love.

The body was beyond the bounds of his experience, and for that very reason it became the subject of countless poems. How many times did the word "womb" appear in his poetry of that period? But through the magic of poetry (the magic of inexperience), Jaromil transmuted that organ of copulation and procreation into an airy conceit of fanciful dreams.

In one poem he wrote that the middle of a girl's body contained *a small ticking clock*.

In another line of verse he imagined that a girl's genitals were *the home of invisible beings*.

Then again he became enthused by the image of a ring and saw himself as a child's marble dropping endlessly through an opening until at last he turned into pure *fall forever falling through her body*.

In another poem a girl's legs turned into two rivers flowing together; at the point of their confluence he imagined a mysterious mountain which he called by the Biblical-sounding name Mount Hereb.

Another poem was about the long wanderings of a velocipede rider (the word *velocipede* seemed as beautiful to him as a sundown) cycling wearily through a landscape. That landscape was a girl's body, and two stacks of hay in which he longed to sleep were her breasts.

It was all so enchanting, this journey over a woman's body, an unseen, unrecognized, unreal body, free of any blemish, without imperfections or diseases, a totally fanciful body—an idyllic playground!

It was wonderful to write about wombs and breasts in the same tone used in telling fairy tales to children. Yes,

Jaromil was living in the land of tenderness, the land of *artificial childhood*. We say "artificial," because real childhood is no paradise, nor is it particularly tender.

Tenderness comes into being at the moment when life gives a person a sudden kick and propels him to the threshold of adulthood. He anxiously realizes all the advantages of childhood which he had not appreciated as a child.

Tenderness is fear of maturity.

It is the attempt to create a tiny artificial space in which it is mutually agreed that we would treat others as children.

Tenderness is also fear of the physical consequences of love. It is an attempt to take love out of the realm of maturity (in which it is binding, treacherous, full of responsibility and physicality), and to consider a woman as a child.

Her tongue is a gaily beating heart, he wrote in a line of verse. It seemed to him that her tongue, her little finger, breast, navel were independent beings conversing in inaudible voices. It seemed to him that a girl's body consisted of thousands of such beings, and that loving the body meant listening to that multitude of beings and hearing *her two breasts whispering in secret signs*.

14

She tormented herself with memories. But at last, as she contemplated the past, she gained a glimpse of the paradise in which she had lived with the infant Jaromil, and she changed her mind. No, it was not true that Jaromil was taking everything away from her; on the contrary, he had given her more than anybody else. He had given her a piece of life unsoiled by lies. No Jewess from a concentration camp could come and reduce that happiness to hypocrisy and emptiness. No, that piece of paradise was her only truth.

And the past (like a shifting kaleidoscope pattern) again looked different: Jaromil had never taken anything valuable from her, he had only torn aside the gilded curtain to reveal lies and hypocrisy. Even before his birth he had helped her to find out that her husband didn't love her, and thirteen years later he had saved her from a crazy adventure which would have brought her nothing but new sorrow.

She used to tell herself that the shared experience of Jaromil's childhood was a pledge and a holy contract for them both. But she came to realize more and more that her son was dishonoring that contract. When she talked to him she saw that he was barely listening and that his head was full of thoughts he had no intention of sharing with her. She learned that he was ashamed to tell her his little secrets, secrets of the body and of the mind, and that he was concealing himself behind veils which she could not penetrate.

It pained and irritated her. That sacred contract they had formed when he was a baby—did it not ensure that he would always trust her and confide in her without shame?

She yearned to resurrect the truth they had once shared during their existence in common. As she had when he was a small child, she told him every morning what clothes to wear, and through her choice of shorts and undershirt she was symbolically present all day long next to his body. When she sensed that this was annoying to him, she revenged herself by taking him to task for minor lapses of cleanliness in his underwear. She enjoyed tarrying in the room where he dressed and undressed, to punish him for his irritating sense of modesty.

"Jaromil, come here, let me see what you look like!" she called out once when guests were visiting the house. "My God, you're a sight!" she said loudly, when she noticed her son's carefully mussed-up hair. She fetched a comb and without interrupting her conversation with her company she proceeded to comb him. The great poet, endowed with diabolic fantasy and a face resembling Rilke's sat still—flushed and furious—and let himself be combed. The only sign of resistance was a cruel sneer (the one he had been practicing for years), frozen on his face.

Maman stepped back to survey the results of her tonsorial efforts, then turned to her guests. "Will somebody please tell me where that child of mine gets those ridiculous grimaces?"

And Jaromil swore eternal allegiance to radical transformation of the world.

15

When he arrived the debate was already in full swing. They were arguing about the definition of progress, and whether such a thing as progress really existed. He looked around and saw that the circle of young Marxists to whose meeting he had been invited by one of his classmates consisted of typical Prague high school students. There seemed to be more seriousness here than in the debates sponsored in his school by his Czech teacher, but even this meeting was not without the usual troublemakers. One of them was holding a wilted lily which he sniffed from time to time, causing waves of giggling, so that the short dark-haired man—in whose apartment they had gathered—at last had to take the flower away from him.

Then Jaromil pricked up his ears, because somebody proclaimed that one cannot talk of progress in art, and that nobody could claim Shakespeare to be inferior to contemporary dramatists. Jaromil was eager to join in the debate, but he found it difficult to address unfamiliar people. He was afraid that everybody would stare at his face, which would turn red, and at his hands, which would gesticulate awkwardly. And yet he was thirsting to *join* this small gathering, and he knew he could not do so without speaking.

To gather courage he thought of the artist, that great authority whom he never questioned, and reminded himself that he was his friend and disciple. That heartened him to such an extent that he finally dared to join the discussion and to repeat the ideas he had heard during his visits to the artist's studio. What was remarkable on this occasion was not that he wasn't speaking his own ideas, but that he wasn't even using his own voice. Jaromil himself was startled to hear that the voice coming out of his mouth resembled the artist's, and that this voice was affecting his hands, too, which began to mimic the artist's characteristic gestures.

Jaromil argued that in art, too, progress was indisputably taking place: modern currents represent a complete revolution in the thousand-year-old development of art. Art has finally been liberated from the duty to propagate political and philosophical views and to imitate reality, so that one could even say that the true history of art was only now beginning.

A few people wanted to break in at this point, but Jaromil refused to yield the floor. At first, he found it unpleasant to hear the artist's words and intonation issuing from his mouth but after a while he felt that this alter ego was a source of safety and reassurance; it concealed him like a shield. He stopped being nervous and shy. He liked the ring of his words, and continued:

He invoked Marx's idea that until modern times mankind had been living in prehistory, and that its real history began only with the proletarian revolution, which was a leap from the realm of necessity into that of freedom. In the history of art, a comparable decisive turning point was the moment when André Breton and other surrealists discovered automatic writing, revealing a hidden treasury of the human subconscious. It is symbolically significant that this occurred at about the same time as the socialist revolution in Russia. The liberation of the human imagination entailed the same leap into the realm of freedom as the liberation from economic thralldom.

At this point, the dark-haired man entered the debate. He praised Jaromil for defending the principle of progress, but expressed doubt that one could link surrealism so closely with the proletarian revolution. He stated his belief that modern art was decadent and that the epoch in art which best corresponded to the proletarian revolution was socialist realism. Not André Breton, but Jiří Wolker—the founder of Czech socialist poetry—must be our model!

Jaromil had come across such views before. In fact, the artist had described them to him, laughing sarcastically. Jaromil, too, now made attempts at a sarcastic laugh and responded that socialist realism was nothing new from an artistic viewpoint, but only a replica of the old bourgeois "kitsch." The dark-haired man said that the only art which is modern is the art that helps in the struggle to build a new world. This could hardly be said of surrealism, which was incomprehensible to the masses.

The discussion was interesting. The dark-haired man voiced his objections with charm and without dogmatism, so that the debate never turned into a quarrel—even though Jaromil, somewhat intoxicated by being the center of attention, occasionally resorted to excessively biting sarcasm. No final verdict was reached. Other people took the floor and the point Jaromil was discussing soon became covered over by other issues.

But was it really so important to determine whether or not progress existed, whether surrealism was a bourgeois movement or a revolutionary one? Did it really matter who was right, he or they? To Jaromil, all that really mattered was that he was now connected to them. He argued with them, but he felt warm sympathy for the group. He didn't even listen any longer, his mind was filled with happiness. He had found people among whom he no longer existed as a mother's son or a student in a class, but as his own self. And it occurred to him that a person can be his own self only when he is fully among others.

The dark-haired man rose and they all realized it was time for them, too, to take their leave because their leader had work to do, which he mentioned with a deliberate vagueness that bestowed upon him an aura of impressive importance. As they were gathered around the hallway door, ready to leave, a bespectacled girl approached Jaromil. Let us note at once that Jaromil had not paid the slightest attention to this girl throughout the meeting. Anyway, she was not at all striking, but rather nondescript—not ugly, just a little dumpy. Her hair was gathered smoothly over her forehead, without any particular hairdo, she was without makeup, and dressed in the kind of clothes worn only to avoid walking around naked.

"That was very interesting, what you were saying before," she told him. "I'd love to thrash it around a bit more with you."

16

There was a park not far from the dark-haired man's apartment. They went there, chatting excitedly. Jaromil found out that the girl was a university student and that she was two whole years older than he (which filled him with enormous pride). They strolled along the circular path, the girl making intellectual conversation, and Jaromil, too, speaking in a weighty manner. They were eager to let each other know what they thought, what they believed, who they were (the girl was oriented toward the sciences, Jaromil toward the arts). They compiled lists of all the great persons they admired and the girl repeated that she was fascinated by Jaromil's unconventional views. She was silent for a while, and she called him an *ephebus*; yes, as soon he walked into the room he seemed to her like an attractive ephebus...

Jaromil did not know exactly what the word meant but it seemed marvelous to get a special designation—and a Greek one to boot. He sensed that the word had something to do with youth; not with the kind of youth he knew from personal experience—awkward and degrading—but strong and admirable. Thus the girl university student was referring to his immaturity but at the same time she deprived it of its painful qualities and made it an advantage. It was encouraging that on their sixth round trip of the park Jaromil performed an act he had contemplated right from the start but for which he needed to gather sufficient courage: he took the girl by the arm.

"Took the girl by the arm" is not quite accurate. It would be more correct to say that he "eased his hand between her hip and her upper arm." He did it unobtrusively, as if he hoped the girl wouldn't even notice, and, indeed, she failed to react to his gesture in any way, so that his hand remained attached to her body as insecurely as some foreign object, a handbag or a package which she had forgotten and which was on the verge of dropping. But then suddenly the hand began to sense that the arm under which it was nestling was aware of its existence. And his legs began to realize that the girl's stride was gradually slowing down. He had experienced such a moment before and knew that something unavoidable hung in the air. And as generally happens when something unavoidable is near, people speed up the inevitable, at least by a second or two (perhaps to prove that they have at least some free will). In any case, Jaromil's hand, which had been limp all this time, came to life and squeezed the girl's arm. At that instant the girl stopped abruptly, lifted her spectacled face toward him and dropped her briefcase to the ground.

This gesture amazed Jaromil. First of all, in his be-witched state he had not even been aware that the girl was carrying anything. The briefcase thus dropped on the scene like a message from heaven. And when Jaromil realized that the girl had come to the Marxist discussion directly from the university, and that the briefcase probably con-tained material of higher learning and scholarly tracts, he became completely intoxicated. It seemed to him that she let all of the sciences and humanities fall to the ground just so she could grasp him in her liberated arms.

The fall of the briefcase was really so dramatic that they began kissing each other in a festive daze. The kissing went on for a long time, and when it finally exhausted itself and they were at a loss as to what to do next, she tilted her bespectacled visage toward his and her voice was full of anxious excitement: "I bet you think I'm like all the others! But let me tell you I'm not! I'm different."

These words were perhaps even more charged with pathos than the fall of the briefcase and Jaromil realized with amazement that he was with a woman who loved him, a woman who loved him at first sight, miraculously, without any effort on his part. And he quickly noted (on the margin of his consciousness, to be read and re-read more carefully later) the fact that she considered him so rich in experience as to cause pain to any woman who loved him.

He assured her that he didn't consider her to be like other women. She picked up her briefcase (now at last Jaromil could take a better look at it: it really was heavy and impressive-looking, full of books), and they set out on their seventh circuit of the park. When they stopped to kiss once more, they suddenly found themselves speared by a beam of bright light. Two policemen were facing them, de-manding identification.

The two abashed lovers fumbled for their identity cards. With trembling fingers they handed them over to the police-men, who were either intent on tracking down prostitutes or merely looking for a little amusement on a boring tour of duty. In any case, for the young couple it was a memorable incident: the whole rest of that evening (Jaromil saw the girl home) they discussed the plight of true love menaced by prejudice, narrow-minded philistine morality, police stupidity, the old generation, outmoded laws, and the general rotten state of the world.

17

It had been a beautiful day and a beautiful evening, but when Jaromil finally got home it was almost midnight and Maman was anxiously pacing from room to room.

"I was worried sick! Where have you been? You have no regard for me at all!"

Jaromil was still overflowing with his great experience and he started to answer Maman in the manner he had used at the Marxist circle, imitating the artist's self-confident voice.

Maman recognized it at once. She heard her son addressing her with the voice of her lost lover. She saw a face that didn't belong to her, she heard a voice that didn't belong to her. Her son was standing before her like a symbol of a double denial. She found it unbearable.

"You're killing me! You're killing me!" she shouted hysterically and ran off into the adjoining room.

Jaromil remained standing in his tracks. He was frightened, and a sense of some dark guilt began to spread over him.

(Alas, dear Jaromil, you will never get rid of that feeling! You are guilty, you are guilty! Every time you leave the house you will carry with you a look of reproach, calling you back! You will walk the world like a dog on a long leash! Even when you are far away you will still feel the collar around your neck! And even when you are with women, even when you are lying in bed with them, a long leash will be attached to your neck and somewhere far, far away Maman will hold its end in her hands, feeling from its vibrations the shameful movements of your body!)

"Maman, please don't be angry, please forgive me!" He was kneeling anxiously at her bedside, stroking her damp face.

(Charles Baudelaire, you'll be over forty years old and you'll still be afraid of her, your mother!)

And Maman waited a long time before forgiving him, to feel as long as possible the touch of his fingers on her skin.

18

(None of this could ever have happened to Xavier, for Xavier had neither mother nor father, and absence of parents is the first precondition of freedom.

But please understand, it is not a question of losing one's parents. Gérard de Nerval's mother died when he was an infant, and yet he spent his whole life under the hypnotic gaze of her beautiful eyes.

Freedom does not begin when parents are rejected or buried; freedom dies when parents are born.

He is free who is unaware of his origin.

He is free who is born of an egg dropped in the woods.

He is free who is spat out from the sky and touches the earth without a pang of gratitude.)

19

During the first week of his love affair with the university student, Jaromil felt himself to be reborn. He heard himself described as an ephebus, he was told that he was beautiful, intelligent, and full of fantasy. He found out that the young lady with glasses loved him and that she trembled with fear lest he leave her (she told him that after they had said good night and she watched him walk away with airy steps, she saw what he was really like: a man moving away, receding, disappearing...). At last he found his real portrait, which he had so long been seeking in both of his mirrors.

That first week they saw each other every day. They spent three evenings taking long evening strolls through the city, one night they went to the theater (they sat in a box, kissed, and paid no attention to the performance), and twice they went to the movies. The seventh day they again went for a walk. It was bitter cold out, he was wearing a light topcoat, no sweater under his jacket (the gray knitted vest which Maman urged him to wear seemed fit only for a country bumpkin), he had no cap or hat (the girl had praised his tousled hair, remarking that it was as unruly as he himself). Because the elastic bands on his long dress socks were loose, and the socks always kept sliding down his calves, he was wearing short gray socks (he had overlooked the lack of harmony between socks and trousers, for such fine points of elegance were beyond him).

They met around seven o'clock and started out on their trek to the outskirts of the city, across vacant suburban lots where the snow crunched under their feet; now and then, they stopped to kiss. Jaromil was enormously impressed by the loyalty of her body. Up till then, his affairs with girls had resembled a tedious climb in which he gradually made his way from one stage to the next: it took a long while before a girl would let him kiss her, another long while before he was allowed to put his hand over her breast, and when at last he managed to touch her rear end he considered himself to have gone quite a way—after all, he never got any further. This affair, however, was different from the very beginning. The girl was completely limp in his arms, defenseless, ready for anything, he could touch her wherever he pleased. He took it as a great sign of love, but at the same time it embarrassed him for he didn't quite know what to do with the unexpected liberty.

And that day (the seventh day) the girl told him that her parents were often away from home, and that she was looking forward to inviting Jaromil to her house. After the dazzling explosion of these words there was prolonged silence; both of them realized what a meeting in an empty house would mean (let us recall that the young lady was quite defenseless in Jaromil's arms). They kept still, and only after a momentous pause did the girl say in a quiet voice, "I believe that in matters of the heart there is no such thing as compromise. Love means that you give each other everything."

Jaromil couldn't agree more, for he, too, believed that love meant everything. But he didn't know what to say; instead of answering he stopped, gazed at the girl with pathos (forgetting that it was night and that pathos is difficult to recognize in the dark), and proceeded to hug and kiss her furiously.

After a quarter of an hour of silence, the girl became talkative once more and told him that he was the first man she had ever invited to her house. She said that she had many male friends, but they were no more than that— friends. They were used to it and jokingly called her *the stone maiden*.

Jaromil was happy to learn that he was to be the stone

maiden's first lover, but at the same time he felt a touch of stage fright. He had heard all sorts of stories about the act of love and he knew that depriving a girl of her virginity was generally considered a rather difficult matter. He found his thoughts wandering, and he had trouble joining in the girl's conversation. He was immersed in the joys and anxieties of that great promised event which would mark the true beginning of his life's history (it occurred to him that this idea was similar to Marx's famous dictum about mankind's leap from prehistory into history).

Even though they didn't talk much, they strolled through the city for a very long time. As night deepened, it was becoming colder and Jaromil felt the cold penetrating his thinly clad body. He suggested they find a place to warm up, but they were too far from the center of town and there was no tavern or other public place anywhere in sight. When he got home at last he was frozen through and through (toward the end of the stroll he had to try hard to keep his teeth from chattering). When he woke up the next morning his throat hurt badly. Maman fetched a thermometer and determined that he had a fever.

20

Jaromil's body was lying sick in bed, while his soul dwelled in contemplation of the great upcoming event. Anticipation of that date consisted of abstract happiness and concrete worry. For Jaromil had no idea at all what making love to a woman was all about, in terms of the various specific details involved. He knew only that such an act required preparation, skill, and knowledge. He knew that behind physical love leered the threatening grimace of pregnancy, and he realized (this had been discussed innumerable times with schoolmates) that there were ways of preventing it. In those barbaric times, men (like knights donning their armor before battle) put on a kind of transparent little sock over their amorous extremity. From a theoretical viewpoint Jaromil was richly informed about such matters. But how can such a little sock be procured? Jaromil would be too ashamed to ask for one in a drugstore! And how could he put it on without the girl noticing it? The little sock seemed embarrassing to him, and he couldn't bear the idea that the girl might find out about it. Was it possible to put it on beforehand, at home? Or was it necessary to wait until he was standing naked before the girl?

He had no answers for such questions. Moreover, he did not have any of those transparent socks, but he told himself he must get one at all cost and try putting it on. He imagined that success in this matter depended largely on speed and skill, and that these could not be achieved without practice.

He was worried about other things, too. What was the love act really like? What does a person feel? What goes on in his body? What if the pleasure is so vast that it makes a person scream out loud and lose control of himself? Wasn't that going to make him look ridiculous? And how long did the whole thing last? Ah, good Lord, was it at all possible to embark on something like that without preparation?

Until that time Jaromil had not yet experienced masturbation. He regarded such activity as something unworthy, which a real man should avoid. He thought of himself as destined not for self-abuse but for great love. All the same, how can great love be consummated without a certain amount of preparation? Jaromil came to believe that masturbation was an indispensable part of such an initiation, and he eased his fundamental opposition toward it. He no longer regarded it as a pitiful substitute for physical love, but as a necessary step toward that goal; it was not a confession of poverty but a foundation for riches.

Thus he came to perform his first rehearsal of the love

act (during a bout of fever two and two-tenths of a degree above normal). He was surprised to learn that it lasted a very short time, and that it failed to stimulate him to any shouts of rapture. This was both disappointing and reassuring. In the next few days he repeated the experiment a few more times but failed to glean any additional information. He felt, however, that he was gaining ever greater control by this means, and that he was now able to face his beloved with utter confidence.

He had been lying in bed with a flannel bandage wound around his neck for some three or four days when Grandma swept into his room shortly after breakfast and said excitedly, "Jaromil! The whole town's gone crazy!" He sat up. "What happened?" Grandma explained that the radio downstairs announced that a revolution had broken out. Jaromil jumped out of bed, ran to the next room, turned on the radio and heard the voice of Klement Gottwald.

He grasped the situation at once, for in recent days he had heard a lot of talk about it (it didn't interest him too much, for as we know he had more serious matters on his mind): the three noncommunist ministers had threatened communist premier Gottwald with resignation. And now he heard Gottwald addressing a throng in Old Town Square. He was denouncing the traitors who had planned to cripple the Communist Party and to block the nation's progress toward socialism. He exhorted the people to insist on the resignation of the ministers, while new revolutionary organs of power under the leadership of the Communist Party were being organized.

The old radio crackled as Gottwald's words were drowned out by the thunderous acclaim of the crowd. All this excited and enthused Jaromil, who was standing in his pajamas in Grandma's room, his neck all bandaged up, shouting hoarsely: "At last! It had to come! At last!"

Grandma was not quite sure whether Jaromil's enthusiasm was justified. "You really think this is a good thing?"

she asked in a worried tone. "Yes, Grandma, it is good. It is excellent!" He embraced her and began pacing excitedly up and down the room. He told himself that the crowd gathered in the square had hurled today's date high into the sky where it would shine like a star for centuries. And it occurred to him what a shame it was that on such a glorious day he was stuck at home with Grandma rather than being out in the streets with the people. But before he had time to think this idea through, the door burst open and his uncle appeared, flushed and excited, shouting: "You hear what's going on? Those whores! Those lousy whores! Pulling off a putsch like that!"

Jaromil glanced at his uncle whom along with his wife and conceited son he had always hated. And it seemed to him that his moment of triumph had come at last. They stood facing each other. The uncle had the door at his back, while Jaromil was backed by the radio, which made him feel supported by an enormous throng a hundred thousand strong, and when he addressed his uncle it was as a hundred thousand address a single individual. "It's not a putsch, it's a revolution," he said.

"Shove your revolution up your ass," the uncle replied. "It's easy to pull off a revolution when you've got the army behind you and the police and a certain big country besides."

When he heard his uncle's pompous voice, talking to him as if he were a snot-nosed little boy, Jaromil's hatred went to his head. "The army and police are needed to keep a handful of bastards from turning the rest of us into a bunch of slaves again."

"You little jackass," replied Jaromil's uncle, "the reds already had most of the power in their hands anyway. They pulled this putsch so they could grab all of it. Christ, I always knew you were a dumb little jerk."

"And I always knew that the working class would sweep capitalist parasites like you into the dust bin of history!"

Jaromil made the last remark in anger, almost without thinking. All the same, let us examine it. He used words which appeared over and over in communist newspapers and in speeches of communist orators, but Jaromil had always disliked them just as he disliked all jargon. He considered himself first and foremost a poet, and even though he held revolutionary opinions he was determined never to give up his own words. And yet he had just spoken of capitalist parasites and the dust bin of history.

Yes, that was remarkable! In the midst of excitement (and thus at a moment of spontaneity when the true self is speaking) Jaromil discarded his own speech and chose to act as a medium for someone else. Moreover, he did so with a sense of intense pleasure; he felt himself to be part of a thousand-headed multitude, one organ of a hydra-headed dragon, and that seemed magnificent. He now felt strong enough to stare down people who only yesterday made him blush and stammer. The raw simplicity of the statement (sweep capitalist parasites into the dust bin) made him happy, because it placed him in the ranks of those direct and simple men who laugh at nuances and whose wisdom lies in their understanding of the ridiculously simple essentials of life.

Jaromil (in pajamas, his neck swathed in flannel), arms akimbo, legs straddled, stood firmly planted in front of the radio which was blaring out an enormous ovation. It seemed to him that this din was flowing into him and filling his body with strength, until he loomed over his uncle like a giant tree or rock roaring with laughter.

And his uncle, who considered Voltaire the father of volts, stepped up and gave Jaromil a resounding slap.

Jaromil felt a stinging pain on his face. He was humiliated, and because he felt as great and powerful as a tree or rock (the hydra-headed dragon was still roaring behind him), he wanted to leap at his uncle and revenge himself. But it took him a while to reach this decision, and in the meantime his uncle had turned on his heel and left the room.

Jaromil shouted after him, "I'll get even! I'll get even, you swine!" and ran toward the door. But Grandma caught him by his pajama sleeve and succeeded in calming him down. Jaromil kept muttering *the swine, the dirty swine* and went back to the bed which he had left—along with his dreams of the girl—less than an hour before. He was no longer able to think about her. He still saw his uncle before his eyes and felt the sting on his face. He reproached himself for not having acted more like a man. In fact, he reproached himself with such bitterness that he began to sob and wet his pillow with furious tears.

Maman came home late that afternoon and anxiously recounted the day's events. They had lost no time in removing the director of her department, for whom she had great respect, and all the noncommunists in the office feared they would soon be arrested.

Jaromil propped himself up on his elbow and passionately joined the conversation. He explained to his mother that what was happening was a revolution, and that revolutions were brief interludes requiring a certain amount of violence so that violence could be done away with once and for all through the establishment of a just society. Mother had to get that through her head.

Mamam responded heatedly, but Jaromil was ready for all her objections. He attacked the stupidity of rich men's rule, the rule of a society of entrepreneurs and tradesmen, and he cleverly reminded Maman that her own family included such types and that they made her suffer. He pointed to the stuffiness of her sister and the vulgarity of her brother-in-law.

Maman began to waver and Jaromil was pleased by the success of his words. He felt avenged for the slap dealt him earlier. When he recalled the incident his bile was again aroused. "Mother, today I made a big decision," he announced. "I'm joining the Communist Party."

When he detected disapproval in his mother's eyes, he elaborated on his statement. He said he was ashamed he hadn't joined a long time ago; only the burden of his family background kept him separated from his true comrades.

"Are you trying to say you're sorry you were born in this house? Are you ashamed of your mother?"

Maman sounded deeply hurt and Jaromil quickly added that she had misunderstood: in his opinion, his mother—her underlying real self—had nothing in common with her sister or the society of the rich.

But Maman said, "If you care for me at all, don't do it. You know how hard it is living here with your uncle. If he found out you'd joined the communists all hell would break loose. Be sensible, I beg you!"

A wave of self-pity rose in Jaromil's throat. Instead of returning his uncle's slap, he had just received another one. He turned his face away, and as soon as Maman left the room he broke once more into sobs.

21

It was six o'clock in the evening. The girl greeted him at the door in a white apron, and led him into a cozy kitchen. The supper turned out to be nothing special—scrambled eggs and salami—but it was the first time that any woman (not counting Maman and Grandma) had cooked a meal for him, so he ate with the self-assurance of a man looked after by his beloved.

Then they went into the next room. It contained a round mahogany table with a knitted cover, weighed down by a massive glass vase: awful pictures hung on the wall. One side of the room was taken up by a couch richly endowed with small pillows. Everything had been settled and arranged for the evening, so that all they had to do was to sink into the soft upholstery. But oddly enough, the girl sat down on a hard chair by the round table and he did the same. For a long, long time they remained sitting on the hard chairs chatting about this and that, until Jaromil's throat became tense with anxiety.

He had to be home by eleven. He had pleaded with his mother to let him stay out all night (he told her his schoolmates were having some sort of party), but his mother's disapproval was so sharp that he didn't dare press the matter further. Now he could only hope that the four hours still remaining would be sufficient to consummate his first act of love.

But the girl talked on and on, and the allotted interval was rapidly dwindling. She talked about her family, about her brother who had once attempted suicide because of unrequited love. "That marked me for life. I can't be like other girls. I can't take love lightly," she said, and Jaromil realized that those words were supposed to add solemnity to the promised enjoyment of physical love. He rose from the chair, bent over her, and said in a very serious voice, "I understand you, yes, I understand." He then helped her get up from the chair, led her to the couch, and eased her down.

They kissed, hugged, and caressed. That took an extremely long time. Jaromil kept thinking it was time for him to undress the girl, but because he had never done such a thing before he didn't know how to begin. First of all, he didn't know whether to turn the light off or leave it on. According to all the reports he had heard about similar situations, he was under the impression that he should turn it off. Anyway, he had a package of the transparent little socks in his jacket and if at the decisive moment he was to put on one of them discreetly and unobtrusively, darkness was essential. But in the midst of the hugging he couldn't seem able to just get up and walk to the light-switch, quite aside from the fact that such an action seemed rather ill-mannered to him (let us not forget that he was well brought up), he was in someone else's house, and after all it was really up to the hostess to turn lights on or off. At last, he managed to ask shyly, "Shouldn't we turn off the light?"

The girl answered, "No, no, please don't." Jaromil didn't know what that meant—whether the girl was rejecting greater intimacy, or whether she did want to make love but not in the dark. Of course, he could have asked her but he was afraid to put such thoughts into actual words.

Then he recalled once more that he had to be home by eleven, and he forced himself to overcome his shyness. He unbuttoned the first female button of his life. It was the top button of her white blouse and he was anxiously awaiting her response. She didn't say anything. He therefore proceeded to unbutton her further, pulled her blouse out from the waistband of her skirt, and at last managed to take her blouse off altogether.

She was now resting on the pillows, clad in a skirt and a bra. Strangely enough, although she had been eagerly kissing Jaromil just a short while before, now that she was partly undressed she seemed petrified. She didn't move, and she held her bosom stiffly like a condemned prisoner defying a firing squad.

Jaromil had no choice but to undress her further. He felt the zipper on the side of her skirt and opened it. The poor fellow knew nothing about the hook which held the skirt at the waist, and for a frustrating few minutes he tried unsuccessfully to pull the skirt down over the girl's hips. The girl, still holding out her chest against an invisible execution squad, was no help at all, probably not even aware of his difficulties.

Ah, let us mercifully skip over some fifteen or twenty minutes of Jaromil's torment. He succeeded at last in disrobing the girl completely. When he saw how devotedly she was lying on the pillows, awaiting the moment they had been planning for such a long time, he realized there was no way of avoiding getting undressed himself. But the chandelier was shining brightly and Jaromil was ashamed to take his clothes off. He thought of an idea: next to the living room he glimpsed the bedroom (an old-fashioned bedroom with large marital beds); the light was turned off there; he could undress there in the dark and even cover himself with a quilt.

"Can't we move to the bedroom?" he suggested reticently.

"Why? What do we need the bedroom for?" the girl laughed.

We don't know why she laughed. It was laughter that was unnecessary, accidental, uneasy. Nevertheless, it hurt Jaromil. He feared that he had said something stupid, that his idea of going to the bedroom had betrayed his ridiculous inexperience. At once he felt completely crestfallen and forsaken, in a strange room under the probing light of a chandelier, with a strange woman who was making fun of him.

At that instant he realized that no love would be possible between them that evening. He sat sulkily on the couch; he was sorry for what had happened, but at the same time he was relieved. There was no longer any need to agonize over putting on the light or turning it off or getting undressed. And he was glad it wasn't his fault. She shouldn't have laughed so stupidly.

"What's the matter?" she asked.

"Nothing," said Jaromil. He knew that if he were to explain the reason for his bad mood, he would only make himself even more ridiculous. He therefore controlled himself, lifted her from the couch, and proceeded to look her over with pretended nonchalance (he wanted to become master of the situation and it seemed to him that the person who examines is master of the person being examined). He said at last, "You're quite pretty, you know."

Once the girl got up from the couch on which she had been waiting in rigid expectation, she felt herself completely liberated. She was restored to her talkative, self-confident self. She didn't at all mind being stared at (perhaps she felt that the person who is examined is master of the one doing the examining). She asked, "Am I prettier dressed or with nothing on?"

There are several classic feminine questions which every man encounters during his lifetime and which young men should be instructed about as part of their education. But Jaromil, like the rest of us, had attended the wrong schools and had no idea what to answer. He tried to guess what answer the girl wanted to hear, but he was confused. A girl generally appears before people with her clothes on, and therefore she ought to be pleased that she is pretty that way. On the other hand, nakedness may be considered a state of physical truthfulness, and from that point of view it should make her happier to be told that she is more attractive in the nude.

"You're beautiful dressed and undressed," he said, but the girl was not at all pleased with that evasion. She skipped about in the room, posed before Jaromil, and urged him to give her a straight answer. "I want to know which way you like me better."

When the question was put in this more personal way, the answer was easier. If other people knew her only as she looked when dressed, it seemed tactless to him to have said that she was less attractive that way. But if she was now asking him for his subjective opinion, he could safely declare that he personally liked her better naked, because this answer implied that he liked her just as she was—that he appreciated her true, unvarnished self that had no need for artificial finery.

His judgment was apparently correct, for when the girl heard his verdict she reacted very favorably. She didn't put her clothes back on until after his departure, she kissed him many times, and as he was leaving (it was a quarter to eleven, Maman would be pleased), she whispered in his ear, "Tonight I found out that you really love me. You're nice, and you really do care for me. Yes, you're right, this way is better. We'll save it for a while, we'll have something to look forward to."

22

In those days he began writing a long poem. It was a narrative poem about a man who suddenly realized that he was old; a man who found himself deserted and forgotten, *beyond the last way-station of fate:*

> *they're whitewashing his walls*
> *and moving out his things;*
> *nothing is left the way it used to be.*

He flees from the house, pursued by relentless Time and he rushes back to where he had lived the most intensive period of his life:

> *back stairs, third floor, second door in rear,*
> *faded name on plate too dim to read.*
> *"Twenty years have passed, please take me in!"*

An old woman opens the door, startled from careless apathy after years of solitude. She bites her lips which had not known color for so long; with a long neglected gesture she tries to fix her sparse, unwashed hair; awkwardly she stretches out her arms to conceal from him the photographs of old lovers hanging on the wall. And then she suddenly realizes that all is well, that appearances no longer matter.

Twenty years and you returned
The last important meeting
of my life...

Yes, all is well. Nothing matters any longer, neither wrinkles, nor shabby clothes, nor yellowed teeth, nor wispy hair, nor sagging skin, nor bloodless lips. There is something far better than beauty or youth:

Certainty.
Life's last
and kindest gift.

And he crosses the room, wearily trailing his hand over the table-top

his limp glove erasing
fingermarks of ancient loves.

He recognizes that she had known many men, throngs of lovers who

squandered all the splendor of her skin.

A long-forgotten song stirs in his soul. Lord, what is that song?

Afloat, afloat on beds of sand...

You are drifting, drifting, until nothing is left but your core, your own heart's core.

She realizes that he, too, has nothing to give her, nothing firm or youthful. But

these moments of fatigue
that now come over me
these testaments to nature's
clean and calm and necessary course
these I bequeath to you alone...

Deeply moved, they touch each other's wrinkled faces. He calls her "my girl," she calls him "my dearest boy," and they cry.

> There was nothing in between
> no mediating look or word
> to conceal his wretchedness—or hers.

It is precisely that mutual wretchedness which they thirst after with their parched tongues. They drink it greedily from each other. They stroke each other's pitiful bodies and hear the engines of death quietly humming under one another's skin. And they know they belong to one another, completely and forever, that this is their last and their greatest love because the last love is always the greatest.

The man thought:

> This love has no door leading out
> this love is like a wall...

And the woman thought:

> Death may still be far away in time
> but its likeness now is near us both.
> Sunk deep in our chairs our work is done.
> Our feet have found their peace, our hands
> no longer need to touch...
> There's nothing more to do
> but wait for spittle at the mouth
> to turn to dew.

When Maman read this strange composition, she was as usual amazed by her son's extraordinary maturity—a maturity that enabled him to comprehend a stage of life so far removed from his own. She did not see that the characters in the poem did not at all express the real psychology of old age. Nor did Jaromil's girl, when he finally showed her the poem, grasp its real nature when she described it as necrophilic.

No, the poem had nothing to do with an old man or an old woman. If we were to ask Jaromil how old the two characters were, he'd stammer in embarrassment and say they were somewhere between forty and eighty. All he knew about old age was that it was a time when a person had passed his maturity; when fate had ended; when there was no longer any need to fear that terrible mystery called the future; when every love that came along was certain and final.

Actually, Jaromil was full of anxiety; he approached the nude body of a woman as if he were treading on thorns. He longed for a body but he was afraid of it. That was why in his erotic poems he fled from the concreteness of the body into a world of childish playfulness. He deprived the body of reality, and imagined the female genital organ as a humming toy. In this poem, he fled in the opposite direction: into old age, where the body was no longer dangerous or exalted, but miserable and pitiful; the wretchedness of an old body reconciled him somewhat to the pride of a youthful female body, destined to become old some day.

The poem was full of naturalistic ugliness. Jaromil did not forget the yellow teeth nor the crust in the corners of the eye nor the sagging belly. But behind the harshness of these details was a deep longing to confine love to its eternal, constant element, to that part of love which could replace a mother's embrace, which is not subject to time, which represents "a true heart" capable of overcoming the power of the body, the treacherous physicality stretching out before him like uncharted terrain rampant with ferocious beasts.

He wrote poems about an artificial childlike love, about an unreal death, and about an unreal old age. These were the three pale bluish flags under which he was nervously marching toward the very real body of an adult woman.

23

When she arrived (Maman and Grandma had gone to the country for a few days), he didn't turn on the lights at all, even though it was already getting dark. They had their supper and then they sat in Jaromil's room. Around ten o'clock (that was the time when Maman generally sent him off to bed), he uttered a phrase he had been practicing all day so as to be able to say it quite simply and casually: "Shall we go to bed?"

She nodded, and Jaromil made the bed. Yes, everything was going according to plan, without a snag. The girl was undressing in a corner and Jaromil was undressing (much more clumsily) in the other. Quickly, he put on his pajamas (the packet with the condoms had already been carefully placed in the pajama pocket), then scrambled under the covers (he knew that the pajamas were not becoming to him, they were too big and made him look small). He watched the girl as she undressed (ah, in the twilight she seemed even more beautiful than last time).

She slid into bed next to him, snuggled up, and proceeded to kiss him furiously. After a while it occurred to Jaromil that it was high time to open the little packet. He reached into his pocket and tried to lift it out as inconspicuously as possible. "What are you looking for?" asked the girl. "Nothing," he answered, and quickly placed the hand that was about to grasp the packet on the girl's breast. Then he decided that the best thing to do was to excuse himself for a moment, go to the bathroom, and prepare himself properly. But as he was going through these deliberations (the girl continued to kiss him), he noticed that the excitement he had felt at first in all its physical obviousness was waning. That threw him into new confusion, for he realized that now there was no longer any point in opening the packet. He therefore tried to caress the girl passionately, at the same time anxiously watching to see whether the lost excitement was returning. It was not. Under his uneasy scrutiny his body seemed to be seized with fear. If anything, it was shrinking rather than growing.

The love play no longer afforded him any pleasure; it was only a screen behind which he was tormenting himself, desperately calling his body to obedience. The stroking, caressing, and kissing went on and on and it was an endless agony, a totally silent agony for Jaromil didn't know what to say and it seemed to him that any word would only call attention to his shame. The girl was silent, too, because she probably began to sense that something shameful was happening without knowing precisely whether the fault was his or hers. In any case, something was going on for which she was unprepared and which she feared to name.

When the terrible pantomime had at last exhausted itself, each of them dropped back on the pillow and tried to go to sleep. It is hard to say how long they slept or whether they actually slept at all or only pretended to, in order to be able to hide from one another.

When they got up in the morning, Jaromil was afraid to look at her; she seemed agonizingly beautiful, all the more beautiful as he had failed to possess her. They went into the kitchen, cooked breakfast, and tried laboriously to conduct a casual conversation.

She said at last, "You don't love me."

Jaromil started to assure her that it wasn't true, but she interrupted: "No, it's useless, I don't want to hear your stories. It's stronger than you are, and last night it all came out. You don't love me enough. You saw it for yourself."

Jaromil intended to convince her that his failure had nothing to do with the strength of his love, but then he changed his mind. The girl's words had given him an unexpected opportunity for hiding his shame. It was a thousand times easier to put up with the reproach that he didn't love her than to accept the idea that there was something wrong with his body. He therefore said nothing and gazed at the floor. When the girl repeated the same accusation, he said in a voice which was intentionally supposed to sound uncertain and unconvincing, "Don't be silly, I do love you."

"You're lying," she said, "you love somebody else."

That was even better. Jaromil bowed his head and sadly shrugged his shoulders, as if admitting there was some truth to this allegation.

"There's no point to it if it isn't the real thing," she said somberly. "I told you that I don't know how to take these things lightly. I can't stand the idea of being just a substitute for someone else."

Although the night he had just lived through had been full of torment, there was still a chance for Jaromil to try repeating it with more success. That's why he said, "No, you're not being fair. I do love you. I love you very much. But there is one thing I should have told you. It is true, there is another woman in my life. That woman loved me and I've done her a terrible wrong. That wrong is now oppressing me like a dark shadow. I'm helpless. Please try to understand. It wouldn't be fair of you to stop seeing me, because I love you and nobody else."

"I didn't say I didn't want to see you anymore. But I won't put up with any other woman, not even a shadow. Try to understand me! For me love is everything, it's the absolute. In love I know no compromise."

Jaromil looked at the girl's spectacled face and his heart ached at the thought that he might lose her; she seemed to be so close to him, she seemed to be able to understand him. All the same, he couldn't risk telling her the truth. He had to pretend to be somebody over whom lay a fateful shadow, somebody torn apart and worthy of pity.

"You talk about absolute love," he said, "but doesn't that mean above all else understanding the other person and loving everything about him—even his shadows?"

That was a well-put argument, and the girl paused over it. It seemed to Jaromil that perhaps everything was not lost after all.

24

He hadn't shown her his poems yet. He had been waiting for the artist to fulfill his promise and have the verse published in some avant-garde journal so that he could dazzle her with the glory of a printed page. But now he badly needed his poetry to come to his aid. He was convinced that once the girl read his poems (especially the one about the old couple), she'd understand and be moved. He was wrong. Perhaps she thought that she owed her younger friend some objective critical advice. Be that as it may, she demolished him by the casual matter-of-factness of her remarks.

What had happened to the marvelous mirror of her enthusiastic admiration in which he had once discovered his uniqueness? In all mirrors, he now saw only the leering grimace of his immaturity and that was unbearable. It was then that the name of a famous poet came to his mind, a poet illumined by the halo of membership in the European avant-garde and participation in local eccentricities. Although he didn't know him and had never even laid eyes on him, Jaromil was seized by a blind faith felt by simple believers toward high priests of their church. He sent him his poems with a humble, pleading letter. He dreamed about the answer he would get, friendly and admiring and this fantasy descended like a balm over his meetings with the girl, which were getting to be rarer and rarer (she claimed she was going through an exam period and had little time) and sadder and sadder.

He was cast back into a period (actually not very distant) when conversation with any woman seemed difficult and required prior preparation. Now, again, he was anticipating every date several days in advance, carrying on imaginary conversations for whole evenings at a time. In these mental dialogues, the figure of the "other woman," about whose existence the girl had expressed her misgivings, loomed ever more mysteriously yet distinctly. She imbued Jaromil with the glow of a richly lived past, she stimulated jealous interest, and she explained his body's lack of success.

Unfortunately, she appeared only in imaginary discussion, for she had quickly and inconspicuously faded from real conversation between Jaromil and the girl, who had lost interest in this supposed rival as unexpectedly as he had first brought her up. That was disquieting to Jaromil. She ignored all Jaromil's little allusions, well-rehearsed slips of the tongue, and sudden silences which were supposed to convey his preoccupation with the memory of another woman.

Instead, she regaled him with long (and, alas, quite merry) stories about the university, and she portrayed various fellow students with such verve that they seemed to Jaromil more real than his own person. The two of them were returning to the situation that had existed when they first met: he was turning back into a shy youth and she into a *stone maiden* conducting learned discourse. Only now and then did it happen (and Jaromil loved and hungrily yearned for those moments) that she suddenly turned pensive or emitted some sad, nostalgic phrase. In vain did Jaromil try to link it up with his own words, for the girl's sorrow was directed only inwardly into herself, and she had no desire to commune with Jaromil's feelings.

What was the source of her sorrow? Who knows; perhaps she lamented the love which she saw disappearing; perhaps she was thinking of someone else. Who knows; on one occasion, that moment of sadness was so intense (they were just coming back from the movies, down a quiet, dark street) that she placed her head on his shoulder.

Heavens! This had happened once before! It had happened to Jaromil as he was walking through the park with a girl he knew from dancing class. That gesture of the head, which had once aroused him so strongly, again had the same effect: he was excited! Enormously and undeniably excited! Only this time he was not ashamed of it—on the contrary, quite on the contrary! This time he was desperately hoping that the girl would notice his excitement!

But her head was resting sadly on his shoulder and she was vaguely staring over her glasses into the distance.

Jaromil's aroused state continued, victoriously, proudly, visibly, and he was eager for it to be recognized and appreciated. He was longing to grasp the girl's hand and to place it where she could feel his manhood, but that was only an impulse, an idea he understood was crazy and hopeless. It then occurred to him that if he stopped and held her close, her body would feel his virile arousal.

But as soon as she sensed from his slowing steps that he wanted to stop and embrace her, she said: "No, please, let's not..." and she said it so mournfully that Jaromil obeyed without a word. And that thing between his legs—that puppet, that clown—seemed like an enemy tormenting and ridiculing him. Jaromil was walking with a strange sad head on his shoulder and a strange sneering jester between his legs.

25

Perhaps he succumbed to the impression that deep sorrow and a longing for consolation (the famous poet still hadn't answered) justified an unconventional step. Be that as it may, Jaromil decided to pay a surprise visit to the artist. As soon as he reached the hall he realized from the sound of voices that the artist was receiving a sizable number of guests, and he felt like excusing himself and leaving. But the artist cordially asked him into the studio where he introduced him to his company—three men and two women.

Jaromil felt his cheeks reddening under the gaze of five strangers, but at the same time he was flattered, because in making the introduction the artist said that he wrote excellent poetry and his tone implied that the guests had already heard something about him before. That was a pleasant feeling. As he sat in the armchair looking around the studio he ascertained with satisfaction that both the women present were far more beautiful than his bespectacled friend. That self-assurance as they crossed one leg over the other, the elegance with which they flicked ashes off their cigarettes, the brilliant way they had of combining scholarly terminology and vulgar expressions into bizarre sentences—Jaromil felt as if he were in an elevator that was zooming with him to splendid heights, far beyond the tormenting voice of his stone maiden.

One of the women turned to him and asked in a warm voice what kind of verse he wrote. "Just... verse," he said in embarrassment, shrugging his shoulders. "Excellent verse," interposed the artist, and Jaromil dropped his head. The second woman looked at him and said in an alto: "The way he's sitting there reminds me of Rimbaud surrounded by Verlaine and his gang, in that painting by La Tour. A child among men. Rimbaud at eighteen was supposed to have looked like a thirteen-year-old. And you, too," she pointed at Jaromil, "look just like a child."

(We can't resist the temptation to point out that this woman leaned toward Jaromil with the same cruel tenderness as the sisters of Rimbaud's teacher Izambard—those famous *huntresses of lice*—leaned over the French poet when he sought asylum with them after one of his long wanderings and they washed, cleaned, and deloused him.)

"Our friend has the good fortune—a rather temporary one—of no longer being a child and not yet being a man," said the artist.

"Puberty is the most poetic of ages," said the first woman.

"You'd be amazed," the artist retorted with a smile, "at the remarkably finished and mature poems of this quite unfinished and virginal young man."

"True," nodded one of the men as a sign that he was familiar with Jaromil's poetry and agreed with the artist's praise.

"Are you going to publish them?" asked the woman with the alto voice.

"This era of positive heroes and busts of Stalin is not very propitious for such things," replied the artist.

The remark about positive heroes switched the conversation back to the track on which it had been moving before Jaromil's arrival. Jaromil was familiar with this topic and could easily have joined the conversation, but he didn't even listen to what they were saying; he looked like a thirteen-year-old, he was a child, a virgin. These words reverberated endlessly through his head. He knew, of course, that nobody wished to insult him, that the artist in particular sincerely liked his poems—but that only made things worse; at a moment like this, what did he care about poetry? He'd sacrifice the maturity of his stanzas a thousand times over if that vouchsafed him his own. He'd trade every line of his verse for one night with a woman.

The debate grew animated and Jaromil would have liked to leave. But he was in such a depressed state that he found it difficult to think of the right words to announce his departure. He was afraid of hearing his own voice; he was afraid that it would tremble or squeak, once more exposing his immaturity and thirteen-ness. He yearned to become invisible, to tiptoe off, somewhere far away, where he could go to sleep and wake after a decade, after his face had had time to age and develop manly creases.

The woman with the alto voice turned to him again: "Good Lord, child, why are you so quiet?"

He mumbled that he'd rather listen than talk (even though he hadn't been listening at all). It seemed to him that the judgment passed on him by his recent experience with the girl was inescapable, and that the sentence condemning him to virginity which he carried on his body like a brand (everybody surely must see that he had never possessed a woman) was confirmed anew.

And because he realized that he was again the target of attention, he became painfully aware of his face and with mounting apprehension felt that its expression was his mother's smile! He recognized it clearly, that delicate, bitter smile; he felt how it stuck to his lips. There was no way of getting rid of it. He felt that his mother was attached to his head, that she had spun herself around him like a cocoon enveloping a larva, depriving him of the right to his own likeness.

He was sitting among a group of adults, cloaked in his mama's visage, pulled by his mama's arms out of a world to which he aspired but which made him feel—gently but definitively—his hateful puerility. This feeling was so painful that Jaromil gathered all his strength to shake off his mother's face, to break loose. He tried to enter the discussion.

They were arguing the same questions that were being heatedly debated at that time by all artists. Modern Czech art had always proclaimed its allegiance to the communist revolution; but when the revolution arrived, it declared itself to be totally committed to a program of readily intelligible, popular realism and modern art was rejected as a monstrous product of bourgeois decadence. "That's our dilemma," said one of the guests. "Should we betray the art we grew up with, or the revolution we admire?"

"The question is badly formulated," said the artist. "A revolution that wants to dig up dead academic art and that manufactures busts of statesmen on an assembly line betrays not only modern art, but itself. Such a revolution has no desire to change the world. Quite the contrary: to preserve the most reactionary spirit of history—the spirit of bigotry, discipline, dogmatism, faith, and conventionality. There is no dilemma. As true revolutionaries we cannot agree with this betrayal of revolution."

Jaromil could easily have expounded on the artist's idea, the logic of which he knew thoroughly, but he had a distaste for acting the role of teacher's pet, an eager boy angling for approval. He was filled with thirst for rebellion. Turning to the artist, he said:

"You love to cite Rimbaud's motto: It's necessary to be absolutely modern. I quite agree. But the absolutely modern is not something we have seen coming for fifty years, but something that shocks and surprises us. Surrealism is in no way absolutely modern—it's been around for a quarter of a century. No, the modern event is the revolution which is now going on. Your failure to understand it only proves how new it really is."

They interrupted him. "Modern art was a movement aimed against the bourgeoisie and the bourgeois world."

"Yes," said Jaromil, "but if it was really consistent in its opposition to the contemporary world, it would welcome its own destruction. Modern art must have anticipated that the revolution would create its own culture—in fact, modern art should have wanted it that way."

"Let me understand you," said the woman with the alto. "You are not disturbed that Baudelaire's poetry is being used for secondhand paper, that all modern literature is prohibited, that the cubist paintings in the National Gallery are carted off to the cellar?"

"Revolution is violence," retorted Jaromil, "that's a well-known fact. Surrealism above all other movements realized that old clowns have to be brutally kicked off the stage, but it didn't have the sense to know that it had turned old and useless itself."

Jaromil's humiliation and anger made him express his ideas with forceful malice, or so it seemed to him. But one thing bothered him with the very first words that issued from his mouth: once again, he was hearing the artist's peculiar, authoritative intonation in his own voice, and he was unable to prevent his right arm from tracing gestures in the air which were idiosyncratic to the artist. It was actually a strange debate of the artist with himself, the artist-man with the artist-child, the artist with his rebellious shadow. Jaromil realized it and felt even more humiliated; and so he expressed himself more and more sharply, in order to revenge himself on his mentor for the gestures and the voice that made him a captive.

Twice the artist retorted to Jaromil's sallies with lengthy rejoinders, but the third time he merely replied with a stern, hard look and Jaromil knew he would never again be a guest in the artist's studio. The painful silence was finally broken by the woman with the alto voice (but now she was no longer speaking with the affection of Izambard's sisters bent over Rimbaud's louse-infested head, but with sadness and disappointment): "I don't know your poetry, but from what I've heard about it it's not likely to be approved by this régime, a régime you defend so vehemently."

Jaromil thought of his last poem, about two old people and their last love. He began to understand that this poem, which he cared about immensely, would never be published in the prevailing epoch of joyful songs and agitprop verse. By renouncing it now, he was sacrificing his most precious possession, his only treasure.

But there was something even more precious than his poems, something which he had never possessed and for which he had been yearning with all his heart: his manhood. He knew that it could be won only through courageous action; and if that courage meant that he was to be totally alone, that he was to renounce his girl, his artist friend, even his poems—so be it; he decided to dare. He said:

"Yes, I know that my poems are completely useless to the revolution. I'm sorry, because I like them. But unfortunately my feelings are no argument against their uselessness."

There was another interval of silence, and then one of the men said, "This is terrible," and he actually shuddered as if a chill ran up his spine. Jaromil felt that his words had produced terror in the whole company, that they were all looking at him as if he symbolized the destruction of everything they loved, everything that made life worthwhile.

It was sad, but beautiful, too: for a moment, Jaromil lost the feeling of being a mere child.

26

Maman read the poems which Jaromil kept silently putting on her table, and through them she tried to gain insight into her son's life. But alas, the poetry did not speak clearly and plainly! Its sincerity was deceptive; it was full of riddles and hints; Maman guessed that her son's head was full of women, but she had no clue as to what his relationship with them was really like.

One day, she opened the drawer of his writing-desk and rummaged around until she found his diary. She knelt down on the floor, and excitedly leafed through it. The entries were for the most part terse and cryptic, but it was clear to her that her son was having a love affair. He designated his beloved only with a capital letter, so that Maman couldn't tell who she was. On the other hand, certain events were described with a passion for detail that Maman found repulsive: the date of their first kiss, how many times they circled the park, the date he first touched her breast, the date he first touched her derrière..

Then Maman came to a date written in red and decorated by numerous exclamation marks. The entry next to the date read: *Tomorrow! Tomorrow! Ah, Jaromil, you old bastard, you bald old fogey, when you read this many years from now, remember that on this day began the Real History of Your Life!*

Impatiently, Maman searched her memory for any significant occurrence connected with that day, and she at last recalled that this was the week she and Grandma were away on their trip to the country. She also remembered that on her return she had found a bottle of her best perfume open on the bathroom shelf. She asked Jaromil about it, and he had said in considerable embarrassment, "I was only playing with it." How stupid she'd been! She recalled that Jaromil as a small child wanted to be an inventor of perfumes, and she was touched. She therefore limited herself to a mild rebuke: "You are too old to be playing with things like that!" But now everything was as clear as day: the perfume was used by a woman with whom Jaromil had slept that night, the night he had lost his virginity.

She visualized his nude body; she imagined the nude body of a woman lying next to him, a female body scented with her perfume and therefore smelling like she did. A wave of nausea swept over her. She glanced once more at the diary and saw that the entries ceased with the exclamation-marked day. How typical—for a man everything ends once he succeeds in sleeping with a woman, she thought with bitter distaste, and her son seemed disgusting to her.

For a few days she deliberately avoided him. Then she noticed that he looked tired and pale; she was convinced this was due to excessive love-making.

It took several more days before she began to notice that Jaromil's face expressed not only fatigue but sadness as well. That drew her closer to him, and gave her hope: she told herself that girls bruise but mothers comfort; she told herself there are many girls but only one mother. I have to fight for him, I have to fight for him, she repeated under her breath, and from that time she began to circle him like a vigilant, loving tigress.

27

_____

He passed his final exams, and with great nostalgia bade farewell to classmates who had been his companions for eight long years. His officially confirmed maturity seemed to stretch ahead of him like a desert. Then one day he found out (quite by accident, from a fellow he knew from meetings in the dark-haired man's apartment) that the stone maiden had fallen in love with a colleague of his.

He made a date with the girl; she told him she was leaving on vacation in a few days; he wrote down her address. He didn't say anything about what he had learned, for fear of putting it into words; he was afraid that this would only bring their break-up nearer; he was glad that she hadn't rejected him completely, even though she had somebody else, that she let him kiss her now and again, and that she at least continued to regard him as a friend; he clung to her desperately, and was ready to cast off all pride; she was the only living being in the lonely desert surrounding him; he clutched at the hope that their dying love might still be rekindled.

The girl left the city and Jaromil faced a scorching summer stretching ahead of him like a long, stifling tunnel. A letter addressed to the girl (a tearful, imploring letter) floated into that tunnel and vanished without a trace. Jaromil thought of the telephone receiver hanging on the wall of his room. Alas, the surrealist art object now took on a very real significance: a disconnected receiver, an unanswered letter, a conversation with nobody listening...

And all this time women floated over the sidewalks in airy dresses, hit tunes streamed into the warm streets out of open windows, trolleys were crammed with people carrying towels and bathing suits, and excursion boats churned down the Moldau, southward, toward the hills and forests...

Jaromil was forsaken, and only his mother's eyes followed him and kept faith with him. But this, too, was agony—to have a pair of eyes constantly probing his loneliness, stripping off his concealment. He couldn't stand his mother's looks nor her questions. He kept fleeing the house, returning late at night and going to bed at once.

We have remarked that Jaromil was not born for masturbation but for great love. During these weeks, however, he masturbated in wild desperation, as if he wanted to punish himself for such base and shameful activity. His nights of self-abuse were followed by days of throbbing headaches, but Jaromil was almost relieved since the pain kept his mind off the beauty of women in summer dresses and dulled the amorous lure of the songs in the streets. His state of drowsy apathy helped him cross the endless expanse of the day.

There was no answer from the girl. If there had at least been a letter from somebody else, if there had been anything at all to break the void! If the famous poet to whom Jaromil had sent his verse had at least written him a few lines! Just a few words of praise! (Yes, it is true we said that Jaromil would gladly have traded all his poetry for assurance that he was a virile man. But let us amplify that: if he was not to be considered a man, only one thing could offer any consolation—to be at least considered a poet.)

He longed to get in touch once more with the famous poet. Not by means of an ordinary letter, but in some outrageously poetic way. One day he left the house with a sharp knife. For a long time he walked up and down in front of a phone booth, and when he was quite sure that nobody was watching he went in and cut off the receiver. Every succeeding day he managed to appropriate another receiver, until he acquired twenty of them (there was no news from either the girl or poet in all this time). He put the receivers in a box which he wrapped and tied, addressed it to the famous poet, and put his own name in the corner. In great excitement he took the package to the post office.

As he was returning from the counter, somebody slapped him on the shoulder. He turned around. It was his old friend from school, the janitor's son. Jaromil was glad to see him (every event was welcome in his monotonous desert); he chatted gratefully and when he found out this former classmate lived nearby, he maneuvered him into an invitation to drop over for a brief visit.

The janitor's son was no longer living with his parents in the school building, but had his own one-room apartment. "My wife isn't home just now," he explained as they entered the hall. Jaromil expressed surprise that his friend was married. "Oh sure, I've been married for over a year," he said, in such a confident and self-evident tone that Jaromil felt a pang of envy.

They sat down and Jaromil saw there was a crib with a small baby on the other side of the room. He realized his friend was a paterfamilias, while he was an onanist.

His friend pulled a bottle of whiskey out of a cabinet and poured out two glassfuls. It occurred to Jaromil that he had no such supply of refreshments at his own house because his mother would frown on it.

"What are you doing these days?" asked Jaromil.

"I'm with the police," said the janitor's son and Jaromil thought of the day when he had been sick at home, listening to the exciting din of the crowd coming over the radio. The police were the most powerful arm of the Communist Party, and his former classmate was probably with the revolutionary crowds, while he—Jaromil—was home with Grandma.

Yes, it turned out that his friend really had been out in the streets those days, on important assignments. He talked about it discreetly but proudly. Jaromil felt a need to make his friend understand that they shared the same political convictions. He told him about the meetings in the dark-haired man's apartment.

"That Jew?" said the janitor's son without enthusiasm. "I'd keep my eyes open if I were you! That's a real strange bird!"

The janitor's son was constantly eluding him, he always seemed to be a step ahead, and Jaromil was anxious to find common ground. He said in a mournful voice, "I don't know if you heard about it, but my dad died in a concentration camp. That really shook me up, and now I know that the world has to be changed, radically changed. And I know where my place is."

The janitor's son finally nodded in agreement; they chatted for quite a while, and when they came to discuss their future Jaromil suddenly declared, "I want to be in politics." He was surprised by his own words; it was as if they rushed ahead of his thoughts, as if they willy-nilly decided the entire course of Jaromil's life. "Naturally," he continued, "my mother wants me to get into esthetics or French or heaven knows what, but I can't see that. That stuff has nothing to do with life. Real life—that's what you're involved with!"

As he was leaving his friend's apartment, he felt the day had been full of decisive insights. Just a few hours ago, he had sent off a package with twenty telephone receivers, thinking it was a daring, fantastic deed, a challenge to a great artist, a symbolic message of vain, fruitless waiting, a plea for the poet's voice.

But the conversation with his schoolmate immediately afterward (and he was certain the timing was no mere accident) gave his poetic act a contradictory significance. It was not a gift nor a pleading request; no, he was proudly *returning* to the poet all his vain waiting for an answer. The decapitated receivers were the severed heads of his loyalty and Jaromil was derisively sending them back, like a Turkish sultan sending the heads of captured crusaders to the Christian commander.

Everything was clear at last. His whole life had been a period of waiting in an abandoned phone booth, listening to a dead receiver. There was only one solution: to get out of the abandoned booth, as quickly as possible!

28

"Jaromil, what's the matter with you?" The intimate tenderness of the question brought tears to his eyes; there was no place to hide, and Maman continued. "It's all right, I know you. You're my child! I know everything about you, even though you don't trust me anymore."

Jaromil looked away, ashamed. She went on, "Don't think of me as your mother, think of me as an older friend. If you told me what's bothering you maybe you'd feel a lot better. I can tell something is bothering you." And she added softly, "And I know it has to do with some girl."

"Yes, Mother, I feel sad," he admitted, because the tender moist atmosphere of mutual understanding surrounded him and there was no way out. "But it's hard for me to talk about it..."

"I understand. And I don't want you to tell me anything right at this moment. I just want you to feel free to talk to me any time you want. Look here. Today is a beautiful day. I have a date with a few friends to go for a boat ride. Come with us and keep us company! It would do you a lot of good to get out a bit!"

Jaromil didn't feel like going, but he couldn't think of any excuse. Besides, he was so tired and dejected that he didn't have enough energy to refuse, and so without quite knowing how it happened he found himself on the deck of an excursion boat with four ladies.

The ladies were all more or less Maman's age, and Jaromil provided them with a rich topic of conversation; they expressed surprise that he'd already finished high school; they declared that he looked like his mother; they shook their heads when they learned he had decided to study political science (they agreed with Maman that this was not the right career for such a sensitive young man) and, of course, they asked him teasingly whether he'd already found himself a girl. Jaromil developed a quiet hatred for all of them, but he saw that Maman was having a good time and for her sake he kept smiling politely.

The boat pulled up alongside a pier and the ladies with their young escort disembarked on a shore covered with half-naked people, and looked for a spot in which to sun themselves; only two of them had bathing costumes; the third undressed her white body down to a pair of pink panties and bra (not at all ashamed to be sporting her undergarments—perhaps she felt chastely concealed by her dumpiness). Maman declared she would tan only her face, and squinting her eyes she tilted her head toward the sky. All four agreed that their young man should take off his clothes, sun himself, and go for a swim. Maman had remembered to bring along Jaromil's trunks.

The sounds of popular music wafted over from a nearby restaurant, filling Jaromil with unrest; tanned boys and girls trotted by, stripped to their bathing suits, and it seemed to

Jaromil that they were all looking at him; their gaze burned through him like a flame; he tried desperately to keep people from knowing he was connected with the quartet of middle-aged ladies. But the ladies eagerly claimed him and acted like one big mother with four chattering heads. They insisted that he take a swim.

"But there's no place to change," he objected.

"Nobody will look at you, silly. Just put a towel around yourself," coaxed the chubby lady in the pink lingerie.

"He's shy," laughed Maman, and the other ladies laughed, too.

"We have to respect his feelings," said Maman. "Come on, you can change behind this and nobody will see you." She was stretching out a large white towel, which was supposed to shield Jaromil from the curiosity of the other bathers.

He stepped back, and Maman followed him. He kept backing away, and she continued to pursue him holding out the towel, so that she looked like a large bird with white wings stalking its prey.

Jaromil kept backing away, and then he suddenly turned and ran.

The ladies looked on in surprise. Maman was still holding the large white bath towel in her outstretched arms as Jaromil wound his way among bare young bodies and slowly disappeared from view.

Part 4:
The Poet on the Run

1

In every poet's life there comes a time when he tears himself away from his mother and starts running.

Not too long ago he was still obediently marching along, his sisters Isabelle and Vitalie up front, he and his brother Frederic in the next rank, and his mother bringing up the rear like a military commander. This is how she paraded her children down the streets of Charleville, week after week.

When he was sixteen, he tore himself out of her grasp for the first time. In Paris the gendarmes caught up with him. He was sheltered for a few weeks by his teacher Izambard and Izambard's sisters (yes, the same ones who hunted for lice in his hair). Then his mother came to fetch him, slapped his face and her arms once more enfolded him in their cold embrace.

But Arthur Rimbaud keeps running away, again and again, a collar securely fastened around his neck, writing poetry on the run.

2

The year was 1870, and the guns of the Franco-Prussian War echoed through Charleville. That was an especially favorable situation for escape; lyrical poets are nostalgically drawn to the sound of battle.

His short body with its crooked legs was fitted out with a hussar's uniform. Eighteen-year-old Lermontov became a soldier, escaping from his grandmother and her troublesome love. He exchanged the pen which is the key to one's soul for a pistol which is the key to the gates of the world. For if we send a bullet into the breast of another being it is like entering that breast ourselves, and the heart of another being—that is the world.

From the moment he tore himself out of his mother's arms, Jaromil had been running and his flight, too, was followed by the echo of battle. It wasn't the rumbling of guns, but the roar of political upheaval. In such an era a soldier is only decoration and the real battle is elsewhere. Jaromil has been diligently attending the faculty of political science. He has stopped writing verse.

3

Revolution and youth are closely allied. What can a revolution promise to adults? To some it brings disgrace, to others favor. But even that favor is questionable, for it affects only the worse half of life, and in addition to advantages it also entails uncertainty, exhausting activity and upheaval of settled habits.

Youth is substantially better off: it is not burdened by guilt, and the revolution can accept young people *in toto*. The uncertainty of revolutionary times is an advantage for youth, because it is the world of the fathers that is challenged. How exciting is the entry into the age of maturity over the shattered ramparts of the adult world!

In the initial period after 1948, communist professors were in the minority in Czech universities. Thus, if revolution was to secure its influence over the academic world, it had to give power to the students. Jaromil was active in the Youth Council, and he acted as the organization's observer at university examinations. He submitted reports to

the Political Council on the professors' methods of examination and on their political opinions, so that in reality it
was the professors rather than the students who were being
examined.

4

But Jaromil was severely tested himself, too, when
he reported to the Council. He had to answer to stern,
zealous young party members and he hoped to find words
that would please them: When young people's education
is at stake, compromise is crime. Teachers with obsolete
ideas are obsolete; the future will be totally new, or it
won't be a future at all. Teachers whose opinions change
overnight cannot be trusted; the future will be pure, or it
will be shameful.

If Jaromil had become a zealous functionary, whose
work affected the fate of adults, can we still maintain that
he was on the run? Does it not seem more likely that he
had reached his goal at last?

Not at all.

When he was only six years old, his mother had already
put him in the position of being a year younger than his
classmates. He is still a year too young. When he is reporting
on a professor's bourgeois attitude, his mind is not on his
subject. Rather, he is anxiously scanning the eyes of the
young people he is addressing, watching his own image.
Just as he inspects his smile and hair in the bathroom mirror,
so he checks the firmness and manliness of his words in the
eyes of his audience.

He is always surrounded by a wall of mirrors, and he
cannot see beyond.

For maturity is indivisible; it is either complete or it

does not exist at all. So long as Jaromil remains a child in any sphere of life, his attendance at examinations and his reports on professors will remain no more than one means of escape.

5

He is continually running, and he cannot get away from her. He has breakfast and supper with her, he says good night and good morning to her. Each morning she hands him a shopping bag. Maman doesn't care that this prosaic household emblem is ill-suited for an ideological supervisor of professors, and she sends him off to do the day's marketing.

Look: there he goes, down the same street we saw him walk at the beginning of the preceding section, when he blushed on seeing an attractive woman coming toward him. Several years have passed, but Jaromil still blushes, and in the store to which his mother sends him is a girl in a white coat whose eyes he is afraid to meet.

He likes the girl enormously, the poor girl who has to sit eight hours a day in the cagelike cashier's booth. The softness of her features, the slowness of her gestures, her imprisonment—all this seems to him mysteriously intimate, appropriate, preordained. Actually, he knows why he feels this way: the girl resembles the maid Magda whose fiancé was shot by the Germans. Magda—"sorrow-lovely face." And the cashier's booth resembles the bathtub in which he saw her.

6

He is hunched over his writing-desk, afraid of his final exams. He is just as scared of them now at the university as he had been during his high school career, for he is accustomed to showing his mother perfect report cards and he does not wish to disappoint her.

His little room seems unbearably close and confined, at a time when the air outside is filled with echoes of revolutionary songs and giant figures with hammers in their hands rise outside the windows.

It is five years since the great Russian revolution and he is condemned to peer into a textbook and to shake with fear because of an exam. What a fate!

At last he pushes the textbook aside (it is late at night) and he muses over his half-finished poem. He is writing about Jan the proletarian, who wants to kill his dream about the beautiful life by making that dream come true. Holding a hammer in one hand, his beloved's arm in the other, he is striding into the revolution, surrounded by legions of his comrades.

And the nervous law student (yes, of course, it is Jiří Wolker) sees the table covered with blood, lots of blood, for

> *terrible are the wounds*
> *of a murdered dream*

but he is not afraid; he knows that a real man must never be afraid of blood.

7

The store closes at six and he watches from the opposite corner. He knows that the girl cashier always leaves a few minutes after six, but he also knows she is always accompanied by a young salesgirl from the same store.

This friend of the cashier is not nearly as pretty; in fact, Jaromil considers her almost ugly. The two girls are opposites: the cashier is dark, the other is a redhead; the cashier is plump, the other skinny; the cashier is quiet, the other noisy; the cashier is mysteriously intimate, the other is repulsive.

He repeats his vigil several times in the hope that one evening the girls might leave separately and he could address the dark-haired girl. But that never happens. One time he follows them; they cross several streets and enter an apartment house; he walks up and down in front of the building for almost an hour, but neither one of them comes out.

8

Mrs. Wolker comes to visit him from their home town and listens to the poem he recites to her. She is satisfied: her son is still her own. Neither other women nor the wide world has succeeded in taking him away from her. On the contrary, women and the world are enclosed in the magic center of poetry, a circle which she herself has drawn around her son, a realm over which she secretly rules.

He is just reading a poem which he wrote in memory of her mother, his beloved grandmother:

I'm off to war my Granny dear
for the glory of this shining world . . .

Mrs. Wolker is at peace. Let her son go off to the wars, let him hold a hammer in one hand and a beloved in the other. There's no harm in that. After all, this world of his encompasses her, and Grandma, and the family kitchen, and all the virtues she has inculcated in him. Let the world see him, hammer in hand. She knows perfectly well that parading *before* the world is an entirely different thing from going out *into* the world.

The poet realizes this difference, too. And he alone knows how melancholy it is to be a prisoner in the house of poetry.

9

Only a true poet knows the enormity of the longing not to be a poet, the longing to leave the mirrored house filled with deafening silence.

A fugitive from the realm of dreams
I'll find my peace in crowds
And to curses change my songs.

But when František Halas wrote these lines he was not with the crowds in the streets; the room in which he was working was quiet.

And it is not at all true that he was an exile from the realm of dreams. On the contrary, the crowds he was writing about were the realm of his dreams.

Nor did he succeed in changing his songs to curses; rather, his curses were continually turning into song.

Is there no way out of the mirrored house?

10

But I
subdued myself
setting my heel
on the throat
of my own song

wrote Vladimir Mayakovsky, and Jaromil understands him.
Poetic language now seems to him like lace which belongs in
Mother's linen closet. He hasn't written any poetry for several
months, and he has no desire to do so. He is on the run. He
goes marketing when Mother asks him, but he keeps the drawer
of his writing-desk locked. He has taken the reproductions of
modern paintings off the walls of his room.

What did he put up instead? A picture of Karl Marx?

No. He put up a picture of his father. It was a photograph from 1938, from the period of the sad mobilization.
His father was wearing an officer's uniform.

Jaromil loved that photograph of a man whom he
hardly knew and who was vanishing from his memory. He
missed that football player, soldier, prisoner. He missed this
man very much.

11

The philosophy auditorium was filled to overflowing.
Several poets were sitting on the podium. A young man
with an enormous head of hair, wearing the blue shirt favored in those days by members of the Youth Union, was
speaking:

"Poetry never plays a more important role than it

does during revolutionary periods; poetry gave the revolution its voice and in return the revolution liberated poetry from isolation; the poet now knows he is being heard by the people, especially young people; for youth, poetry and revolution are one and the same."

Then the first poet rose to his feet and recited a poem about a girl who broke off with her beloved, a young man working at the lathe next to her own, because he was lazy and failed to fulfill his production quotas. The young man did not want to lose his girl, and so he proceeded to work with such enormous zeal that the red star of a socialist hero of labor was soon pinned to his machine. Other poets gradually took the floor and recited poems about peace, Lenin and Stalin, martyrs in the antifascist struggle, and workers who surpass quotas.

12

Young people have no inkling what enormous power there is in youth. But the poet who now got up to recite his poem, a silver-maned man in his sixties, knew it.

That person is young, he proclaimed in a musical voice, who marches in step with the youth of the world, and the youth of the world is socialism. That person is young who is walking with the future, and who refuses to look back.

In the view of the silver-haired poet, youth was not a designation of a particular period of life but a *value* that transcended any concrete age. This thought, clothed in appropriate verse, nicely fulfilled a double purpose: it flattered the youthful audience, and it magically erased the poet's wrinkles and made him a peer of the young boys and girls (for he made it clear that he was one of those pioneers walking hand in hand with the future).

Jaromil was sitting in the audience and watched the poets with interest, although he felt like someone on the other shore, so to speak, who no longer belonged among them. He was listening to their compositions with the same cool detachment with which he listened to the words of the professors when he was about to make a report to the Council. Jaromil paid special attention to the famous poet who was now getting up from his chair (the applause that rewarded the silver-haired poet for his compliments had died down). Yes, the man now striding to the podium was the same poet who had once received a package with twenty telephone receivers.

13

My dear Master, We are now in the month of love; I am seventeen years old: the age of hopes and illusions, as they say... And if I send you some of these verses... it is because I love all poets, all good Parnassians. Don't sneer too much when you read these verses: you'll make me deliriously happy, dear Master, if you'll be so kind and have my poem published! I am unknown; what difference does that make? Poets are brothers. These lines believe, love, hope. That's all. Dear master, reach down to me, lift me up; I am young, give me your hand...

He was lying; he was fifteen years and seven months old. It was even before the first time he ran away from Mother, from Charleville. But that letter would long ring in his head like a litany of shame, like a document of weakness and dependence. He would get even with his dear master, with that old bald-headed fool Théodore de Banville! Only a year later he would ridicule all his poetizing, all the precious hyacinths and lilies that filled his verse; he would send a mocking letter like a postal slap in the face.

But at the moment, the dear master who is reciting on the podium has no idea of the hatred lying in wait for him. He is reading a poem about a Russian town destroyed by fascists and rising out of the ruins. The poem is full of fantastic, surrealistic scenes: bosoms of Soviet girls float through the streets like multicolored balloons; a petroleum lamp drops from the sky to light up the white town, while helicopters land on the roofs like so many descending angels.

14

Seduced by the famous poet's personal charm, the audience burst into applause. But among the unthinking throng was a thoughtful minority who knew that a revolutionary audience must not wait like a humble supplicant for gifts from the podium. On the contrary, nowadays it is the poems that are supplicants, begging to be admitted to the socialist paradise, but young revolutionaries guarding the gates of this paradise must be vigilant: the future must be radically new or it won't be a future at all; it must be totally pure or it will be totally shameful.

"What kind of nonsense is he trying to sell us?" shouted Jaromil, and others soon joined in. "Is he trying to link socialism with surrealism? Is he trying to pair a horse with a cat, yesterday with tomorrow?"

The famous poet grasped what was going on, but he was proud and had no intention of giving in. From his earliest days he was used to shocking the bourgeoisie and to standing his ground against an audience. His face flushed. He chose as his last poem one different from that which he had originally planned. It was a poem full of wild images and unbridled erotic fantasy. Whistling and shouting broke out when he finished.

The students whistled derisively at the old scholar who

had come because he liked them; in their angry rebellion he saw glimmers of his own youth. He was under the impression that his love entitled him to tell them what was on his mind. It was the spring of 1968, in Paris. Alas! The students were completely unable to perceive the visage of youth behind his wrinkled face, and the old scholar watched with surprise as he was booed by those he loved.

15

The famous poet raised his hand to calm the din. And then he began shouting at the students that they were a bunch of puritan schoolmistresses, dogmatic priests, and stupid policemen, that they protested against his poems because at bottom they hated freedom.

The old scholar listened silently to the whistles and catcalls. He recalled that when he had been young he, too, had liked to hoot and whistle, surrounded by a band of his comrades. But the band had broken up long ago, and now he stood alone.

The famous poet was shouting that it was the duty of poetry to safeguard freedom, and that even a metaphor was worth fighting for. He declared that he would go right on pairing horses with cats and modern art with socialism, and if this was a quixotic undertaking then he was glad to be Don Quixote, for he regarded socialism as an epoch of joy and freedom and he rejected any other kind of socialism.

The old scholar was watching the noisy young people around him and it suddenly occurred to him that he was the only one in the whole audience who had the privilege of freedom, for he was old. Only when a person reaches old age can he stop caring about the opinions of his fellows, or of the public, or of the future. He is alone with approaching death and death has no ears and does not need to be pleased. In the face of death a man can do and say what pleases his own self.

They whistled and demanded the floor to answer him. After a while Jaromil rose to his feet, too. His eyes were filled with rage, and the crowd was at his back. He said that only the revolution was modern whereas the decadent eroticism and unintelligible images of surrealist art were junk that had no connection with the people. "What is truly modern?" he challenged the famous poet. "Your obscure lines, or we who are building a new world?" He answered his own question: "There is nothing absolutely modern in the world except the masses of the people, building socialism." Thunderous applause greeted his words.

The applause was still ringing in the old man's ears as he left, walking down the corridors of the Sorbonne. The inscriptions on the walls read: *Be realists—demand the impossible*. And a bit further: *The emancipation of man must be total or nothing*. And further still: *No regrets*.

16

The benches in the large classroom are stacked against the walls; brushes and paints are scattered all over the floor. Several students of political science are busy painting paper banners with May Day slogans. Jaromil, author and editor of the slogans, is supervising the work, glancing now and then into his notebook.

But what's going on? Did we make a mistake in our dates? He is dictating the very same slogans which were read a moment ago by the old scholar on the walls of the rebellious Sorbonne. No, we made no mistake. The slogans Jaromil is dictating to his colleagues are exactly the same as those scrawled some twenty years later by French students on the walls of the Sorbonne and Nanterre.

Dream is reality, proclaims one of the banners. Another one: *Be realists—demand the impossible*. And another: *We are ordering permanent happiness*. And: *No churches*. (Jaromil is especially proud of that one. Those two brief words reject two millennia of history.) Further: *No freedom for the enemies of freedom!* and: *Power to the imagination!* and: *Death to the lukewarm!* and *Revolution in politics, in the family, in love!*

His colleagues are tracing out the letters, and Jaromil is proudly strolling among them like a grand marshal of words. He is happy to be needed and to have found a use for his verbal gifts. He knows that poetry is dead (*Art is dead*, says a Sobonne wall), but it died in order to rise again from its grave as agitprop, proclamations on banners, and slogans on city walls (*Poetry is in the street*, says a wall of the Odéon).

17

"Have you looked at the newspaper? The first page listed a hundred suggested slogans for May Day. It was put out by agitprop of the Central Committee. Didn't a single one appeal to you?"

A stocky young man from the District Council was facing Jaromil. He introduced himself as chairman of the May Day committee for higher education.

"*Dream is reality*—why, that's the coarsest kind of idealism! *No churches*—I quite agree with you, comrade, but for the moment that conflicts with the party's clerical policy. *Death to the lukewarm*—since when do we have the right to threaten people with death? *Power to the imagination*—that's all we need! *Revolution in love*—would you mind telling me what you mean by that? Do you want free love in contrast to bourgeois marriage, or monogamy in contrast to bourgeois promiscuity?"

Jaromil declared that the revolution must change the world in all its components, including love and the family, or else it would not be a revolution.

"All right then," admitted the stocky youth, "but that can be put much better: *Long live socialism, long live the socialist family!* You see, that's a slogan straight out of the newspaper. You could have saved yourself the trouble."

18

Life is elsewhere, French students wrote on the wall of the Sorbonne. Yes, he knows that very well, that's why he is leaving London for Ireland, where the people are rebelling. His name is Percy Shelley, he is twenty years old, and he is carrying hundreds of leaflets and proclamations as passports which will ensure his entry into real life.

For real life is elsewhere. The students are pulling up cobblestones, overturning cars, making barricades; their entrance into the world is noisy and magnificent, illuminated by flames and glorified by explosions of tear gas grenades. Life was so much harder for Rimbaud, who dreamed about the barricades of the Paris commune but was unable to leave Charleville. But in 1968, thousands of Rimbauds have their own barricades. Standing behind them they refuse to make any compromise with the temporary owners of the world. Liberation of man must be total or nothing.

A mile away, on the other bank of the Seine, the present owners of the world continue to live their normal lives and think of the turmoil in the Latin Quarter as something happening far away. *Dream is reality*, the students wrote on the walls, but it seems that the opposite was true: their reality (the barricades, the overturned cars, the red flags) was a dream.

19

But that is never clear at any moment in time—whether reality is a dream, or the dream a reality. The students who gathered at the university with red flags fluttering overhead came gladly, but at the same time they knew what difficulties they would face if they stayed home. For Czech students the year 1949 marked that interesting transition when a dream is no longer just a dream. Their jubilation was still voluntary and yet it was already compulsory as well.

The students marched through the streets with Jaromil at their side; he was responsible for the slogans on the banners and for the declamation of his colleagues; this time he no longer thought up beautifully provocative aphorisms but simply copied several slogans recommended by central agit-prop. He was leading the shouting like a corporal counting out cadence, and his colleagues rhythmically yelled out the slogans after him.

20

The marchers had already passed the reviewing stand on Wenceslas Square and the blue-shirted young people were dancing to hastily improvised bands. Everything was gay and free, and people who were strangers just moments before joined in hearty camaraderie. But Percy Shelley is unhappy, Percy is alone.

He's already been in Dublin for several weeks, he's handed out dozens of flyers, the police know all about him, but he has not succeeded in befriending a single Irishman. Life always seems to be somewhere else.

If there were at least a barricade to climb on, the sound of gunfire! It seems to Jaromil that festive parades are only pale imitations of great revolutionary demonstrations, that they have no substance, and vanish like smoke in the air.

He thinks of the girl imprisoned in the cashier's cage and a terrible sadness comes over him; he dreams of a daring feat: he breaks the store window with a hammer, pushes terrified shoppers aside, opens the cashier's cage, and carries off the liberated brunette, to the amazed stares of onlookers.

He dreams that they are walking arm in arm through crowded streets, deeply in love, pressing close to each other. And the dance whirling all around them is not merely a dance but a procession to the barricades, the year is 1848 and 1870 and 1945, the scene is Paris, Warsaw, Budapest, Prague, and Vienna, the participants are the same throngs eternally leaping from barricade to barricade, and he leaps with them, holding his beloved by the hand...

21

He could still feel the warmth of her hand in his, when he saw him. He was walking toward him, massive and imposing. A young woman was tripping along at his side. She was not wearing a blue shirt like most of the girls dancing in the street. She was as elegant as a fashion model.

The massive man was absentmindedly darting his eyes over the crowd, nodding greetings this way and that. When he was but a few steps away from Jaromil, their eyes met for a moment, and in an instant of confusion Jaromil, too, bowed his head like all the other people who had recognized and greeted the famous man. The man returned the gesture with an absent look (the way we greet someone we don't know) and his companion made a slight, noncommittal movement of the head.

Ah, that woman was so lovely! And she was no fantasy, she was so real that in the radiance of her real body the girl from the cashier's booth/bathtub faded to phantoms and disappeared from Jaromil's side.

Jaromil stood on the sidewalk, ignominiously alone, and stared with hate after the receding couple. Yes, it was he, his *dear master*, the recipient of the package with twenty telephone receivers.

22

Dusk was slowly falling on the city and Jaromil yearned to meet her. Several times he followed a woman whose back reminded him of hers. It was exciting to go on a make-believe chase after a woman vanishing in an infinity of people. Then he decided to take a stroll past the apartment house he had once seen her enter. It seemed unlikely he would meet her there again, but he didn't feel like going home as long as his mother was up. (He could bear his home only at night, when his mother was asleep and his father's photograph woke to life.)

And so he walked up and down the lonely suburban street on which the gaiety of May Day with its banners and lilac bouquets did not seem to have left any traces. Lights began to go on in the apartment house windows. The windows of the ground-floor apartment lit up, too, and Jaromil saw a girl with a familiar face!

No, it wasn't his dark-haired cashier. It was her friend, the skinny redhead. She was just moving toward the window to let down the blinds.

Jaromil could barely manage to swallow his disappointment. He realized that the girl saw him. He blushed, and behaved just the way he did when the mournful, beautiful maid had looked up from the bathtub toward the bathroom door:

He ran away.

23

It was the second day of May, six o'clock in the evening. The salesgirls poured out into the streets, and something unexpected happened: the redhead was coming out alone.

He tried to hide behind a corner, but it was too late. She saw him and rushed up to him. "You know, sir, it isn't very polite to peek into people's windows at night!"

He blushed, and tried to talk his way out of the embarrassing affair of the previous night. He was afraid the presence of the redhead might spoil his chances of meeting the brunette. But the redhead was very talkative and had no intention of letting Jaromil go. She even invited him to accompany her home to her apartment (escorting a young lady to her door, she said, is far more polite than staring at her through the window).

Desperately, Jaromil kept his eyes glued on the doors of the store. "Where is your girl friend?" he asked at last.

"You're behind the times. She's gone."

They walked together toward the girl's house and Jaromil learned that the two girls had come from the country, got jobs in the store, and shared an apartment. But the brunette had left Prague because she was getting married.

When they stopped in front of the apartment house, the girl said, "Don't you want to come up for a moment?"

Surprised and confused, Jaromil went up to her place. And without knowing how it happened, they were embracing, kissing, and in no time at all they were sitting on a bed covered by a wool bedspread.

It was all so quick and simple! Before he could think about the difficult and decisive existential task ahead of him, she put her hand between his legs. He was overjoyed, for his body reacted just the way a young man's body should.

24

"You're terrific, you're terrific," she kept whispering in his ear. He was lying next to her, sunk deep in pillows and enormously happy.

"How many women have you had before me?"

He shrugged his shoulders and smiled mysteriously.

"You won't tell?"

"Guess."

"I'd say somewhere between five and ten," she ventured an estimate.

He was filled with happy pride; it seemed to him as if a moment ago he had made love not only to her but to five or ten other girls as well. She not only liberated him of his virginity, she made him feel like a man of great prowess and experience.

He smiled at her gratefully, and her naked body filled him with enthusiasm. How could he have been so blind as to consider her ugly? Her chest was adorned by a pair of real, unquestionable breasts and her underbelly boasted a clump of real, unquestionable hair!

"You're even more beautiful naked than dressed," he said, and went on to praise her charms.

"Have you liked me for a long time?" she asked.

"Oh yes, you know that."

"Yes, I know. I noticed the way you used to come to

the store. You always used to wait for me out in the street afterward."

"That's right."

"You were afraid to start up anything with me, because I was never alone. But I knew that someday we'd get together. Because I liked you, too."

25

He gazed at her, letting her last words reverberate in his mind. Yes, that's how it was. The whole time when he was tormented by loneliness, when he kept throwing himself desperately into meetings and parades, when he kept running on and on, his manhood had already been prepared for him. This modest little room with peeling walls had been quietly waiting for him, this room and this commonplace woman whose body had finally created a physical bond between him and the crowds.

The more I make love, the more I want to make revolution—the more I make revolution the more I want to make love, proclaimed a Sorbonne slogan, and Jaromil penetrated the redhead's body a second time. Maturity must be total or not exist at all. He made love to her long and beautifully.

And Percy Shelley who like Jaromil had a girlish face and looked younger than his age, ran through the streets of Dublin and kept running on and on, because he knew that life was elsewhere. Rimbaud, too, kept running—to Stuttgart, to Milan, to Marseille, to Aden, to Harar, and then back to Marseille, but by then he had only one leg and it is hard to run on one leg.

He slid off her body. As he lay stretched out next to her, tired and content, it occurred to him that he was not resting after two bouts of love but after a long, long run.

Part 5:
The Poet
Is Jealous

1

Jaromil kept on running, and the world kept changing: his uncle, who thought that Voltaire was the inventor of volts, was falsely accused of fraud (along with hundreds of other businessmen). They nationalized both his stores and sentenced him to several years in jail. His wife and son were expelled from Prague as enemies of the working class. They left the house in icy silence, determined never to forgive Maman for Jaromil's defection to the family's enemies.

The government assigned the vacated ground floor of the villa to a family who immediately adopted a surly, belligerent attitude. The new tenants had moved from a dingy basement apartment and considered it the height of injustice for anyone to have owned such a spacious and pleasant villa. They felt that they didn't come to the villa merely to live but to settle an old historical wrong. Without asking anyone's permission, they made themselves at home in the garden, and demanded that Maman have the walls of the house repaired since peeling plaster could endanger their child when he played out in the yard.

Grandma was getting older, she was losing her memory, and one day (almost imperceptibly) she turned into crematorium smoke.

It was no wonder that under these conditions Maman found her son's growing alienation especially hard to bear. He was studying subjects for which she had an antipathy and he stopped showing her his poems. When she tried to open his drawer she found it locked. It was like a slap in the face. To think that Jaromil suspected her of prying into his affairs! She resorted to a spare key which Jaromil had no idea existed, but when she examined his diary she discovered no new entry or new poem. Then she noticed her late husband's picture on the wall and she recalled how she had once implored the statuette of Apollo to erase all traces of his likeness from the infant growing in her womb. Alas, was her husband to contest her claim to Jaromil even from the grave?

At the end of the preceding section, we left Jaromil in the redhead's bed. About a week later, Maman again opened the drawer of his desk. She found in his diary several laconic remarks which she didn't understand, but she also discovered something far more important: new poems. It seemed to her that Apollo's lyre was again victorious over her husband's military uniform, and she quietly rejoiced.

After reading the poems this favorable impression was enhanced, for she sincerely liked them (this was actually the first time she had honestly enjoyed Jaromil's verse!). They were rhymed (deep down, Maman always suspected that unrhymed verse was not really poetry at all), they were completely intelligible, and full of beautiful words. There was no trace of decrepit old men, corpses moldering in the earth, sagging bellies, or rheumy eyes. Instead, the poems referred to flowers, sky, clouds, and in a few places (this had never occurred before) there was even the word "mother."

Jaromil was coming home; when she heard his steps on the stairs, all the hard years of suffering suddenly rose to her eyes and she could not hold back her tears.

"What is it, Mother? What's the matter?" he asked softly, and Maman drank in the tenderness which had long been absent from his voice.

"Nothing, Jaromil, nothing," she answered, weeping all the harder as a result of her son's solicitude. Once again, her tears were of many kinds: tears of sorrow for her loneliness; tears of reproach for her son's rejection; tears of hope (stimulated by the melodic line of his new poems) that he might be coming back to her; tears of anger for the clumsy way he was standing over her (couldn't he at least stroke her hair?); tears of deceit, intended to soften and to capture him.

At last, after awkward hesitation, he took her by the hand. That was beautiful. Maman stopped crying, and her words began to flow as generously as had her tears a moment earlier. She talked about everything that was wrong with her life: her widowhood, her loneliness, the tenants trying to chase her out of her own house, her sister who was no longer speaking to her ("because of you, Jaromil!"), and finally, the most important thing of all—the only close friend she had in the world was turning away from her.

"But that's not true. I am not turning away from you!"

She would not settle for such an easy answer. She laughed bitterly; How could he say that? He was always coming home late at night, there were whole days on end when the two of them didn't exchange a single word, and even when they talked a little now and again she knew perfectly well that he wasn't really listening and that his mind was somewhere else. Yes, he was becoming a stranger.

"But, Mother, that's not true."

Again she smiled bitterly. Oh no? Did she have to prove it to him? Did he want to know what really hurt her more than anything else? Was he interested? All right, then. She had always respected his privacy, even when he was a little boy. What a struggle she had with the rest of the family to get him his own room! And now—what an insult! How does he think she felt when she found out, purely by accident, sweeping out his room one day, that he locked the drawer of his desk on her! Why lock it? Who could possibly want to interfere with his privacy? Does he imagine she had nothing better to do than to stick her nose into his affairs?

"Oh, Mother, that's a misunderstanding! I hardly ever use that drawer! If it's locked it's just by accident!"

Maman knew her son was lying, but that wasn't important. More significant than his words was the submissiveness in his voice, which was like an offering of peace.

"I want to believe you, Jaromil," she said, and squeezed his hand.

As he gazed at her, she became conscious of her tear-stained face. She rushed off to the bathroom to examine herself in the mirror, and she was horrified: her weepy face looked ugly, and the dowdy gray dress she was wearing only made matters worse. She briskly washed her face with cold water, changed into a pink dressing gown, and fetched a bottle of red wine from the cabinet. She began telling Jaromil once more that the two of them should get to know each other better, for they had nobody but each other in the whole world. She talked on this theme for a long time and it seemed to her that Jaromil's eyes expressed warmth and agreement. She was thus encouraged to say that she had no doubt that he—now a grown-up university student—had his private secrets which she respected, but all the same, she was hoping that the women in Jaromil's life would not spoil their good relationship.

Jaromil listened with patient understanding. The reason why he had avoided his mother during the past year was that his sorrow required solitude and darkness. But since the time of his happy landing on the sunny shores of the redhead's body, he had been longing for peace and light; his estrangement from his mother marred the harmony of life. Aside from emotional considerations, there was also a more practical need for good relations with Maman: the redhead had a room of her own, whereas he—a grown man—was still living with his mother and could effect an independent existence only through his mistress's independence. This disparity was painful to him, and he was glad that Maman was sitting with him now, wearing a pink dressing gown and sipping wine, like a pleasant young woman with whom he could amicably discuss his rights and privileges.

He declared that he had nothing to hide (Maman's throat tightened with anxious expectation), and he began telling her about the redhead. He didn't mention, of course, that Maman already knew the girl by sight from the store where she did her shopping, but he explained that the young lady in question was eighteen years old, that she was no university student but a simple working girl (he said this almost belligerently) who was earning her living with her own hands.

Maman poured herself another glass of wine; it seemed to her that things were taking a turn for the better. The picture of the girl painted by Jaromil dissipated her anxiety. The girl was very young (the terrifying thought of an experienced, corrupt woman happily dissolved), she was rather uneducated (Maman thus had no need to fear the strength of her influence), and Jaromil stressed her simplicity and kind-heartedness with such vehemence that she suspected the girl was not much of a beauty (so that it could be assumed her son's infatuation would not last very long).

Jaromil sensed that his mother did not disapprove of his redhead's portrait, and he was happy. He toyed with the fantasy that he might soon be sitting at one table with his mother and his redhead; with the angel of his childhood and the angel of his maturity. It all seemed as beautiful as peace; peace between his own home and the outside world, peace under the wings of his two angels.

Thus, after a long period of estrangement, mother and son were savoring their intimacy. They chatted merrily, but Jaromil continued to keep his modest practical objective in mind: to win the right to his own room where he could take the girl any time he liked, where they could do as they pleased and stay as long as they pleased. For he rightly perceived that only that person is truly adult who is master of some clearly defined space, the owner of complete privacy. He expressed this thought to his mother, in a roundabout, careful way. He said he would stay home that much more readily if he could consider himself his own master there.

Maman emerged from the pleasant wine-induced haze as alert as a tigress. She realized at once what her son was after. "What do you mean, Jaromil, don't you feel at home here?"

He retorted that he liked his home very much but that he wanted the right to invite anyone he pleased and to live as independently as his girl.

Maman became aware that Jaromil was unwittingly offering her a great opportunity: after all, she too had several admirers whom she could not ask to her house because she feared Jaromil's condemnation. Was this not an excellent chance to trade Jaromil's freedom for a little freedom of her own?

But when she visualized a strange woman in Jaromil's childhood room, an insurmountable distaste rose up in her. "You have to admit there is some difference between a mother and a landlady," she said heatedly and she knew she was about to ruin her own chances of living the full life of a woman. Her disgust over her son's physicality was stronger than the longing of her own body for physical gratification, and this insight terrified her.

Jaromil, who was still stubbornly pursuing his goal, did not understand his mother's inner turmoil and he continued to press his lost cause, bringing up further useless arguments. Only after a while did he notice that his mother was crying. He was frightened at the thought that he had hurt the angel of his childhood, and he lapsed into silence. In the mirror of his mother's tears he suddenly saw his demand for independence as impudence, arrogance, even lewd shamelessness.

Maman was desperate: she saw the gulf between the two of them opening once more. She had gained nothing, and lost everything! She quickly tried to think of some way to preserve that precious thread of understanding between her son and herself. She took his hand, and said through her tears:

"Please don't be angry, Jaromil! It's just that I'm so upset by the way you've changed. You've changed so much lately!"

"Changed? I don't know what you mean, Mother."

"Yes, you've changed, you're different, and what hurts me more than anything else is that you've stopped writing poetry. You used to write such beautiful poems! Now you've given it up completely. And that hurts me."

Jaromil wanted to say something, but she didn't let him. "Believe your mother," she continued. "I have a feeling for these things; you have tremendous talent! It's your vocation. It's a shame to sell it short. You're a poet, Jaromil, a born poet. And I'm sorry it means so little to you."

Jaromil was drinking in his mother's words, overjoyed. It was true. The angel of his childhood understood him better than anybody else! How depressed he had been because he had stopped writing!

"But I'm writing poetry again now, Mother! Really! I will show you!"

"It's no use, Jaromil," Maman sadly shook her head. "Don't try to fool me. I know you've stopped."

"You're wrong! Just wait one second!" he shouted. He ran off to his room, unlocked the drawer, and returned with a sheaf of poems.

Maman looked at the same words she had read a few hours earlier in Jaromil's room.

"Oh, Jaromil, these poems are really beautiful! You've made great progress. Great progress! You're a poet, and I am so happy for you..."

2

Everything seemed to indicate that Jaromil's enormous yearning for newness (the religion of the New) was only the disguised longing of a virginal youth for the unimaginable experience of the sex act. When he first reached the blissful shore of the redhead's body, a peculiar idea occurred to him: he now knew at last what it meant to be absolutely modern; it meant to lie on the shore of the redhead's body.

On that occasion, he was so happy and full of enthusiasm that he wanted to recite poetry to her. Mentally, he quickly reviewed all the poems he knew by heart (his own and other poets') but he concluded (with considerable amazement) that the redhead probably wouldn't care for any of them. This brought forth a disturbing thought. It became clear to him that the only poems that were absolutely modern were those which could be readily accepted and understood by the redhead, a girl of the crowd.

It was a sudden illumination; why was he so foolish as to want to step on the throat of his own song? What was the sense of giving up poetry for the sake of revolution? After all, he had at last reached the realm of real life (by "real life" Jaromil understood a whirling world of parading throngs, physical love, and revolutionary slogans), all he had to do now was give himself entirely to this new life and become its violin string.

He felt full of poetic spirit and tried to write a poem the redhead would like. That was not a simple task. Heretofore he had written only free verse and he did not have the technical skill for more structured verse forms. He was sure the girl would not consider an unrhymed composition to be true poetry. Even the victorious revolution was of the same opinion. Let us recall that in those days unrhymed verse was not even deemed worthy of publication. All modern poetry was declared to be the product of a rotten bourgeoisie and free verse was the surest stigma of literary decadence.

Was the revolution's fondness for rhyme only an accidental preference? Hardly. In rhyme and rhythm resides a certain magic power. An amorphous world becomes at once orderly, lucid, clear, and beautiful when squeezed into regular meters. If a woman *weary of breath* has *gone to her death*, dying becomes harmoniously integrated into the cosmic order. Even if such a poem were intended as a bitter protest against mortality, death becomes justified as an occasion for beautiful protest. Bones, funeral wreaths, gravestones, coffins—everything in a poem becomes transmuted into a ballet in which both the reader and the poet perform their dance. The dancers, of course, cannot disagree with the dance. Through poetry, man realizes his agreement with existence, and rhyme and rhythm are the crudest means of gaining consent. Can a revolution dispense with repeated affirmation of the new order? Can a revolution dispense with rhyme?

Rave along with me! Nezval exhorted his readers, and Baudelaire wrote, *One must always be drunk ... on wine, on poetry, on virtue, according to taste ...* Poetry is intoxication and man drinks in order to merge more easily with the world. Revolutions have no wish to be examined or analyzed, they only yearn to merge with the masses. For that reason, revolutions are lyrical and in need of lyricism.

Of course, the lyricism sought after by the revolution was different from the kind of poetry composed by Jaromil in his early phase. At one time, he had eagerly followed the quiet adventures and enticing intimations of his own inner self. Now, however, he cleared out his soul and turned it into a huge arena for the noisy circus of the real world.

He exchanged the beauty of singularity which only he understood for the beauty of generality understood by everyone.

He was passionately eager to popularize the old-fashioned wonders at which art (in its renegade pride) had turned up its nose: sunset, roses, morning dew, stars, nostalgic longing for the native soil, mother love. What a beautiful, intimate, intelligible world! Jaromil was returning to it with happy surprise, like a prodigal son coming home after years of wandering.

Oh, to be simple, absolutely simple, as simple as a folk-song, a child's game, a murmuring brook, a redheaded girl!

Oh, to return to the source of eternal beauty, to love simple words like *star* and *song* and *lark*—even the word *oh*, that despised and ridiculed little word!

Jaromil was beguiled by certain verbs, too, especially those that described simple motions: *walk*, *run*, but especially *float* and *fly*. In a poem which he wrote in celebration of Lenin's anniversary, an apple branch was cast upon a stream. The branch floated all the way to Lenin's homeland. No Czech river flows to Russia, but a poem is a magical land where rivers change their course. In another poem he wrote that the world would soon be as free as the *scent of pines drifting over mountaintops*. In another he summoned up the aroma of jasmine which became so powerful that it turned into an invisible schooner sailing through the air. He imagined himself aboard this aromatic boat, floating far, far away, all the way to Marseille. According to a newspaper article, Marseille dock-workers were on strike, and Jaromil wished to join them as a comrade and brother.

His poems were also filled with that most poetic of all means of locomotion, *wings*; the night *pulsed* with the *quiet beat of wings*. Longing, sorrow, even hatred had wings. And of course time was steadily pursuing its *winged course*.

All these lines intimated a wish for *a vast embrace*,

reminiscent of Schiller's famous lines: *Seid umschlungen, Millionen! Diesen Kuss der ganzen Welt!* This cosmic embrace encompassed not only space but time as well, not only the docks of Marseille but that magical far-off island— *the future*.

Jaromil had always regarded the future as an awesome mystery. It comprised everything unknown, and for that reason it lured and terrified. It was the opposite of certainty, the opposite of home (this is why during periods of anxiety he dreamed about the love of old people, who were happy because they no longer had a future). The revolution, however, gave the future an entirely different meaning. It was no longer a mystery; a revolutionary knew the future by heart. He knew all about it from brochures, books, lectures, agitprop speeches. It didn't terrify; on the contrary, it offered a haven of certainty in an uncertain present, so that the revolutionary reached out to it like a child reaching out to its mother.

Jaromil wrote a poem about a communist functionary who fell asleep on a couch in the secretariat office, late one night when *the bustling council gave way to morning dew* (in those days, a fighting communist was always conceived as a debating communist). The ringing of trolley-car bells under the windows became in the party functionary's dream the joyous peal of all the bells in the world, announcing that there would be no more war and that the globe belonged to the working people. The official realized that by a magical leap he was somehow in a distant future. He was standing in the middle of a field and a woman was riding toward him on a tractor (the woman of the future was habitually depicted as a tractor driver). With wonder she recognized the official as the socialist hero of the past—the working man of former times who had sacrificed himself so that she could now freely and happily till the soil. She descended from her machine to greet him. "This is your home, this is your world," she says, and wants to reward him. (For heaven's sake, how could that pretty young woman reward a tired old functionary?) At this point the trolleys under the windows ring out with special vigor and the man sleeping on the narrow couch in the corner of the party office awakens...

Jaromil wrote a number of similar new poems, but he remained unsatisfied. Nobody ever saw them except Jaromil and his mother. He sent all of them to the literary editor of the daily newspaper, and diligently examined the paper every morning. One day he finally found five four-line stanzas on the top of page three, with his name printed in bold type under the title. That same day he proudly handed an issue of the paper to the redheaded girl and asked her to look through it carefully. The girl was unable to find anything remarkable (she normally ignored poetry, so she paid no attention to authors' names) and Jaromil finally had to point his finger at the poem.

"I had no idea you were a poet!" She looked admiringly into his eyes.

Jaromil told her he had been writing poetry for a long time, and pulled a sheaf of handwritten poems out of his pocket.

The redhead proceeded to read them and Jaromil told her he had given up poetry some time ago, but that she had inspired him to go back to it. Meeting her was like meeting Poesy herself.

"You mean it?" she asked, and when Jaromil nodded she embraced him and kissed him.

"The magical thing about it is," continued Jaromil, "that you're not only the queen of my recent poems but even of those I wrote before knowing you. When I saw you for the first time it seemed to me that my old poems sprang to life and were personified in a woman like you."

Encouraged by her curious, uncomprehending face he proceeded to tell her how he had once written a long prose poem, a fantastic tale, about a boy named Xavier.

Actually, he hadn't really written it, he only dreamed about it and longed to write it down one day.

Xavier lived completely differently from other people; his life was a dream. He slept, and had a dream, and in that dream he fell asleep and had another dream, and from that dream he awoke to find himself in the previous dream. And so he passed from one dream to another and lived several different lives simultaneously. He crossed from one life to another—isn't that a beautiful existence, not to be tied down to a single life? To be a mortal and yet to live many lives?

"Yes, I suppose it would be nice . . . ," said the redhead.

And Jaromil continued: when he had seen her in the store for the first time he had been amazed, because she looked exactly the way he had imagined Xavier's greatest love to look: fragile, redheaded, with delicate freckles . . .

"But I'm ugly," the redhead protested.

"No! I love your freckles and your flaming hair! I love all that because it is my home, my old dream!"

The girl kissed him and he continued. "Just imagine, the whole story started like this: Xavier loved to wander through sooty suburban streets. He always passed a certain ground-floor window. He'd stop in front of it and dream about a beautiful girl who perhaps lived there. One day the window was lit and he saw a tender, delicate, redheaded girl. He couldn't resist. He opened the window and jumped into the room."

"But you ran away from my window!" laughed the girl.

"Yes, that's true," replied Jaromil, "I ran away because I was afraid that I was passing from reality into fantasy. Do you know what it's like to find yourself in a situation you had known previously from a dream? It gives you such a fright that you want to take to your heels!"

"That's true," agreed the redhead happily.

"So in the story, Xavier jumped through the window

after the girl, but then her husband came and Xavier locked him up in a heavy oak wardrobe. That husband is there to this day, a skeleton. And Xavier took his beloved far away, just as I will take you!"

"You're my Xavier," whispered the girl gratefully into Jaromil's ear. She playfully nicknamed him Xavy and Xavik and she hugged him and kissed him long into the night.

3

Of Jaromil's numerous visits to his redheaded girl's flat we wish to recall the time when the redhead was wearing a dress with a row of large white buttons in front. Jaromil began to try to unbutton them; the girl laughed, for they served only as decoration.

"Wait, I'll take it off myself," she said, and reached up for the zipper at the back of her neck.

Jaromil was embarrassed by his clumsiness, and having at last grasped the principle of the dress he was eager to make up for his faux pas.

"No, no, I'll take it off myself. Leave me alone!" she backed away from him, laughing.

He could not insist without appearing ridiculous, but he was upset by the girl's behavior. He believed that a man had to undress his mistress—otherwise the whole operation was no different from ordinary, everyday dressing and undressing. This opinion was not based on experience, but on literature and its suggestive phrases: *he was a connoisseur at disrobing women*; or, *he unbuttoned her blouse with expert fingers*. He could not imagine an act of physical love that was not preceded by an eager, excited flurry of unbuttoning, unzipping, and unhooking.

"What's the idea of taking your clothes off yourself? You're not visiting a doctor!" The girl had already slipped out of her dress and was wearing only her underclothing.

"Doctor? What do you mean?"

"Yes, that's how the whole thing seems to me. Like a doctor's examination."

"I see!" the girl laughed. "Maybe you're right."

She took off her bra and stood in front of Jaromil, sticking out her small breasts. "I have a pain, doctor, right here under my heart."

Jaromil didn't seem to get the joke. "Excuse me," she said apologetically, "you're probably used to examining your patients lying down," and stretched out on the couch. "Please take a close look at that heart of mine."

Jaromil had no choice but to comply. He leaned over the girl's chest and put his ear over her heart. His earlobe rested against the soft cushion of her breast and from the depths of her body he heard rhythmic thumping. It occurred to him that this was precisely what a doctor would feel when he was examining the redhead's body behind the closed, mysterious doors of his office. He lifted his head, glanced at the naked girl and felt a hot, painful surge of jealousy. He was seeing her through the eyes of a strange man, a doctor. He quickly put both his hands on her breasts (not at all the way a doctor would) in order to put an end to the tormenting game.

"Doctor, that's naughty of you! What are you doing? That's not part of the examination!" protested the girl.

Jaromil was seized with anger. He saw the face of his girl as she would look when a stranger's hands were touching her. He saw her frivolous protest and longed to strike her. But at the same moment he realized how excited he had become and tore off the girl's panties and entered her body.

His excitement was so great that the jealous anger quickly melted, especially when he heard the girl's moans and sighs (that marvelous homage) and the words of endearment which had become a permanent part of their intimate ritual: "Xavy! Xavik!"

Then he lay peacefully next to her, gently kissed her shoulders, and felt good. But it was Jaromil's folly never to be satisfied with a beautiful *moment*. A beautiful moment was meaningful to him only as a token of a beautiful eternity; a beautiful moment that had fallen out of a polluted eternity was a deceptive lie. He wanted therefore to make sure their eternity would be a totally pure, unsullied one. He asked, more pleadingly than aggressively, "Tell me that it was only a silly joke, that business with the doctor."

"Yes, of course," replied the girl. What else was there to say to such a silly question? Yet it didn't satisfy Jaromil. He pressed on:

"I couldn't stand it if anybody else touched you. I simply couldn't stand it!" He cupped his hands over the girl's poor underdeveloped breasts, as if his future happiness depended upon their inviolability.

The girl laughed (quite innocently). "But what should I do if I get sick?"

Jaromil realized he could not rule out all medical examinations and that his position was untenable. But he also knew that if a stranger's hands were to touch the girl's breasts, his whole world would fall to pieces. He repeated:

"I couldn't bear it! You understand? I simply couldn't bear it!"

"So what do you want me to do when I need a doctor?"

He said quietly and reproachfully, "You could always find a woman doctor."

"What choice have I got? You know how it is these days!" she burst out bitterly. "We're all assigned to a certain doctor, whether we like it or not. You know what socialist medicine is all about. They give the orders and you do as you're told. Take gynecologic examinations, for instance..."

Jaromil's heart skipped a beat, but he said calmly, "Why, is there anything wrong with you?"

"Oh no, that's just for prevention. Because of cancer. That's the law."

"Stop it, I don't want to hear about it!" said Jaromil, and placed his hand over her mouth. The gesture was so vehement and abrupt that he feared the girl might mistake it for a slap and get angry; but her eyes were looking at him so humbly that Jaromil felt no need to apologize for the unwitting brutality of his movement. In fact, he began to enjoy it and kept his hand over the girl's mouth.

"Let me inform you," he said, "that if anybody ever lays a finger on you I will never touch you again."

He was still pressing his palm against the girl's lips. It was the first time he had ever used physical violence on a woman, and he found it intoxicating; he put both of his hands around her neck as if he was about to choke her. He felt the fragility of her throat under his fingers and it struck him that he could easily strangle her by merely pressing down his thumbs.

"I'd strangle you if anybody touched you," he said, and continued holding her by the throat; he enjoyed the feeling that the girl's possible nonexistence was in his hands. It seemed to him that at this one moment, at least, the girl belonged to him completely, and this filled him with a joyous sense of power, a feeling so alluring that he entered her a second time.

In the course of love-making he squeezed her roughly several times, put his hand on her throat (how exciting it might be to choke a beloved during intercourse!), and bit her several times.

Then they rested, lying side by side, but the love act had not lasted long enough perhaps, for it had not been capable of dissipating Jaromil's bitter anger; the girl was lying next to him, unstrangled, alive, her nudity reminding Jaromil of doctors' hands and gynecological examinations.

"Don't be angry," she said, caressing his hand.

"I can't help it. A body pawed over by a bunch of strangers disgusts me."

The girl at last understood that he was in earnest. She implored, "For heaven's sake, I was only joking!"

"It was no joke. It was the truth."

"No, it wasn't."

"Don't tell me that! It was the truth and I know there is nothing to be done about it. Gynecological examinations are compulsory and you've got to go. I don't blame you. But a body that has been handled by somebody else disgusts me. I can't help it. That's how I am."

"I swear I made it all up! I haven't been sick since I was a child. I never go to the doctor. I did receive a card about the gynecological examination, but I threw it away. I never went there."

"I don't believe you."

She tried to reassure him.

"All right, then. But suppose they call you again?"

"Don't worry, they're too disorganized to notice that I didn't show up."

He believed her, but his distress was not to be assuaged by reason. After all, it wasn't really a matter of medical checkups. He was tormented by the sense that she was eluding him, that she was not totally his.

"I love you," she repeated. But this brief moment could not satisfy him. He wanted to possess eternity, or at least the eternity of this girl's life. And he did not possess it. Even that small segment of her life during which she had passed from virginity to womanhood belonged to someone else.

"It's unbearable to me that somebody else is going to touch you. And that somebody already has."

"Nobody's going to touch me."

"But somebody's already been inside you. And that's disgusting."

She hugged him.

He pushed her away.

"How many?"

"One."

"You're lying!"

"I swear it!"

"Did you love him?"

She shook her head.

"How could you go to bed with somebody you didn't love?"

"Stop tormenting me!" she said.

"Answer me! How could you do such a thing?"

"Stop tormenting me! I didn't love him, and it was awful."

"What was awful?"

"Don't ask."

"What is there to hide?"

She broke into tears and confided to him that it had been an older man from her village, that he was repulsive, that he had had her in his power ("Don't ask me, you wouldn't want to know about it!"), that by now she had managed to forget all about him ("If you love me, never remind me of that man again").

She wept so pitifully that Jaromil's anger at last subsided. Tears are an excellent solvent.

He stroked her cheek. "Don't cry!"

"You're my dear Xavy," she sobbed. "You came in through the window and locked the bad man in a chest and he'll turn into a skeleton and you'll take me far, far away."

They embraced and kissed. The girl swore that she couldn't bear anyone else's hands on her body and he swore that he loved her. They made love once more, and this time they loved each other gently, their bodies filled with tender spirit.

"You're my Xavy," she kept repeating afterward, stroking his hair.

"Yes, I'll take you far away where you'll be safe," he said, and he knew exactly the right place. He had a pavilion

waiting for her under peaceful skies, with birds flying overhead toward a bright future and scent-filled boats gliding
through the air toward Marseille; he had a haven waiting
for her, watched over by the guardian angel of his childhood.

"You know what? I want to introduce you to my
mother," he said, and his eyes were full of tears.

4

The mother of the family occupying the ground floor
of the villa had been exhibiting an increasingly swollen belly;
her third child was on the way, and the father stopped
Jaromil's Maman one day to tell her it would be extremely
unjust if two people were to occupy the same space as five;
he suggested she give up one of the three rooms on the
second floor. Maman answered that this was not possible.
The tenant said that he intended to turn the matter over to
the proper authorities who would determine whether or not
the living space in the villa was equitably distributed. Maman countered that her son was about to get married, and
that there would soon be three persons on the second floor,
perhaps even four.

Thus, when Jaromil told her a few days later that he
wanted to introduce his girl to her, Maman was not dis-
pleased. At least the tenants would be convinced she was
sincere when she spoke of her son's upcoming marriage.

However, when Jaromil admitted to Maman that she
already knew the girl and that she was the redheaded salesgirl
from the store where Maman did her shopping, Maman
was unable to hide an expression of unpleasant surprise.

"I trust you don't mind that she's only a salesgirl,"
Jaromil said belligerently. "I told you before that she was
just a simple working woman."

For a few moments, Maman was unable to accept the

idea that the awkward, surly, and unattractive girl from the store was the great love of her son's life, but at last she managed to control herself. "Forgive me if I seem surprised," she said, determined to put up with anything her son had in store for her.

A painful, three-hour visit duly came and went. Everyone was nervous, but managed to weather the ordeal.

"How did you like her?" Jaromil asked his mother anxiously as soon as the girl had left.

"Well, yes, she seems quite nice. Why shouldn't I like her?" she answered, knowing perfectly well that the tone of her voice was at odds with her words.

"You mean you didn't like her?"

"I just told you that I did."

"No, I could tell from the way you spoke that you weren't being honest with me."

In the course of her visit the redhead had been guilty of numerous awkwardnesses (she was the first to reach out her hand to Maman, she was the first to sit down, the first to take a sip of coffee), she made numerous other faux pas (she kept interrupting when Maman was talking), and uttered numerous tactless remarks (she asked Maman how old she was). When Maman was in the midst of recounting these shortcomings, she suddenly realized that Jaromil might think her narrow-minded (he regarded excessive concern for good manners as a sign of bourgeois pettiness) and she quickly added:

"Don't get me wrong, I don't think those things are all that terrible. Just keep inviting her to the house. Contact with an atmosphere like ours is bound to be good for her."

But the idea that she might have to face that redheaded, homely, hostile body with any regularity released a new wave of distaste in Maman. She said in a soothing voice, "After all, you can't really blame her for what she is. You have to imagine the kind of environment in which she was brought up and consider the place where she works now. In a place like that you've got to put up with everything, you've got to please everybody. If the boss wants to have a little fun it's hard to refuse him. In such an atmosphere one little amorous escapade more or less is not taken too seriously."

She watched Jaromil's face and saw it flush. A hot wave of jealousy rose in his body, and it seemed to Maman she could almost feel that heat herself. (And why not? It was the same hot wave she had felt when Jaromil first introduced the girl to her, so that the two of them were like two connected vessels through which flowed the same caustic humors.) Jaromil's face had again become childlike and submissive. Maman was no longer facing a strange, independent man but her own beloved child, a child who was unhappy, a child who had once upon a time run to her for comfort. She could not tear herself away from this splendid spectacle.

Jaromil left the room and after a few minutes of solitude, Maman caught herself beating her head with her fists. She kept repeating to herself in a whisper, "Stop it, stop it, stop this stupid jealousy, stop it!"

All the same, the damage was done. Their brave pavilion, their tent of harmony guarded by the angel of childhood was torn to shreds. An epoch of jealousy opened before mother and son.

His mother's words about amorous escapades which are not taken seriously continued to ring in his head. He imagined the redhead's colleagues in the store telling dirty jokes; he imagined the climactic, lewd moment of contact between narrator and listener as the punchline approached; and he was in agony. He visualized the boss rubbing up against her body, covertly touching her breast or slapping her rear end, and he was furious that such gestures were not taken seriously, whereas for him they meant everything. Once, when he was visiting her, he noticed that she forgot to close the toilet door behind her. He made a big scene about it, for he immediately conjured up the image of the girl's similar carelessness in her place of employment, with a strange man accidentally surprising her while she was sitting on the bowl.

When he aired his jealous imaginings in the girl's presence, she was capable of calming him with gentleness and reassurance. But no sooner did he find himself alone in his room than the tormenting thoughts recurred. There was no guarantee that the girl was telling him the truth. After all, wasn't he himself inducing her to tell lies? When he reacted with such fury to the idea of an ordinary medical checkup, had he not frightened her forever from telling him what was on her mind?

Gone was that happy early era when love-making was merry and he was full of gratitude to her for having led him so simply and surely out of the labyrinth of virginity. But the very cause of his former gratitude he now subjected to anxious analysis. Over and over again he summoned up the unchaste touch of her hand which had excited him so fabulously the first time he had been with her. He was now scrutinizing it with suspicion; it was not possible, he told himself, that she had never touched anybody that way before; if she had dared use such a lewd gesture within half an hour of meeting him, a total stranger, then this gesture must have been something quite routine and mechanical for her.

That was a terrible thought. True, he had already made peace with the idea that he was not the first man in her life, but he accepted this thought only because the girl's words had suggested some sort of painful, bitter affair in which she had been nothing but a mistreated victim. This awakened pity in him, and pity dissolved his jealousy somewhat. But if this had been a relationship in which the girl learned such obscene gestures it could not have been a totally one-sided affair. After all, the gesture was far too joyous. It contained a whole little history of amorous pleasure!

It was too painful a subject to talk about. The very sound of her lover's name caused him great suffering. Nevertheless, he tried in a roundabout way to track down the origin of the gesture that preyed on his mind (and which he continued to experience with his body, for the girl seemed to have a great fondness for that particular caress) and at last he soothed himself with the idea that a great love bursts out of the blue like a bolt of lightning, freeing the woman at one stroke of all shame and inhibition. Precisely for that reason, precisely because she is pure and innocent, she gives herself to her lover as readily as if she were a harlot; and not only that: love unlocks in her such treasures of unexpected inspiration that her spontaneous playfulness may resemble the practiced tricks of a shameless slut. In one blinding flash the genius of love reveals all knowledge and skill. Jaromil found this idea beautiful and profound. In its light his girl appeared a patron saint of love.

Then one day a classmate remarked sarcastically, "Tell me, who was that raving beauty I saw you with last night?"

He denied her as readily as Peter denied Christ. He said she was just a casual acquaintance; he waved his arm in deprecation. But like Peter, deep in his heart he remained true. He did cut down on their strolls together through certain well-traveled streets, and he felt relieved when nobody he knew saw the two of them, but he did not agree with his classmate and developed a distaste for him. He was moved by his redhead's meager, shabby wardrobe and he saw the plainness of her clothes as part of her charm (the charm of simplicity and poverty), as well as the charm of his own love. He told himself that it was not too difficult to love somebody sophisticated, lovely, elegantly dressed: such a love was a meaningless reflex automatically stimulated by the accident of beauty. But a great love seeks to create a beloved being out of an imperfect creature, a creature all the more human for her imperfections.

One day as he was in the midst of declaring his love for her (no doubt after some bitter quarrel), she said, "I really don't know what you see in me. There are so many prettier girls around."

With considerable animation, he explained that beauty had nothing to do with love. He declared that he loved precisely those things about her which others might find ugly. Carried away by his fervor he even began to itemize. He said that her breasts were small and underdeveloped and she had big wrinkled nipples that tended to arouse pity rather than enthusiasm. He told her that her face was freckled and her hair red and her body thin, and these were the very reasons he loved her.

The redhead broke into tears, because she understood the physical facts (small breasts, red hair) and failed to understand the abstract conclusion.

Jaromil, however, was quite entranced with his concept. The girl's weeping over her homeliness warmed and inspired him. He resolved to devote his whole life to wiping away those tears and to enveloping her in his love. In this outburst of sentiment he now even conceived of her former lover as one of the blemishes that made her all the more lovable. That was a truly remarkable achievement of will and of intellect. Jaromil realized as much, and launched into writing a poem:

speak of the maid who's always on my mind (that was a line that kept returning as a refrain). He expressed the longing to possess her with all her blemishes, in all her human totality and eternity, *even old loves that molder in her flesh*...

Jaromil was enthusiastic about his composition because it seemed to him that in place of the great shining pavilion of harmony, in place of the artificial space where all antinomies were eliminated, where mother and son sat at a common table of peace, he had found another edifice—an absolute one, a sterner and more truthful absolute. For if the absolute of purity and peace did not exist, there was still the absolute of feeling in which everything foreign and impure was dissolved.

He was enormously pleased with the poem even though he knew no newspaper would print it, since it had nothing to do with the joyful building of socialism. But he had not written it for the newspapers, he had written it for himself and his girl. She was moved to tears when he read it to her, but she was also frightened once again by all the references to her ugliness, to hands that tore at her body, to old age.

Jaromil did not mind her uneasiness. On the contrary, he enjoyed it and savored it. He liked to dwell on her apprehensions and to assuage them with lengthy explanations and reassurances. To his chagrin, however, the girl did not share his fondness for the subject, and soon directed the conversation elsewhere.

Jaromil might have forgiven the girl her meager breasts (actually, he had never been angry at her on their account), and he might even have overlooked the strangers' hands squeezing her body, but one thing he found impossible to dismiss: her endless chatter. He had just read her some lines embodying a distillate of everything he thought and believed and he had hardly finished before she was chattering merrily about something entirely different.

Yes, he was ready to dissolve all her faults in the *aqua regia* of his love, but only under one condition: that she obediently lower herself into this solvent bath, that she immerse herself completely in this tub of love, that not a single thought stray elsewhere, that she be content to stay submerged beneath the surface of his words and thoughts, that she belong totally to this world, body and soul.

Instead, she was once again prattling on and on, about her childhood and her family, a subject which Jaromil found particularly odious, because he did not know how to voice his objection (it was a perfectly innocent family, in fact, a proletarian family). It was on account of them that she kept jumping out of the tub he had prepared for her, the vessel he had filled to the brim with the all-forgiving waters of love.

He was forced to listen yet once more to stories about her father (a worn-out old worker from the country), about her siblings (it wasn't a family so much as a rabbit-hutch, Jaromil thought: two sisters, four brothers) and she seemed to be especially fond of one of her brothers (his name was Jan and he seemed to be something of a queer duck—in the pre-February era he had had a job as chauffeur for an anticommunist cabinet minister); no, it was not just a family, it was a distasteful, alien nest, traces of which still clung to the redhead, estranging her from him and keeping her from being entirely his. And that brother Jan, he was not a mere brother but first and foremost a man, a man who had been watching her for eighteen years, a man who knew dozens of her little intimate secrets, a man with whom she had shared a bathroom (how many times she must have forgotten to lock the door!), a man who had been living with her at the time of her transition to womanhood, a man who had surely seen her naked many times . . .

You must be mine to die upon the rack if I want you, a sick and jealous Keats had written to his Fanny, and Jaromil, back home again in his childhood room, started writing a poem to calm himself. He thought about death, that great embrace which stills everything. He thought about the death of strong men, great revolutionaries, and he was seized by the idea of writing a great dirge that would be sung at the funerals of communist heroes.

Death. In those days of compulsory joy it too belonged among the forbidden topics. But Jaromil was confident of finding a special viewpoint that would free death of its customary aura of gloom (after all, he had written beautiful lines about death before; in his own way he was an expert on the beauty of death). He felt he had the power to write *socialist* poetry of death.

He was musing about the death of a great revolutionary: *like the sun's farewell / to mountain crests...*

And he began writing a poem entitled "Epitaph": *Must I die? / Then let it be by fire...*

5

Lyrical poetry is a realm in which any statement immediately becomes truth. Yesterday the poet said *life is a vale of tears*; today he said *life is a land of smiles*; and he was right both times. There is no inconsistency. The lyrical poet does not have to prove anything. The only proof is the intensity of his own emotion.

The genius of lyrical poetry is the genius of inexperience. The poet does not know much about the world, but he arranges the words that stream out of his being into structures as formal as crystals. The poet himself is immature, yet his verse has the finality of a prophecy before which he stands in awe.

Alas, my aquatic love. When Maman read Jaromil's first poem it occurred to her (with a feeling akin to shame) that Jaromil knew more about love than she did. She didn't know anything about his attempts to spy upon Magda while she was taking her bath. For Maman, the words "aquatic love" signified something far more general, some sort of mysterious category of love, something as opaque and elusive as the pronouncement of a sibyl.

We can scoff at the poet's lack of maturity, but there is something amazing about him, too: his words sparkle with droplets that come from the heart and that give his verse the luster of beauty. These magic dewdrops need not be stimulated by real-life events. On the contrary, we suspect that the poet sometimes squeezes his heart with the same detachment as a housewife squeezing a lemon over her salad. Actually, Jaromil was not terribly concerned about the dockworkers of Marseille; but at the moment he wrote about the love he bore them, he was truly moved by their plight and generously poured out his heart over his words, so that they took on a flesh-and-blood reality.

By means of his poetry the lyric author creates his self-portrait. But no portrait is completely accurate, and the poet retouches his true likeness.

Retouches? Yes, he makes it more expressive, for he is tormented by the vagueness of his own features. He longs for a form of his own and hopes his poetry will bestow upon his features a firm outline.

And he tries to make his portrait striking, for his real life is uneventful. The face incarnated in his verse often wears a passionate, fierce expression, making up for the lack of dramatic action in the poet's life.

But if the poet's self-portrait is to see the light of day, his poetry must first be published. The newspaper had printed several of Jaromil's works, but he remained dissatisfied. In the letters accompanying his submitted manuscripts he addressed the anonymous editor in a warm, intimate tone, to cajole him into an answer and an invitation to meet. However (and this was almost humiliating), even after Jaromil's poems were published nobody seemed interested in meeting him personally or in approaching him as a fellow man of letters; the editor never responded.

The reaction to his poems among his classmates also was not up to his expectations. Perhaps if he had belonged to the élite of contemporary poets whose voices were carried by loudspeakers and whose pictures shone in illustrated weeklies—perhaps then he might have aroused some interest among his university classmates. But the handful of his poems published on the back pages of a newspaper hardly created a stir. For his fellow students who yearned after brilliant diplomatic or political careers, Jaromil had become a person who was uninterestingly odd rather than oddly interesting.

And all this time Jaromil so passionately thirsted for glory! He longed for it like all poets. *Oh glory, you mighty divinity, may your great name inspire me and may my verse conquer you,* prayed Victor Hugo. *I am a poet, I am a great poet and one day I shall be loved by the whole world; it is important to repeat this to myself, to pray to my unfinished monument,* Jiří Orten consoled himself.

An obsessive longing for admiration is not a vice appended to the poet's talents (as may be true of a mathematician or an architect); rather, it is part of the very essence of the lyrical temperament, it virtually defines the lyrical poet: the poet is he who shows his self-portrait to the world in the hope that the face projected upon the screen by his poetry will be loved and worshipped.

My soul is an exotic flower with a strange and sensuous aroma. I have great talent, perhaps even genius, Jiří Wolker wrote in his diary and Jaromil, disgusted by the unresponsive newspaper editor, selected several poems and sent them off to a respected literary journal. What happiness! In two weeks he received a note telling him his poetry was considered promising and inviting him to visit the editorial offices. He prepared himself for that visit as meticulously as he had rehearsed for a rendezvous with a girl. He decided that he wanted to "present" himself to the editors in the deepest sense of the word, and he tried to clarify his identity in his own mind. Who was he as a poet and as a man, what were his dreams, his origins, his loves, his hates? He picked up pencil and paper and wrote down some of his opinions, viewpoints, stages of development. Then, one day, he knocked on the door and entered.

A thin little man with glasses was sitting behind the table and asked him what he wanted. Jaromil introduced himself. The editor asked him once more what he wanted.

Jaromil repeated his name, louder and more distinctly. The editor said it was his pleasure to meet Jaromil but that he still did not understand what it was he wanted. Jaromil explained that he had sent some poems to the journal and that he had been invited for a visit. The editor said that poetry was handled by a colleague who was out at the moment. Jaromil replied that this was a pity, as he would have liked to know when his poems were scheduled for publication.

The editor lost his patience. He rose from his chair, took Jaromil by the arm, and led him to a big cabinet. He opened it and showed Jaromil the tall stacks of manuscripts piled on the shelves. "My dear comrade," he said, "in an average day we get verse from twelve new authors. What does that add up to in a year?"

"I don't know," Jaromil mumbled in embarrassment, when the editor pressed him for a guess.

"Per year, that makes four thousand three hundred eighty new poets. Would you like to go abroad?"

"Yes, I suppose so," said Jaromil.

"Then keep on writing," said the editor. "I am certain that sooner or later we will start exporting poets. Other countries export their mechanics, engineers or wheat and coal, but our greatest export asset is poets. Czech poets could give a valuable boost to developing countries. In return for our poets, we'll get electronic instruments or bananas."

A few days later, Jaromil's mother told him that the janitor's son had been at the house looking for him. "He said you should visit him at police headquarters. And he asked me to tell you that he congratulates you on your poems."

Jaromil blushed with pleasure. "Did he really say that?"

"Yes. As he was leaving he made a point of saying, 'Tell him that I congratulate him on his poems. Don't forget.'"

"That makes me happy. Yes. That really makes me happy," Jaromil said with special emphasis. "You know, I really write my poems for people like him. I am not writing for some snob of a litterateur. After all, a carpenter doesn't make chairs for other carpenters, but for the people."

And so one day the following week he entered the great building of the National Security, announced himself to the armed guard in the lobby, waited a while, and finally shook the hand of his old cohort who had come dashing down the stairway and greeted him warmly. They went into his office, and the janitor's son repeated, "Listen, I had no idea I had such a famous schoolmate! I was saying to myself: it's him, it isn't him, it's him, but in the end I told myself, it must be him, it couldn't be a coincidence, not with a name like that!"

Then he led Jaromil out in the hall and showed him a big bulletin board with several photographs (policemen training with dogs, with weapons, with parachutes) and several printed circulars. In the middle of it all was a clipping of one of Jaromil's poems, decoratively outlined in red ink, which dominated the whole board.

"What do you say?" asked the janitor's son. Jaromil didn't say anything, but he was happy. It was the first time he had ever seen one of his poems living an independent life of its own.

The janitor's son took Jaromil by the arm and led him back to his office. "I bet you wouldn't have dreamed that fellows like us read poetry," he laughed.

"Why not?" said Jaromil, who was enormously impressed by the idea that his verse was not being praised by old maids but by men with revolvers on their backsides. "Why not? Today's police officer is a different breed from the uniformed cutthroat of the bourgeois days."

"You're probably thinking that police work and poetry don't mix, but you're wrong," mused the janitor's son.

Jaromil elaborated on this thought. "After all, today's

poets are different from the old type, too. They aren't spoiled, moonstruck milksops."

The janitor's son continued. "We're in a tough trade— let me tell you, my friend, how tough it can be—but we enjoy something delicate once in a while. Sometimes a man can hardly stand what he has to put up with in the course of a day's work."

Then (his day's duty was just ending) he asked Jaromil to join him for a few beers across the street.

"Believe me, security work is no picnic," resumed the janitor's son after they had settled themselves in the tavern. He took a long gulp from his stein. "Remember what I said the last time about that Jew? Well, he turned out to be quite a swine, let me tell you. It's a good thing we've got him under lock and key."

Of course, Jaromil had no idea that the dark-haired man who had led the Marxist youth circle had been arrested. He did have a vague sense that people were being rounded up, but he did not know that there were tens of thousands of them, including many communists; that many were tortured; and that their guilt was mostly fictitious. That's why he reacted to his friend's announcement with mere surprise, untinged by either approval or condemnation. Nevertheless, Jaromil's reaction did contain a trace of sympathy, such that the janitor's son felt called upon to say firmly, "There's no room for sentimentality in our work."

Jaromil feared his friend was again eluding him, was again a few steps ahead. "Don't be surprised that I feel sorry for him. I can't help it. But you're right, sentimentality could cost us dearly."

"Very dearly," added the janitor's son.

"None of us wants to be cruel," insisted Jaromil.

"That's right."

"But we'd commit the greatest cruelty of all if we didn't have the courage to be cruel toward those who are," said Jaromil.

"Damn right," agreed the janitor's son.

"No freedom for the enemies of freedom. It's cruel, I know, but that's how it's got to be."

"Damn right," reiterated the janitor's son. "I could tell you a lot of stories about that, but my lips are sealed. It's my duty. Listen, my friend, there are some things I can't even tell my wife about. Even my own wife doesn't know some of the things I do here."

"I understand," said Jaromil and once again, he was envious of his classmate's manly occupation, his secrecy, his wife, even the idea that he kept secrets from her and she could not object. He envied his friend's *real life*, with its rude beauty (and beautiful rudeness) which continually surpassed Jaromil's existence (he had no idea why they arrested the dark-haired man, he only knew that it had to be done). Face to face with a friend his same age, he once again bitterly realized that he had not yet penetrated into real life.

While Jaromil was engaged in these envious ruminations, the janitor's son looked him deep in the eyes (at the same time his mouth broadened into a dull smile) and began to recite the verse tacked to the bulletin board. He knew the whole poem by heart and didn't skip a single word. Jaromil was at a loss as to how to react (his friend kept his eyes glued on him throughout). He blushed (aware of the painful naiveté of the recitation), but his sense of happy pride was infinitely stronger than his embarrassment—the janitor's son loved his poetry and had learned it by heart! His poems had thus entered the world of men, independently, on their own, as his emissaries and advance guard!

The janitor's son droned the recitation to its end. Then he said that for a whole year he had been attending a special school in a villa on the outskirts of Prague, and that the school occasionally invited interesting people to address the police students. "We're thinking of asking some poets to come over some Sunday for a special poetry night."

They ordered another round of beer, and Jaromil said, "That's a beautiful idea, having policemen arrange a poetry night."

"Why not policemen? What's wrong with that?"

"Nothing at all," replied Jaromil. "On the contrary. Police and poesy, poesy and police. Perhaps the two are closer than anyone thinks."

"Sure, why not?" said the janitor's son, and declared that he'd love to see Jaromil among the invited poets.

Jaromil demurred at first, but in the end was happy to acquiesce. If literature had hesitated to reach out its fragile, bloodless hand to him, he was now being clasped by the hard, rough hand of life itself.

6

Let's keep Jaromil's picture before us a while longer. He is sitting across the table from the janitor's son, a stein of beer in his hand. Behind him, in the far distance, is the closed world of his childhood; in front of him, in the personification of a former classmate, is the world of action, the alien world which he fears and for which he desperately yearns.

This is the basic situation of immaturity. The lyrical approach is one way of dealing with this situation: the person banished from the safe enclosure of childhood longs to go out into the world, but because he is afraid of it he constructs an artificial, *substitute* world of verse. He lets his poems orbit around him like planets around the sun. He becomes the center of a small universe in which nothing is alien, in which he feels as much at home as an infant inside its mother, for everything is constructed out of the familiar materials of his own soul. Here he can achieve everything which is so difficult "outside." Jiří Wolker, a shy adolescent student, can lead revolutionary throngs to the barricades; here, in cruel verse, virginal Arthur Rimbaud vicariously lashes his "little mistresses." But those revolutionary throngs and those mistresses are not constituted out of the hostile material of an alien outer world but they are part of the poet's own being, the material of his own dreams, and do not disturb the unity of the universe which he has constructed for himself.

Jiří Orten wrote a beautiful poem about a child who was happy inside its mother's body and perceived birth as a terrifying death, *a death full of light and horrid faces*. The infant desperately wanted to go back, back into the mother, back into the *sweet-scented night*.

In immature man the longing persists for the safety and unity of the universe which he occupied alone inside his mother's body. Anxiety (or anger) persists as well—toward the adult world of relativity in which he is lost like a drop in an alien sea. That's why young people are such passionate monists, emissaries of the absolute; that's why the poet weaves his private world of verse; that's why the young revolutionary (in whom anger is stronger than anxiety) insists on an absolutely new world forged from a single idea; that's why such a person can't bear compromise, either in love or politics, the rebellious student hurls his *all or nothing* in the face of history, and twenty-year-old Victor Hugo rages when he sees his fiancée Adele Foucher holding the hem of her skirt so high over the muddy sidewalk that her ankle is exposed. *It seems to me that modesty is more important than a skirt,* he reprimands her in a letter, adding, *pay heed to my words or I will box the ears of the first insolent lout who dared look at you!*

The adult world, on hearing this majestic threat, bursts into laughter. The poet is wounded by the betrayal of his beloved's ankle and by the laughter of the crowd. The dramatic struggle between the poet and the world begins.

The adult world knows perfectly well that the absolute

is an illusion, that nothing human is either great or eternal and that it is perfectly normal for a sister to sleep with her brother in one room. But Jaromil was in torment! His redhead announced that her brother was coming to Prague and planned to stay with her for a week; she asked Jaromil not to come to her flat during that time. That was too much for him, and he became angry: he couldn't be expected to give up his girl for a whole week just because "somebody or other" was coming to town.

"You're not being fair!" countered the redhead. "I am younger than you, but I have a place of my own and we've always been meeting there. Why can't we ever stay at your house?"

Jaromil knew the girl was right, and his irritation mounted. He became more aware than ever of his shameful lack of independence, and blinded by anger he announced to his mother that very day (with unprecedented forcefulness) that he was going to invite his young lady to the house because that was the only place where they could have some privacy.

How they resembled each other, mother and son! Both equally bewitched by nostalgia for the monistic period of unity and harmony. He wants to return to the sweet-scented night of her maternal depths, and she wants to be that sweet-scented night, now and forever. When her son was growing up, Maman had tried to surround him like an airy embrace. She had accepted all his opinions: she became a disciple of modern art, she converted to communism, believed in her son's glory, denounced the hypocrisy of professors who took one position one day and another the next. She still wanted to surround her son like the sky, still wanted to be of the same matter as he.

How then could she tolerate the intrusion of the foreign body of a strange woman into this harmonious unity?

Jaromil saw the opposition in her face, and this increased his obstinacy. Yes, he wanted to search for the sweet-scented night, he was seeking the old maternal universe, but he no longer looked for it in his mother. On the contrary, in his search for his lost mother his mother was the biggest obstacle.

She recognized her son's determination and she yielded. One evening, the redhead found herself for the first time in Jaromil's room; it would have been a beautiful occasion if both of them hadn't been so nervous; Maman had gone to the movies, but her spirit still seemed to hover over them, watching and listening. They talked much more softly than usual. When Jaromil embraced the girl he found her body cold and realized that it was best not to go further. And so instead of the expected joys, they spent the evening in distracted conversation, constantly looking at the hand of the clock that announced Maman's approaching return. The only way out of Jaromil's room led through his mother's room, and the redhead was vehement about not wanting to meet her. She therefore rushed off some half an hour before Maman's arrival, and left Jaromil in a very bad mood.

Far from discouraging him, however, this experience only made him more determined. He came to the conclusion that his position in the family house was unbearable; it wasn't his home, it was his mother's, and he was a mere tenant. He was goaded to the point of willful obstinacy. He invited the redhead again, and greeted her with forced jocularity, which was supposed to banish the uneasiness that had oppressed them the first time. He even had a bottle of wine standing on the table and because neither of them was used to alcohol they soon drank themselves into a state in which they could succeed in ignoring Maman's omnipresent shadow.

All that week, Maman kept coming home late in the evening, as Jaromil had hoped. In fact, she exceeded his wishes and was out of the house even on days when he hadn't asked her to be. It was neither goodwill nor a concession, but a protest demonstration. Her exile was intended to demonstrate to Jaromil his cruelty, her late hours were supposed to say to him: you're behaving as if you were lord and master here, you're treating me like a housemaid, I can't even sit down and catch my breath when I'm through with a day's hard work.

Unfortunately, she couldn't utilize those long afternoons and evenings when she was out of the house for any good purpose. The co-worker who had once been interested in her had grown tired of the fruitless courtship. She tried (with little success) to reestablish ties with some of her old friends. She went to the movies. With morbid satisfaction she savored the bitter emotions of a woman who had already lost her parents and her husband and who was being chased out of her own house by her son. She sat in the dark movie theater, watching two strangers kissing on the distant screen, and tears slowly trickled down her face.

One day she came home a little earlier than usual, ready to put on an aggrieved face and to ignore her son's greeting. She had hardly entered her room and closed the door behind her when the blood rushed to her head. From Jaromil's room, just a few steps away, she heard the loud panting of her son mixed with feminine moaning.

She stood paralyzed, and yet it occurred to her that she couldn't possibly remain in that spot and listen to the amorous exclamations—that would be tantamount to standing right next to them and staring (at that moment she actually did see them in her mind's eye, quite distinctly), and that would be unbearable. She was overwhelmed by a wave of mindless anger made all the more rabid as she realized her utter impotence, for she could nether scream nor stamp her feet nor break furniture nor barge in and beat the two of them; she could do nothing at all except stand stock-still and listen.

And then the little bit of lucid sense that was left in her brain joined with the blind surge of anger into a sudden, insane inspiration. When the redhead moaned once more from the next room, Maman called out in a voice filled with anxious solicitude, "Jaromil, for heaven's sake, what's wrong with your young lady?"

The moans ceased immediately and Maman rushed to the medicine cabinet. She took out a little bottle and ran back to the door of Jaromil's room. She pushed down on the door handle; the door was locked. "For God's sake, don't scare me like this. What's wrong? Is the young lady all right?"

Jaromil was holding the redhead's body, which was trembling with anxiety in his arms. He muttered, "No, it's nothing..."

"The young lady had cramps?"

"Yes..."

"Open the door, I have something to make her feel better," Maman said, once more pushing down the handle of the locked door.

"Wait a minute," said her son, quickly rising from the girl's side.

"Such pains!" said Maman. "It must have been awful!"

"One second," said Jaromil, hastily pulling on his trousers and shirt. He threw a blanket over the girl.

"It must be the stomach, don't you think?" Maman asked through the door.

"Yes," answered Jaromil, who opened the door slightly and reached out for the bottle of stomach drops.

"Won't you let me in?" said Maman. A kind of madness was driving her further and further; she didn't let herself be put off and pushed into the room. The first thing she saw was a bra draped over a chair and lingerie scattered about. Then she saw the girl. She was cowering under the blanket and she really looked as pale as if she had just passed through a severe abdominal attack.

Now Maman had to brazen it out; she sat down next to the girl. "What happened to you? I came home and heard such terrible sounds ... poor thing!" She shook out twenty drops on a cube of sugar. "But I know all about these stomach cramps! Just suck on this and you'll be fine in no time..." She lifted the lump of sugar to the redhead's mouth. The girl's lips reached for it as obediently as they had for Jaromil's kisses a little while earlier.

Maman had been driven into her son's room by intoxicating anger. The anger was now dissipated, but the intoxication remained: she gazed on that small, gently opening mouth and felt an enormous urge to pull the covers off the redhead and to see her completely naked. To disrupt the unity of that small, hostile world formed by the girl and Jaromil; to touch what he touched; to claim it as her own; to occupy it; to enfold both bodies in her airy embrace; to immerse herself in their ill-concealed nudity (she noticed Jaromil's shorts lying on the floor); to come between them, insolently and innocently, as if it was all a matter of stomach cramps; to be with them the way she was with Jaromil, when she gave him drink from her naked breast; to cross over the bridge of this ambiguous innocence into their play-making and their love; to be like a sky vaulting over their naked bodies, to merge with them...

She was frightened by her own excitement. She advised the girl to breathe deeply, and quickly left the room.

7

_____

A small, locked bus was standing in front of the police headquarters building with a number of poets clustered around it waiting for the driver. Two police officials who were among the organizers of the poetry evening were in the group, too, as was Jaromil. He knew several of the poets by sight (for example, the silver-maned poet who had once taken part in a meeting at Jaromil's school and recited a poem about youth). Jaromil didn't quite dare address any of them, although his diffidence was somewhat eased by the recent publication of five of his poems in a literary journal. To be on the safe side he had stuck the journal into the breast pocket of his jacket. This made half his chest look flatly masculine and the other half provocatively feminine.

The driver appeared at last and the poets (there were eleven of them, including Jaromil) scrambled into the bus. After an hour's drive, the vehicle stopped in the midst of pleasant countryside, the poets got out, the two officials showed them a river, a garden, a villa, took them through the whole building, the classrooms, the auditorium (where the festive evening would soon commence); they were forced to peer into a row of three-bed dormitories where participants in police courses were housed (startled, these men jumped to attention with the same exaggerated military bearing used during official inspections), and at last the poets were led into the director's offices. Awaiting them were a tray of sandwiches, two bottles of wine, the director in uniform, and, to top it all off, an exceptionally beautiful girl. One after another, they shook the director's hand and mumbled their names. He pointed to the girl. "This young lady is in charge of our film circle," and he proceeded to explain to the eleven poets (who were meanwhile one after another shaking the girl's hand) that the people's security forces had their own club where a rich cultural life was being cultivated. They had a drama group, a choral group, and recently had started a film circle under the young lady's direction; she was currently a student at the film school and she had been nice enough to offer her help to the young policemen. They were trying to provide her with everything she needed: an excellent camera, the latest in lighting equipment, and, above all, enthusiastic young men; the director quipped that he wasn't quite sure whether this enthusiasm was stimulated by interest in cinema or in the pretty young cinematographer.

After shaking everyone's hand, the young lady nodded

to several youths standing behind huge reflectors, and instantly the poets and the director found themselves chewing their sandwiches in the glare of spotlights. The director tried to make spontaneous, relaxed conversation, but it was continually being interrupted by the girl's orders to her crew. The lights were shifted several times, and at last the camera began its soft buzz. After a few minutes of filmed conviviality the director thanked the poets for their participation, looked at his watch, and said that the public was already eagerly awaiting them.

"If you please, comrade poets, step this way," said one of the organizers, and proceeded to read their names from a slip of paper. The poets lined up in alphabetical order and at his signal marched to the stage. A long table stood on the platform, with a chair for each of the poets marked by a place card. As they sat down the crowded auditorium rang with applause.

This was Jaromil's first appearance before a crowd of people. He was filled with elation, and this sense of intoxication did not leave him all night. In any case, everything went off splendidly. After the poets sat down on their assigned chairs, one of the organizers stepped up to the lectern positioned at one end of the table, greeted the eleven poets, and introduced them. One by one, the poets named rose to their feet, bowed, and the hall burst into applause. Jaromil, too, bowed, and was so stunned by the applause that it took him a few seconds to notice that the janitor's son was waving at him from the front row. He nodded back, and this small gesture seen by the eyes of all gave him a delightful sense of informality, so that during the course of the evening he nodded at his friend several more times like someone who felt totally free and comfortable on the stage.

The poets were sitting in alphabetical order and Jaromil found himself to the immediate left of the silver-haired poet. "My dear boy! What a surprise! I saw your poems in the journal the other day." Jaromil smiled politely and the poet continued. "I made it a point to remember your name. They are truly excellent poems, I really enjoyed them." Before he could continue, the organizer again stepped to the microphone and asked the poets to recite selections from some of their latest work.

And so one poet after another stepped up to the lectern in alphabetical order, read a few poems, acknowledged the applause, and returned to his seat. Jaromil anxiously awaited his turn; he was afraid of stuttering, he was afraid his voice might quaver, he was afraid of everything; he got to his feet and walked to the lectern like a sleepwalker; he had no time to think. He started to recite and after a few lines of verse his sense of confidence increased. The applause at the conclusion of the poem was the longest accorded anyone thus far.

The accolade added to Jaromil's self-assurance, such that he recited the second poem with even greater confidence than he had the first. He did not mind in the least that two large reflectors suddenly burst into light and a camera started to buzz only a few steps away. He pretended to be unaware of this activity, continuing his recitation without a hitch. He even succeeded in lifting his eyes from the paper and in looking not only at the vague dark expanse of the hall but at the very specific spot near the camera where the pretty young filmmaker was standing. There was another wave of applause, Jaromil read two more poems, heard the buzz of the camera, saw the face of the cinematographer, bowed, and returned to his place. At that moment, the silver-maned poet rose from his chair and, tilting back his majestic head, opened his arms and clasped Jaromil's back. "My friend, you're a poet! You're a poet!" Then because the applause still continued, he turned toward the audience and bowed his silver head.

After the eleventh poet had finished his presentation, the organizer once more stepped to the podium, thanked everyone, and announced there would be a small intermission, after which anyone in the audience who was interested could return to chat with the poets. "That part of the program is not compulsory. It is voluntary, and concerns only those who are interested."

Jaromil was enchanted; people squeezed his hand, clustered around him; one of the poets identified himself as the editor of a publishing house and expressed surprise that Jaromil had not yet published a book; he invited Jaromil to send him a selection of his verse; another cordially asked him to take part in a meeting arranged by a student organization. The janitor's son, of course, clung close to Jaromil and made it known that they had been close friends ever since childhood. The director shook Jaromil's hand and said, "It looks like this evening's laurels belong to the youngest!"

He then turned to the other poets and announced that to his great regret he would be unable to join in at the discussion session, because he had to officiate at the dance scheduled to begin next door at any moment. With a jocular smile, he remarked that girls from neighboring villages were all flocking to the dance because his policemen were such a handsome group of lads. "Never mind, comrades, I'm sure this won't be your last visit here. Thank you for your beautiful and inspiring poems! Come to see us again soon!" He shook everyone's hand and left for the adjoining hall where the sounds of a dance band already could be heard.

The auditorium which just a few minutes earlier resounded to deafening applause was silent and almost empty. The poets, still animated by the response to their performance, waited up front in a small cluster. One of the functionaries stepped to the microphone and announced, "Comrades, intermission is over and I am returning the floor to our honored guests. Will all those who want to take part in the discussion please sit down?"

The poets returned to their chairs on the podium. Facing them, in the front row of the empty auditorium, about ten people took their seats. Among them were the janitor's son, both organizers who accompanied the poets on the bus, and an old gentleman with a wooden leg and crutches as well as several unremarkable-looking men and even two women. One seemed to be about fifty (perhaps a secretary from the office). The other was the cinematographer who had finished her shooting and was now watching the poets with large, calm eyes. The presence of the beautiful woman was all the more significant and encouraging to the poets as the merry sounds of the dance next door grew louder and more seductive. The poets sitting on the stage and the people in the first row of the auditorium were about equally matched in number, and the two groups eyed each other warily like opposing soccer squads lined up on the field before the kickoff. As the painful silence continued, Jaromil felt a growing sense of uneasiness about his team's capabilities.

But Jaromil had underestimated his colleagues. Some of them were veterans of hundreds of similar occasions, so that discussion had become their specialty. Let us also recall the historical context: this was an era of discussions and meetings. The most diverse institutions, party and youth organizations, workers' and social clubs were busily arranging cultural evenings to which they invited all sorts of painters, poets, astronomers, agronomists, and economists. The organizers of such events were honored and rewarded for their endeavors, for the epoch required revolutionary activity, and lacking revolutionary barricades such fervor had to be channeled into meetings and discussions. And the painters, poets, agronomists, and economists loved to participate because this was their way of proving they were not merely esoteric specialists but true revolutionaries in living touch with the masses.

The poets were therefore thoroughly familiar with questions posed by audiences; they knew that these questions recurred repeatedly with the crushing regularity of statistical law. They knew that somebody was sure to ask: Comrade, how did you first start to write? They knew that somebody else would ask: How old were you when you wrote your first poem? They knew that somebody was sure to inquire: Who is your favorite author? There was also sure to be somebody in the audience intent on showing off his familiarity with Marxist thought by means of questions such as: Comrade, how would you define socialist realism? And they knew that in addition to questions they would also be treated to exhortations to write more poetry about (1) the occupations of the people present at the discussion, (2) youth, (3) the evils of life under capitalism, (4) love.

The initial minute of silence then was not caused by inexperience; on the contrary, it was to be accounted for by the poets' excessively routine, professional approach. To some extent it may have also been the fault of bad teamwork, because this group of poets had never appeared together before and they had no prearranged kickoff pattern. At last the silver-maned poet broke the silence, talked beautifully and inspiringly, and after ten minutes of improvisation challenged the row of listeners to voice any questions that came to their minds. Now that the poets had warmed up to the game they exhibited an eloquence and spontaneous teamwork that were flawless. They made sure that everyone got his proper turn, they complimented one another cleverly, they alternated serious answers with witty anecdotes. All the basic standard questions were duly posed and the standard answers duly given. (Who wouldn't be fascinated by the silver-maned poet's response to the question of how and when he wrote his first poem? He explained that if it hadn't been for his cat Mitzi he would never have become a poet, for it was she who inspired him to compose his first lines of verse, at the age of five. He proceeded to recite the poem, and because the opposite row had no idea whether to take it seriously or not, he started giggling himself, so that every-one—poets and questioners alike—enjoyed a good loud laugh.)

The expected exhortations materialized, too. It was Jaromil's former classmate who got up first and launched into a sober discourse. Yes, the poetry evening was excellent and all the poets were first-rate. But had anyone noticed that despite the fact that approximately thirty-three poems had been presented (assuming an average of three poems per poet), not a single one of them dealt with the national security force, even indirectly? And could anyone honestly maintain that the people's police did not play a role in our lives that deserved at least one thirty-third of our attention and respect?

Then the middle-aged lady rose to her feet. She said she agreed completely with the sentiments just expressed by Jaromil's former schoolmate, but that she had an entirely different question: Why was so little written these days about love? Muffled laughter could be heard on the questioners' squad. The lady continued: After all, people loved one another under socialism, too, and they'd enjoy some poems about love.

The silver-maned poet rose, bowed his head, and said that the lady was absolutely right. Why should a socialist be ashamed of love? Is there anything wrong with love? I am an old man, he said, but I am not afraid to admit that when I see women in their light summer dresses, revealing their young attractive bodies, I cannot help turning my head. The row of questioners tittered with the conspiratorial sympathy of fellow sinners. The poet went on: What have I to offer these beautiful young women? Shall I hand them a hammer tied with a red ribbon? Or when I come to pay my respects, shall I bring a sickle to put in their vases? No, I offer them roses; love poetry resembles the roses which we offer to lovely women.

Yes, that's right, the lady assented eagerly. The old

poet, encouraged by the response, pulled a sheaf of manuscripts out of his breast-pocket and recited a long love
poem.

Yes, yes, that was so beautiful, gushed the lady. But
at that moment one of the police officials who had been
acting as organizer for the evening rose to his feet and said
that those lines were indeed beautiful but one should be
able to tell even from a love poem that it was written by a
socialist poet.

But how can a socialist love poem be different from
any other? asked the lady, still fascinated by the pathetically
lowered silver head of the old poet, and by his poem.

Jaromil kept silent while all the others had their turn,
and yet he knew that he must speak. It seemed to him that
his moment had come at last. After all, he had thought out
this question long ago, way back in the days when he had
visited the artist and devotedly listened to his talk about the
new art and the new world.

Alas, once again it was the artist, it was the artist's
voice and words that issued from Jaromil's mouth!

What did he say? That in the old bourgeois society
love was so deformed by money, social considerations, prej-
udices, that it could never be itself, that it was always but
a shadow of genuine love. Only the new era, by sweeping
away the power of money and influence of prejudice, would
enable man to be fully human and restore love to its glory.
Socialist love poetry is the voice of this great, liberated
emotion.

Jaromil was pleased by his own eloquence and noted
a pair of calm, dark eyes fixed upon him. It seemed to him
that the words "genuine love" and "liberated emotion" flowed
from his mouth like brave ships sailing into the harbor of
those big, dark eyes.

But when he finished one of the poets smiled sarcastically and said, "You really think that there is more feeling
in your lines than in the poems of Heinrich Heine? Do the

loves of Victor Hugo seem too petty to you? Are you trying to tell us that the love of a man like Neruda was deformed by money and prejudice?"

That was an unexpected blow. Jaromil didn't know what to say; he reddened, as a pair of dark eyes witnessed his humiliation.

The middle-aged lady was gratified by the scornful attack of Jaromil's colleague. She said: "Why do you want to meddle with love, comrades? Love will be the same till the end of time, thank goodness."

The organizer replied: "Oh, no, comrade, you are mistaken!"

"No, that's not exactly what I meant to say," the poet quickly interjected, "but the difference between love poetry in the old days and modern love poetry will not lie in the power and truthfulness of the emotion."

"Then where's the difference?" asked the lady.

"Here: that in the past, love—even the greatest love— was always a kind of escape from social life which was distasteful. But the love of today's man is closely connected with our social duties, our work, our struggle for unity. And that's where its new beauty lies."

The opposing row expressed agreement with this formulation. Jaromil, however, broke into a contemptuous laugh: "That kind of beauty, my dear friend, is not very new at all. Didn't the great writers of the past connect love with social struggle? The lovers in Shelley's famous poem were both revolutionaries who died a common death at the stake. Is this what you mean by love isolated from social life?"

A painful lull ensued. A moment ago Jaromil didn't know how to answer his fellow poet's objections, and now his colleague was at a loss for words, such that the impression might arise (an inadmissible impression) that there was no real difference between yesterday and today, and that the new world was really an illusion. In fact, the lady rose to her feet once more and announced with an eager smile,

"We're waiting, comrades. Tell us—how is love today any different from love in the old days?"

At that decisive moment, when everyone was disconcerted, the man with the wooden leg intervened. He had been following the debate carefully, but with evident impatience. Now he struggled to his feet, propped himself up against the chair, and stood up erect. "Allow me to introduce myself, comrades," he said, and the people in his row began to shout at him that this was not necessary since they knew him very well. "I am not introducing myself to you, but to the comrade poets, our guests," he retorted, and because he realized that his name alone would not mean much to the poets, he proceeded to give them a brief account of his life's history. He'd been working in this place for almost thirty years; he was already employed there way back in the days of Mr. Kocvara, the manufacturer who had used the villa as a summer home. He had been there all during the war, after the Gestapo arrested Mr. Kocvara and took over the house as a recreation center. After the war it had been given to the Catholics and now it was owned by the police. "But from everything I've seen no government takes such good care of us working people as the communists." Still, even nowadays everything was not as it should have been. "In the days of Kocvara, in the days of the Gestapo, in the days of the Catholics the bus stop was always right across from the villa." That was extremely convenient. All he had to do was to step out of his door and he was at the bus stop. All of a sudden, for no good reason, they moved the bus stop two blocks down the street. He had protested to every office and bureau he could think of. No use. He pounded the floor with his crutch. "The villa is now supposed to belong to the working people! So you tell me why it is that a working man like me has to walk two blocks to get to the bus stop!"

The people in the front row replied (partly with impatience, partly with a certain amusement) that they had already explained to him a hundred times that the bus now stopped in front of the plant which had recently been built.

The man with the wooden leg replied that he knew all that, but he proposed that the bus stop at both places.

The people in his row said it was nonsense for a bus to make two stops within two blocks.

The word "nonsense" insulted the man with the wooden leg. He said that nobody had the right to speak to him that way. He struck the crutch against the floor and his face flushed with anger. Anyway, it wasn't true that you couldn't have two stops two blocks apart. He had seen buses make such stops on other routes.

One of the organizers rose and repeated word for word (apparently he had done so many times before) the decision of the Czechoslovak autobus transportation bureau specifically prohibiting bus stops closer than a specified minimum distance.

The man with the wooden leg pointed out that he had suggested a compromise solution. Why not put the stop halfway between the villa and the new plant?

That would only mean that both the workers and the policemen would be inconvenienced, they responded.

The dispute had already gone on for twenty minutes and the poets were vainly trying to join the debate. The people in the row opposite were immersed in the topic they were thoroughly at home with and didn't give the poets a chance to speak. Only after the man with the wooden leg became tired of his fellow employees' opposition and sat down sulkily in his chair did the discussion die down. In the ensuing silence the band music from the dance next door echoed through the hall.

Nobody had anything more to say. One of the officials rose, thanked the poets for their visit, and for the interesting discussion. The silver-maned poet spoke on behalf of the visitors and said that the discussion was more valuable for the poets than for the audience (as was usually the case) and that it was the poets who were grateful for the opportunity.

In the adjoining room, a singer's voice launched into a popular tune; members of the opposite row clustered around the man with the wooden leg to soothe his anger, and the poets found themselves alone. Only after a while the janitor's son approached with the two organizers and took them to the bus.

8

The beautiful cinematography student was going back with the poets. As the bus sped through the night toward Prague, the poets surrounded her and each of them tried to win her interest. By an unfortunate coincidence Jaromil found himself seated too far away to take part in the entertainment. He was thinking about his redhead and he realized more and more clearly how incorrigibly ugly she was.

The bus stopped somewhere in the middle of Prague and some of the poets decided to drop in at a tavern. Jaromil and the beautiful cinematographer accompanied them. They sat around a large table, talked, drank, and then the girl suggested they come up to her place. By then, only a handful remained: Jaromil, the silver-maned poet, and the publishing house editor. They made themselves comfortable in a beautiful room on the first floor of a modern villa which the girl was subletting. They chatted and sipped wine.

The old poet devoted himself to the girl with a verve with which nobody could compete. He sat next to her, praised her beauty, recited poems to her, improvised odes celebrating her charms, now and again sinking on one knee before her and clutching her hands. The editor lavished virtually the same attention on Jaromil. He didn't extol his beauty, but he repeated over and over: You are a poet, you are a poet! (Let us note that if a poet calls someone else a poet, it isn't the same thing as an engineer calling someone an engineer or a farmer calling someone a farmer. A farmer is a person merely engaged in farming. A poet is not merely a man writing verse, but a man *elected* to write verse. Only a poet is capable of detecting this touch of grace in a fellow poet. Let us recall Rimbaud's letter: *all poets are brothers*. And only a brother is capable of detecting the secret family sign.)

The filmmaker, before whom the silver-maned poet was kneeling and whose hands were victims of his ardent admiration, kept gazing at Jaromil. Jaromil soon became aware of the girl's interest, was enchanted, and stared back. What a beautiful rectangle! The old poet gazed at the girl, the editor at Jaromil, and Jaromil and the girl at one another.

Only once was this visual geometry disturbed, and only for a brief moment. The editor took Jaromil by the arm and led him to the balcony adjoining the room. He then requested that Jaromil join him in urinating over the railing into the courtyard below. Jaromil gladly obliged, for he was anxious that the editor remember his promise to publish a collection of his poems.

When the two of them returned from the balcony, the old poet rose from his knees and said it was time to go. He could see perfectly well, he said, that he was not the one the girl was longing for. He asked the editor (who was far less observant and considerate) to leave the young couple alone, for this was what they wanted and deserved. As the old poet put it—they were the prince and princess of the evening.

When at last the editor, too, grasped the situation and was ready to leave, the old poet had already taken him by the arm and was pulling him to the door. Jaromil saw himself about to be alone with the girl, who was sitting in a big armchair, her legs crossed, her dark wavy hair falling over her shoulders and her eyes gazing straight at him . . .

The story of two people about to become lovers is so eternal that it almost made us forget History. How pleasant it is to recount such love stories! How sweet it would be to forget the monster that saps our brief lives as cement for its vain monuments. How sweet it would be to forget History!

But it knocks on the door and enters our story. It is not coming in the guise of secret police, nor in the guise of a sudden revolution. History does not always make a dramatic entrance, it often seeps through every-day life like dirty dishwater. In our story, History makes its appearance in the guise of underwear.

During the epoch we have been describing, elegance was considered a political crime in Jaromil's homeland. The clothes worn at that time were awful (it was just after the war and everything was still in short supply). Elegance of underwear, especially, was considered in that dour epoch almost as a luxury deserving of severe punishment! Men who were bothered by the hideousness of the underwear then being sold (the shorts were extremely wide, reached down to the knees, and left a comical open wedge over the belly) resorted to brief linen trunks intended mainly for sports and gymnastics and called "training shorts" or "trainers." That epoch thus witnessed the peculiar spectacle of men all over Bohemia climbing into the beds of their wives and sweethearts garbed like soccer players. Bedrooms in those days resembled a sports stadium, but from the viewpoint of sartorial elegance this was not so bad: the "trainers" had a certain sporty rakishness and came in gay colors— blue, green, red, yellow.

Jaromil generally paid little attention to his clothing, for he was under his mother's care. She picked out his suits and his underwear, she made sure his underwear was sufficiently warm that he wouldn't catch cold. She knew precisely how many sets of underwear Jaromil owned, and by a mere glance into the linen closet could tell which particular pair Jaromil was wearing that day. When she noticed that no regular underwear was missing from the closet, she became angry. She didn't like Jaromil to wear the "trainers," for she believed these shorts were not underwear proper and should be worn exclusively for sports. When Jaromil objected that the standard underwear was ugly, she answered with barely concealed irritation that nobody would ever see it on him anyway. And so whenever Jaromil went to call on his redhead, he always pulled a pair of underpants out of the linen closet, hid them in his writing-desk and secretly put on his colorful "trainers."

This time, however, he had no inkling of what the night would bring and he was wearing a horrible pair of drawers, wide, shabby, dirty gray!

You might think this an insignificant complication, for he could have easily put out the light so that the girl couldn't see his underwear. But a small lamp with a pink shade was casting an amorous glow over the room, and was impatiently waiting to light the two lovers' way toward mutual ecstasy; Jaromil couldn't imagine asking the girl to turn off the lamp.

Or perhaps it occurred to you that he could pull his ugly underwear off together with his trousers. But this thought never crossed Jaromil's mind, for he had never done such a thing before. Such a sudden leap into nakedness frightened him. He always undressed gradually; when he was with the redhead, he made love to her in his shorts until the very last moment, when he pulled them off under the cover of excitement.

And so he stood terrified, facing the large dark eyes, and announced that it was time for him, too, to take his leave.

The old poet was enraged. He told Jaromil that he must never insult a woman, and in a whisper he described to him the pleasures that awaited. But the poet's words only seemed to emphasize the hideousness concealed under his trousers. Watched by the beautiful eyes, his heart aching, Jaromil backed toward the door.

The moment he reached the street he was overcome by tearful regret; he couldn't get the picture of the beautiful woman out of his mind. And the silver-haired poet (they said good night to the editor at a tram stop and were now walking alone through the dark streets) was tormenting him by taking him to task over and over again for having committed both an insult against good sense and and a breach of gallantry.

Jaromil retorted that he had no intention of insulting the young lady, but that he was in love with his own girl who loved him passionately in return.

You're crazy, said the old poet. After all, you're a poet, a lover of life: you won't harm your girl by making love to another. Life is short and missed opportunities never recur.

That was painful to hear. Jaromil answered that in his opinion a single great love on which we stake everything is worth more than a thousand petty affairs; that his one girl encompassed all the women of the world; that his girl was so fascinating, so endlessly lovable, that it was easier for him to live a thousand unexpected adventures with this one girl than it had been for Don Juan to experience with a thousand and one girls.

The old poet stopped; Jaromil's words clearly touched him. "Perhaps you're right," he said, "but I am an old man and I belong to an old world. I must admit that even though I'm married, I'd have loved to stay with that woman."

When Jaromil continued to expound his views on the superiority of monogamous love, the old poet bowed his head. "Perhaps you're right, my friend. I know you're right, in fact. Didn't I, too, dream about a great love? About one single great love? A love as boundless as the universe? But I missed my chance, dear friend, because that old world, that lousy old world of money and whores, wasn't made for love."

Both of them were drunk. The old poet put his arm

around the young poet's shoulders. They stopped in the middle of the road. The old man lifted his arm. "Death to the old world! Long live love!"

Jaromil found this a magnificent, bohemian, and poetic gesture. Both of them yelled long and enthusiastically into the dark recesses of Prague: "Death to the old world! Long live the glory of love!"

The silver-haired poet suddenly knelt down in front of Jaromil and kissed his hand. "My friend, I salute your youth! My age salutes your youth, because only youth can save the world!" He was silent for a few moments; then, his bare head touching Jaromil's knees, he added in a melancholy voice, "And I salute your great love."

They parted at last and Jaromil soon found himself back in his room. Before his eyes he saw the image of a beautiful, rejected woman. Driven by an impulse for self-punishment, he examined himself in the mirror. He took off his trousers in order to see himself in his ugly, shabby underwear. Consumed with loathing, he continued to gaze for a long time at his ridiculous homeliness.

Then he realized that his anger was not directed at himself at all. He was thinking of his mother—who chose his underwear, who made it necessary for him to resort to surreptitious tricks, who knew about every last shirt and sock. With hate he thought about his mother who was holding him by a long invisible rope cutting into his neck.

9

He started to treat the redheaded girl with even greater cruelty than before. Of course, this cruelty was masked in the guise of wounded love: Why don't you try to understand me a little? Can't you see the mood I'm in? Have we become such strangers that you can't guess what's bothering me? If you really loved me, the way I love you, you'd sense what I am thinking. How come you're always interested in things I don't like? Why are you always telling me about brother number one and brother number two and sister number three? Don't you see that I have lots of things on my mind just now, that I need your help and support instead of this eternal egocentric gibberish?

The girl of course defended herself. What's wrong with talking about my family? Don't you talk to me about yours? Is my mother less of a person than yours? And she reminded him (for the first time since it happened) how his mother had invaded their privacy and forced herself on them.

Jaromil loved and hated his mother. Now he sprang to her defense. What's wrong with Mother offering to help us? That only shows that she liked you, that she accepted you as a member of the family.

The redhead laughed: surely Mother knows the difference between the groans of stomach cramps and the sighs of love! Jaromil was insulted, sulked, and the girl had to ask his forgiveness.

One day they were walking down the street, the redhead's arm tucked under Jaromil's, and they were stubbornly silent (whenever they weren't reproaching each other they were silent, and whenever they spoke they reproached each other). Jaromil saw two beautiful women walking toward them. One was quite young, the other older; the younger one was prettier and more elegant-looking, but the other one was rather chic, too, and surprisingly attractive. Jaromil knew them both: one was the young filmmaker and the other was his mother.

He blushed and greeted them. Both women returned the greeting (Mother did so with exaggerated gaiety). Arm-in-arm with his homely girl, Jaromil felt as if the beautiful filmmaker had seen him in his shameful underwear.

When he came home he asked his mother how she had become acquainted with the cinematographer. She answered with coquettish playfulness that she had known her for some time. Jaromil pressed her for details, but Maman continued to evade him, like a girl teasing her beau; in the end, she told him: the pleasant and intelligent woman had first visited her about two weeks ago. She had said that she admired Jaromil as a poet and wished to shoot a short film about him; it would be an amateur film produced under the auspices of the national police film club, but all the same it would be assured a sizable viewing public.

"Why did she come to you? Why didn't she see me directly?" asked Jaromil.

Mother explained that the girl wanted to get all the background information from her first, rather than bother Jaromil. Actually the girl was so nice that she asked Mother to work on the script! Imagine! The rough draft is already done, the story of a young poet's life.

"Why didn't you tell me anything about it?" demanded Jaromil, annoyed. The association between his mother and the film student instinctively struck him as unpleasant.

"We intended the whole thing as a surprise. It was a piece of bad luck that we met you in the street. You were supposed to come home one day, open the door—and everything would be ready to roll: the girl, the crew, the camera, all set to shoot the film."

Jaromil had no choice in the matter. He came home one day and found the young cinematographer in the house. This time, he was wearing red "trainers" (since the fateful poetry evening he had stopped wearing ugly underwear), but he felt as clumsy and unsure of himself as he had the first time he had met her.

The film-girl declared (nobody bothered to ask Jaromil for his opinion) they would spend the day shooting documentary background material, such as childhood photographs; Maman would speak the commentary. Jaromil was casually informed that the entire film was conceived as a mother's reminiscences about her poet-son. Jaromil felt like asking just what his mother had in mind, but he was afraid of the answer; his face was red. Besides the two women, three men were in the room, grouped around the lighting equipment; it seemed to Jaromil that they were watching him with a sneer; he didn't dare speak.

"Those childhood photos are marvelous. I'd love to use them all," said the girl, leafing through the family album.

"How will they show up on the screen?" Maman asked with professional interest, and the girl assured her there was no need to worry. She then explained to Jaromil that the first sequence of the film would be merely a montage of photographs of him, with his mother recounting her reminiscences off-camera. Then the camera would focus on Maman, and finally the poet would come into the picture: the poet in his native house, the poet writing, the poet strolling through the garden, and finally the poet in open nature amid his favorite surroundings; in a beloved, secluded part of the country, he would recite a poem which would close the film. ("And just where is this beloved landscape of mine supposed to be?" he asked sullenly. They answered that his favorite spot was of course the romantic region near Prague, full of hills and wild crags. "That's not true! I hate those stupid rocks," said Jaromil, but nobody took him seriously.)

Jaromil didn't like this scenario at all and suggested he would like to do some work on it himself; he objected that the script contained much that was banal and conventional (to show a photograph of a one-year-old infant was ridiculous!); he claimed to know of far more interesting problems which could be treated in the film; they asked him to be more specific. He answered that he couldn't spell it all out right then and there, and that he would like some time to think it over.

He wanted to have the shooting postponed at all costs, but his efforts were in vain. Maman put her arm around him and said to her dark-haired collaborator, "He's my eternal troublemaker! He was never satisfied..." She playfully stuck her face close to his. "Isn't that true?" Jaromil didn't answer, and she repeated, "You're my little troublemaker. Admit it!"

The cinematographer said it was great for an author to be a perfectionist, but this time Jaromil was not the author. His mother and she were the authors of the script, and they were ready to take the responsibility. Let Jaromil allow them to make the kind of film they saw fit, just as they were ready to let him write the kind of poetry he liked.

And Maman added that Jaromil needn't be afraid that the film wouldn't do him justice, for both of them—the cinematographer and herself—had the deepest respect and affection for him. She said this in a coquettish way, and it was not clear whether she was flirting with him or with her new-found friend.

Be that as it may, she was definitely flirtatious. Jaromil had never seen her act that way before. This very morning she had gone to the hairdresser and had her hair done in a strikingly youthful fashion; she talked louder than usual, kept laughing and giggling, used all the witticisms she had ever heard, and with great aplomb played the role of hostess, supplying the men of the film crew with a steady stream of coffee and refreshments. She addressed the dark-haired girl with the easy intimacy of a close friend (thus suggesting a sisterhood of sophistication) while condescendingly putting her arm around Jaromil and calling him her troublemaker (thus kicking him back into his adolescence, his childhood, his babyhood).

(What a remarkable sight, mother and son, in their tug-of-war! She is pulling him into his diapers, he is pulling her into her shroud. Ah, what a lovely sight!)

Jaromil bowed to the inevitable; he saw that the two women were as full of steam as two locomotives and that he was in no position to resist their eloquence; he saw the

three men of the crew as a derisive audience likely to jeer
at any false step he might take; he spoke in a whisper while
Maman and the girl talked with hearty zest, because the
presence of the audience was an advantage to them and a
handicap to him. He therefore announced that he was ca-
pitulating, and started to leave. But they countered (again
in a coquettish manner) that he really ought to stay; it would
give them pleasure, they cajoled, if he watched them while
they were working; and so he stayed, idly watching the men
fussing with their lights and removing snapshots from the
family album; now and again he went off to his room,
pretending to be reading or working; confused thoughts filled
his mind; he tried to find something pleasant in the dismally
unpleasant situation and it occurred to him that the girl
might have thought up the whole business just to have an
opportunity to meet him again; he told himself that in such
a situation his mother was merely an unfortunate impedi-
ment to be patiently avoided; he tried to calm himself and
to think of a way to utilize the horrid film affair for his own
benefit, and to make up for the episode that had tormented
him ever since the night he had fled like a coward from the
cinematographer's villa; he tried to overcome his embarrassment and went out to observe periodically how the
shooting was going, hoping that he and the girl might reestablish that magic link of eyes that captivated him at their
first meeting; but the filmmaker seemed absorbed in her
work, going about her job in a sober, matter-of-fact way,
such that their eyes met only accidentally and fleetingly.
Jaromil therefore gave up any attempt to get a response from
the girl while filming was in progress; instead, he decided
he would offer to see her home after the day's shooting.

At last the trio of crew members dismantled their
equipment and hauled their cameras and lights to the
panel truck parked outside. Jaromil was just coming out
of his room when he heard his mother saying to the
girl, "Let's go, I'll come with you. We might still have

time to sit down somewhere and have a little chat."

Jaromil felt as if his prize had been whisked away from under his very nose. Coldly he said goodbye to the girl and as soon as the two women left the house he, too, walked out and strode quickly and angrily toward the redhead's apartment building. She was not home. He paced up and down the block for about half an hour, his mood darkening. Finally he saw her coming. Happy surprise registered on her face, angry rebuke on his. How come she hadn't been home? Hadn't it occurred to her that he might drop over? Why had she stayed out so late?

She hardly had time to close the door behind her before he started pulling off her clothes. He pretended that he was making love to the beautiful film student; soon he heard the redhead's sighs and in his imagination he connected them with the dark-haired girl and this excited him so much that he entered the redhead several times in close succession, but he never stayed inside her longer than a few seconds. The redhead found this so peculiar that she began to laugh. But Jaromil was especially sensitive to ridicule that day and he didn't perceive that the laughing was that of friendly amusement. He was greatly insulted, and slapped the girl's face; she broke into tears and this made Jaromil happy; she wept, and he hit her a few more times. A woman's tears shed for us—this is redemption, Jesus Christ dying for us on the cross. Jaromil savored the redhead's tears for a while, then he kissed and caressed her and went home somewhat soothed.

A few days later the filming resumed. The panel truck came, out of it scrambled three young men (another contemptuous audience) followed by the beautiful girl whose vicarious sighs still breathed in Jaromil's ears. And of course, Maman was present, too, getting younger and younger, resembling a musical instrument that sang, thundered, laughed, and coyly skipped away from the orchestra for solo passages.

This time the eye of the camera was scheduled to focus on Jaromil; he was supposed to be shown in his native surroundings, at his writing-desk, in the garden (for according to the script he loved the garden, the flower-beds, the lawn, the flowers); he was to appear with his mother, who had already recounted her reminiscences in the lengthy introductory segment of the film. The girl posed the two of them on a bench in the garden and prodded Jaromil to initiate a natural, casual chat with his mother. This rehearsal for spontaneity lasted about an hour, but Maman was not discouraged. She kept up a steady stream of chatter (in the actual film, the conversation would not be heard; mother and son would be shown talking to each other, with the soundtrack carrying Maman's prerecorded commentary) and when Maman noticed that Jaromil's expression was not sufficiently positive, she began telling him it wasn't easy to be the mother of a boy like him, a shy lonely boy always sulking about one thing or another.

Then they shoved him in the panel truck and drove him to the romantic countryside near Prague where according to Maman's conviction Jaromil had been conceived. Maman was far too reticent to have ever confided to anyone why she found this landscape so precious. She didn't want to say it—and yet she did. She talked excitedly, in a roundabout, ambiguous way, claiming that this part of the country always had a special meaning for her personally, that she regarded it as a land of love. "Just look at that landscape, how it resembles a woman. There is something maternal about those rich soft curves. And look at those rocks, those wandering, solitary boulders! Isn't there something masculine about the way those stark harsh boulders jut against the sky? Isn't this the land of man and woman? Isn't this an erotic land?"

Jaromil kept planning rebellion; he wanted to tell them that their film was a banal piece of trash; his sense of good taste was outraged; perhaps he might have been able to create a small scene or at least run away, the way he had once run from the river-boat excursion with his mother and her friends, but this time he could not escape. He was held captive by the filmmaker's dark eyes, afraid of losing her a second time.

They posed him in front of a huge boulder, and asked him to recite his favorite poem. Maman was extremely excited. How long it has been! Precisely at this spot she had once made love to a young engineer, long, long ago; precisely here her son was now looming up as if he had sprung out of the ground like a mushroom. (Ah yes, as if on the spot where parents scattered their seed children sprung up like mushrooms!) Maman was carried away by the image of this strange, beautiful, impossible mushroom, speaking in a quaking voice about his yearning to die by fire.

Jaromil sensed that he was doing a poor job of recitation, but he couldn't help it. He reminded himself that he was not subject to stagefright, that he had recited the same poem to an audience of policemen and had performed smoothly and successfully. But this time the words stuck in his throat; standing in front of a ridiculous rock in a ridiculous landscape, afraid of being stared at by some passerby airing his dog (his mother had felt similar uneasiness twenty years earlier), he was unable to concentrate on his verse and performed awkwardly and unnaturally.

They forced him to repeat his poem over and over again, but in the end they gave up. "My big hero!" sighed Maman. "Even when he was going to school he was afraid of every exam. Often he was so scared I had to literally chase him to school."

The filmmaker said they might be able to dub in an actor's voice. She asked Jaromil to stand once more in front of the rock and to move his lips as if he were reciting.

He did as he was told.

"For God's sake!" she shouted impatiently. "You have to move your mouth as if you were speaking, not just any old way! The actor has to synchronize with the movement of your lips!"

And so Jaromil stood before the rock, opening and closing his mouth, and the camera began buzzing at last.

10

Two days ago he had been facing the camera wearing only a light topcoat; now he had to put on his scarf, hat, and heavy winter overcoat; snow had fallen. He was supposed to meet the redhead in front of her house at six o'clock, but it was already a quarter past and there was still no sign of her.

A few minutes of waiting would be no great tragedy, but Jaromil had undergone so much humiliation in the preceding days that he had reached the limit of his endurance; he had to parade up and down a street full of pedestrians, all of whom could clearly tell he was waiting for someone who was in no hurry to see him, and his ignominy was thus made public.

He was afraid to glance at his watch, for such an expressive gesture would clearly convict him in the eyes of the whole street as a lover waiting in vain; he pulled up the sleeve of his overcoat slightly and tucked the edge of it under his watchband in such a way that he could keep glancing inconspicuously at his watch; when he saw that the big hand was already showing twenty minutes after, he became furious; why was it he always managed to be a few minutes early, and this dumb, ugly one could never be on time?

At last she appeared and was met by Jaromil's stony face. They went up to her room, sat down, and the girl tried to excuse herself: she had been with a girl friend. That was the worst thing she could have said. Actually, of course, probably nothing could have mollified Jaromil, least of all the idea that he was kept waiting because of some obscure girl friend—the very essence of insignificance. He told the redhead that he was sorry she had to break off an important discussion with a girl friend on his account, and he suggested that she turn right around and go back.

The girl saw that Jaromil was severely upset. She said that the meeting with her friend had been urgent: her friend was breaking up with her fiancé, she was terribly depressed, and the redhead hadn't the heart to leave until she was in a little better frame of mind.

Jaromil said it had been very noble of her to dry her girl friend's tears, and he hoped her girl friend would return the favor, now that Jaromil was about to put an end to their whole affair. That's right. He was ready to break off, for he refused to have anything to do with someone to whom a stupid girl friend's stupid tears meant more than he.

The redhead saw that things were going from bad to worse; she said that she was very sorry, and that she was asking his forgiveness.

But all this did not alleviate the insatiable demands of his humiliated pride; he declared that her excuses did not alter one iota his conviction that what the redhead was calling love was not love at all; perhaps she thought he was making too much of an apparently petty episode; but it was precisely these small details that revealed her true attitude toward him; that unbearable casualness, that careless matter-of-fact attitude of hers. Why, she was treating him the same way she treated a girl friend, a customer in the store, a passerby in the street! Let her never again say that she loved him! Her love was only a pitiful parody of love!

The girl realized that things had got as bad as they could possibly be. She tried to break through Jaromil's hateful sadness with a kiss; he pushed her away with a near-brutal gesture; she fell to her knees and pressed her head against his stomach; Jaromil wavered, but then lifted her up and coldly asked her not to touch him anymore.

Hatred was going to his head like alcohol; it was a seductive, enchanting feeling. What made it even more intoxicating was the way it bounded back from the girl to hurt and punish him; it was a self-tormenting hate, for Jaromil knew perfectly well that by chasing away the red-headed girl he was losing the only woman he had; he sensed that his anger was unjustified, and that he was being unfair; but for those very reasons he was all the more cruel, for what attracted him was the abyss: the abyss of solitude, the abyss of self-condemnation. He knew that without the girl he would be unhappy (he would be alone) and dissatisfied with himself (knowing that he wronged her), but all this knowledge was impotent against the splendid intoxication of anger. He told her that what he had just said applied forever; her hand must never touch him again.

The girl had encountered Jaromil's anger and jealousy before, but this time she recognized an almost furious determination in his voice. She realized that Jaromil was capable of doing almost anything to satisfy his baffling anger. Almost at the last moment, at the very edge of the chasm, she said, "Don't be angry with me, I beg you! Don't be angry. I lied to you. I wasn't with a girl friend at all."

That startled him. "Where were you then?"

"You'll be mad at me, you don't like him, but I can't help it—I simply had to see him."

"Whom are you talking about?"

"I went to see my brother. Jan, the one who stayed at my place."

He flared up. "Why are you always making such a fuss about your brother?"

"Don't be angry, he means nothing to me. Compared with you he means nothing. But you've got to understand—he's still my brother, we spent more than fifteen years together. He's going away. For a long time. I had to say goodbye to him."

The idea of this sentimental farewell was repugnant

to Jaromil. "Where can your brother be going that it deserves throwing everything else overboard? Is he going on a business trip for a couple of weeks? Or is he off for a weekend in the country?"

No, it was not a business trip, nor a weekend in the country. It was something far more serious, but she couldn't tell Jaromil about it because he would get too angry.

"Is that what you call love? Hiding things from me? Keeping secrets from me?"

Yes, she knew perfectly well that love meant being open with each other. But he must try to understand. She's scared, she's simply scared to death...

"Scared of what? Where could your brother be going that you're afraid to tell me?"

"Can't you guess?"

No, Jaromil couldn't guess. (At this point, his anger was stumbling far behind his curiosity.)

At last the girl confided in him. Her brother had decided to leave the country, secretly, illegally; the day after tomorrow he expected to be over the border.

What's that? Her brother wants to betray our young socialist republic? To betray the revolution? Her brother wants to become an emigrant? Doesn't he realize what he's doing? Doesn't he realize that all emigrants automatically become employees of foreign espionage services trying to undermine our country?

The girl nodded in agreement. Instinct assured her that Jaromil was more likely to forgive her brother's treason against the state than her fifteen minutes of tardiness. That's why she kept nodding. She agreed with everything Jaromil was saying, she said.

"What good is your agreeing with me? You should have talked him out of it! You should have stopped him!"

Yes, she had tried to talk him out of it. She had done everything she could to make him change his mind. That's why she had been late. Perhaps now Jaromil would understand why she was late. Perhaps now Jaromil would forgive her.

And Jaromil really did forgive her lateness. But he told her he could not forgive her brother's desertion. "Your brother took his stand on the other side of the barricades. That's why he is my personal enemy. If a war were to break out, your brother would shoot at me and I at him. Do you understand that?"

"Yes, I do," replied the redhead and she assured Jaromil that she stood firmly on his side, and had no other loyalties.

"How can you say that? If you were really on my side, you'd never let him leave the country!"

"What could I do? I am not strong enough to hold him back!"

"You should have informed me at once. I would have known what to do. But instead, you lied to me! You made up a story about your girl friend! You wanted to fool me. And now you have the gall to say you're on my side!"

She swore that she was on his side, and that she would remain true to him under any circumstances.

"If you meant that, you would have called the police!"

"What do you mean, the police? Surely you don't think I'd turn my own brother over to the police! That would be impossible!"

Jaromil couldn't bear any opposition. "Impossible? If you don't call the police right now, I will!"

The girl repeated that a brother was a brother, and she simply couldn't imagine denouncing him to the police.

"So a brother means more to you than I do?"

Certainly not. But that's quite a different thing from betraying him to the police.

"Love means all or nothing. Love is total or it doesn't exist. I am here, and he's on the other side. You have to take your stand on my side, and not in the middle. And if you're with me, you have to want what I want, do what I do. The fate of the revolution and my fate are one and the same. Anybody who is against the revolution is against me. And if my enemies are not your enemies then you are my enemy!"

No, no, she was not his enemy; she wanted to be united with him in everything. She knew perfectly well love means all or nothing.

"That's right. Love means all or nothing. Next to real love everything else becomes pale, everything else fades away."

Yes, she agreed completely, that's precisely the way she felt, too.

"That's the best test of real love—that it is completely deaf to what the rest of the world thinks. But you're always listening to others, you're full of all kinds of scruples and you beat me over the head with those scruples."

She has no wish to beat him over the head, far from it. But she was scared of doing her brother harm, terrible harm; she was afraid he could pay dearly.

"And what if he does? Suppose he pays dearly—it would be a just price to pay. Or are you by any chance afraid of him? Are you afraid of leaving him? Are you afraid of leaving your family? You want to be stuck to them all your life? You have no idea how I hate your lukewarmness, your half-heartedness, your awful inability to love!"

No, that's not true, she loves him as well as she knows how.

"Yes, that's right," he laughed sarcastically. "As well as you know how! The trouble is that you don't know how! You don't know how to love at all!"

She said that was not true.

"Could you live without me?"

She swore that she couldn't.

"Could you go on living if I died?"

No, no, no.

"Could you go on living if I left you?"

No, no, she shook her head.

What more could he ask? His anger faded, but the excitement remained. Death was suddenly here, sweet, sweet death, to which they had pledged each other in the event of separation. He said in a voice that trembled with emotion, "I couldn't live without you, either." She reiterated that she couldn't live without him and they repeated this over and over, until they were afloat on a cloud of vague yearning; they took off each other's clothes and made love. He stroked her face and felt the moistness of tears. That was beautiful, that had never happened to him before—a woman crying because of love for him. Tears signified to him a magic elixir that brought release and transcendence of the human condition; tears dissolved all physical limitations, and created union with infinity; Jaromil was moved by the dampness of the girl's face and realized that he himself was weeping; they loved one another and their faces and bodies were drenched with moisture, they dissolved into each other, their fluids flowed into one another like two rivers, they wept and made love and were outside this world, like a lake that had left the earth and floated toward the sky.

Then, resting calmly side by side, they continued to caress each other's faces; the girl's rusty hair was matted into comical strands and her face was puffy and red; she was ugly, and Jaromil thought of his poem in which he described how he longed to drink of his beloved, how he thirsted even for her ugliness and her tangled carroty hair and her freckle-stained skin and the old loves that moldered in her flesh; he caressed her and lovingly savored her pitiful wretchedness. He vowed that he loved her, and she vowed the same.

And because he didn't want to let go of this moment of absolute fulfillment, this moment of intoxication with mutually pledged death, he said again, "I really couldn't live without you. I simply couldn't."

"Yes, I would be terribly lonely too if I lost you. It would be awful."

He stiffened. "You mean you can imagine a situation in which you would go on living without me?"

The girl didn't seem to notice the hidden trap. "I'd be awfully sad."

"But you would be able to go on living."

"What else could I do if you left me? But I'd be terribly lonely."

Jaromil realized he had been the victim of a misunderstanding; the redheaded girl had not really pledged her death. When she had said that she couldn't live without him, she had meant it merely as a bit of conventional love-patter, a pretty phrase, a metaphor; poor fool, she had no idea what it was all about—pledging a little sadness to him—who knew only absolutes! All or nothing, life and death! Full of bitter irony, he inquired, "And how long would you be sad? A day? Or even a whole week?"

"A week?" she smiled. "My dear Xavy, I couldn't get over it in a week…" She pressed close to him, to indicate with the touch of her body that her sorrow could hardly be measured by weeks.

But Jaromil reflected upon the matter. What's her love really worth? A few weeks of sorrow. Very well! And what's sorrow, anyway? A bit of frustration. And what is a week of sorrow? After all, nobody is capable of grieving all the time. She'd mourn for a few minutes in the morning, a few minutes in the evening. How many minutes would that make altogether? How many minutes of sorrow was her love worth? How many minutes of sorrow was he worth?

He tried to imagine her life after his death, unruffled, undisturbed, calmly spanning the abyss of his nonbeing.

He had no desire to resume the stormy, jealous dialogue; he heard her voice, asking why he looked so troubled; he didn't answer; the tenderness of that voice was like an ineffectual salve.

Then he rose and began to dress. He was no longer angry; she kept asking him why he was so sad, and instead of an answer he wistfully stroked her cheek; and he said, gazing into her eyes, "You want to go to the police yourself?"

She was under the impression that their beautiful love-making had forever banished his ill will toward her brother. She was therefore startled by his question, and didn't know what to say.

He asked her again (sadly and quietly), "Are you going to tell the police yourself?"

She stuttered something. She wanted to challenge him, and at the same time she feared a confrontation. The meaning of her stuttered words was obvious, however, and Jaromil said, "I understand. You don't want to go there. I'll take care of it myself." He touched her face again (compassionately, sadly, disappointedly).

She was confused and couldn't speak. They kissed, and he left.

When he woke the next morning, Maman had already left the house. While he was still sleeping she had laid out all his clothes on a chair: his shirt, necktie, trousers, jacket, and, of course, his underwear. It was not possible to eliminate this twenty years' habit, and Jaromil had resigned himself to it. But that morning, when he saw the folded, light gray drawers with their absurdly shapeless cut and the gaping fly that was virtually a command to urinate, he was overcome by majestic fury.

Yes, he had risen that morning as one rises to a great, decisive day. He picked up the drawers and examined them in his outstretched arms; he scrutinized them carefully, with hatred that bordered almost on affection. Then he bit down on one end, firmly grasped the other and gave a sharp pull. He heard the sound of ripping cloth. He threw the torn underwear on the floor. He hoped his mother would see it lying there.

Then he pulled on a pair of yellow "trainers," put on the shirt, tie, jacket, and trousers that Maman had prepared for him, and left the house.

11

He turned in his identity card in the lobby (as was the custom upon entering the great building of National Security) and climbed the stairs to the second floor. Look at the way he climbs. He is conscious of every step! He looks as if he is carrying his fate on his shoulders; he is climbing the stairs as if he is climbing not merely to a higher level of a building but to a higher level of his own life, whence he would be able to survey an entirely new panorama.

All the signs were auspicious; when he stepped into the office of his old schoolmate and saw his face he saw that it was the face of a friend; it smiled at him; it registered pleasant surprise; it was cheerful.

The janitor's son said how glad he was Jaromil had come to visit him, and Jaromil's soul surged with bliss. He sat down on the chair that was offered him and for the first time he felt he was truly facing his former schoolmate as one tough-minded adult faces another; equal to equal; man to man.

For a while they indulged in the usual small talk of old friends, but for Jaromil this was only a pleasant overture during which he eagerly waited for the curtain to rise. "The main reason I came to see you," he said at last in a grave voice, "is that I want to tell you something important. I know of a man who is about to flee the country in the next few hours. We've got to do something to stop him."

The janitor's son became extremely attentive and asked Jaromil a number of questions. Jaromil answered them quickly and precisely.

"This is a very serious matter," said the janitor's son. "I can't handle this by myself."

He led Jaromil down a long corridor into another

office, where he introduced him to an older man in civilian clothes. After the janitor's son described Jaromil as an old schoolmate, the man gave Jaromil a comradely smile; they called a secretary and took down a statement; Jaromil had to give exact information: the girl's name; her occupation and place of work; her age; her family background; the occupations of her father, her brothers, her sisters; the precise time and date she informed him of her brother's intended defection; what sort of person is her brother; what does Jaromil know about him?

Jaromil said that he knew quite a bit, since the girl often talked about him. That's exactly the reason why he considered the whole matter so important and why he rushed to inform them, as his comrades and fellow citizens. The girl's brother hates our form of society. How sad that is! He comes from a humble, poor family, but because he was once employed as a chauffeur for a bourgeois politician he is now a willing tool of people who are plotting treason against our country. Yes, he can say that with utter certainty, for the girl conveyed to him her brother's opinions quite explicitly. According to her, he was ready to shoot down communists. One could well imagine what this type of individual—a man whose only aim was to destroy socialism—would do once he crossed the border.

With masculine matter-of-factness the three men dictated the statement to the secretary, and the older official then told Jaromil's friend to go quickly and make the necessary arrangements. After the janitor's son had dashed out, the official thanked Jaromil for his help. He told him that if the whole nation were as vigilant as he, the socialist fatherland would be invincible. And he said that he hoped their meeting would not be the last. "You surely realize how many enemies our fatherland has," said the man. "You spend a lot of time at the university among students, and no doubt you know a lot of literary-type individuals. Of course, the majority of them are honest people, but there are quite a few troublemakers among them, too."

Jaromil gazed with admiration at the policeman's face. It looked beautiful to him, crisscrossed with deep wrinkles testifying to a hard, two-fisted life. Yes, Jaromil too hoped their meeting would not be the last. He was glad to be of help. He knew where he stood.

They shook hands and smiled at each other.

With this smile etched on his mind (the beautiful, wrinkle-creased smile of a real man), Jaromil left police headquarters. He paused at the top of the flight of stairs leading to the sidewalk. A sunny, frosty morning was vaulting over the city rooftops. He breathed in the cold air and felt himself to be filled to the brim with virility and he all but burst into song.

First he wanted to go straight home, to sit down at his desk and write poetry. But after a few steps he halted; he didn't feel like being alone. It seemed to him that during the past hour his features had hardened, his step become firmer, and his voice more decisive. And he longed to be seen in his new incarnation. He went by the university and spoke to everyone he knew. Nobody commented that he seemed any different from usual, but the sun was still shining and an unwritten poem was still soaring over the rooftops. He went home, locked himself in his room, covered a few sheets of paper, but was not satisfied with the results.

And so he put down his pen and gave himself over to daydreams; he dreamt of a mysterious threshold which a youth must cross in order to become a man; he knew the name of that threshold: its name was not love, it was duty. It is hard to write poetry about duty. What image does that word call forth? But Jaromil felt that precisely this harsh, stark word could summon up new and unexpected imagery. After all, he wasn't writing about duty in the old sense of the word, imposed by external authority, but duty which man creates for himself, which he chooses freely, a duty which is voluntary and represents human daring and dignity.

These reflections permeated Jaromil with enthusiasm, for they helped him sketch an entirely new self-portrait. He longed once again to be seen in this new metamorphosis and rushed over to the redhead's place. It was again around six o'clock and she should have been home long ago. But her landlord informed him she had not yet returned home from work. He said that two men had been looking for her about half an hour earlier and that he had told them the same thing.

Jaromil had time to kill, and he ambled up and down the redhead's street. After a while he noticed two men who also seemed to be strolling up and down. It occurred to Jaromil they might be the same pair mentioned by the landlord; then he saw the girl approaching from the opposite side of the street. He didn't want her to see him, so he ducked into a dark doorway and watched her walking briskly toward her building and disappearing inside. He felt uneasy and afraid to move. Then he saw the two men follow after her. A minute or two later, all three of them emerged; only then did he notice a car parked a few steps from the entrance; the two men and the girl climbed in and drove off.

Jaromil knew that the two gentlemen were most likely policemen; but in addition to an icy sense of fear he also felt amazement that his behavior earlier that day had been a real act which had set in motion a real train of events.

The next day he hurried to the girl's house, to catch her as soon as she came home from work. But the landlord told him that since the time the two men took her away the young lady had not come back.

That disturbed him very much. Early next morning he went again to police headquarters. The janitor's son continued to behave in a friendly manner, cordially pressed his hand, smiled cheerfully. When Jaromil inquired about his girl, who had not yet returned home, he told him not to worry. "You put us on the track of a very serious matter. We've got to get those bugs under a magnifying glass," he said with an equivocal smile.

Once again, Jaromil walked out of the police building into a sunny, frosty morning; once again he sucked in the icy air and felt big and filled with destiny. One thing, however, was different from the previous day. It now occurred to him that through his decisive act he had *entered the realm of tragedy.*

Yes, that's literally what he told himself as he descended the long flight of stairs toward the street: I have entered the realm of tragedy. His friend's cheerfully terrifying phrase, *we've got to get those bugs under a magnifying glass,* fired his imagination. He was aware that his girl was now in the hands of strange men, that she was at their mercy, that she was in danger, and that interrogation lasting several days was surely no laughing matter. He also remembered what his friend had told him about the dark-haired Jew and about the more grim aspects of his work. All these ideas and images filled him with a kind of sweet, fragrant and majestic substance, so that he felt himself growing bigger and striding through the streets like an animated monument of grief.

It occurred to him that now he knew at last why the poetry he had tried to write two days before had been worthless. Two days ago he hadn't yet understood his own act. Two days ago he had wanted to write poems about duty, but now everything had become clear: the majesty of duty grows out of the bloody, split head of love!

Jaromil walked the streets dazed by his own fate. Then he returned home and found a letter. You are invited to come next week on such and such a day to meet some people I think you will find congenial. It was signed by the girl cinematographer.

Even though the invitation did not promise anything definite, Jaromil was greatly pleased, for it proved that the beautiful filmmaker was not a lost opportunity, that their story was not yet finished. The strange idea was going through his head that it was no coincidence this letter came on the day it did, on the day he first fully understood the tragedy of his situation; surely, there was some deeper significance to all that. He was filled by a vague, inspiring feeling that everything he had experienced during the last two days had qualified him to gaze unabashed at last upon the dazzling beauty of the dark-haired filmmaker and to attend her party with manly self-confidence.

He felt better than ever before. His head was swimming with poetry, and he sat down at his desk. No, love and duty were not antithetical concepts, he told himself. That was the distorted, old way of looking at the problem. Love or duty, love or revolution—no, no, there was no such dilemma. He did not expose his girl to danger because love meant little to him—quite to the contrary, he wanted to effect a world in which people would love each other more than ever. Yes, that's how it was. Jaromil had risked the safety of his own beloved precisely because he loved her more than other men love their women; precisely because he knew what love and the bright new world of pure feeling were all about. Of course, it is terrible to sacrifice a concrete living woman (redheaded, petite, talkative, freckle-faced) for the sake of the future world. Such a sacrifice, the only genuine tragedy of our time, was worthy of a great poem!

He sat down at his desk and wrote and paced the room and it seemed to him that the poem he was creating was the greatest he had ever composed.

It was a bewitching night, more intoxicating than all the amorous nights he could imagine; it was a magical night even though he was all alone in his old childhood room. Maman was next door and Jaromil had completely forgotten that he had ever been angry at her. In fact, when she knocked on the door to ask what he was doing, he spoke to her tenderly. He explained that he needed quiet and concentration. "I am writing the greatest poem of my life," he said. Maman smiled (maternally, receptively, sympathetically) and left him in peace.

Eventually he went to bed. It occurred to him that at that very moment his girl was no doubt surrounded by men—policemen, interrogators, guards. They could do with her whatever they wanted. Watch her change into prison clothes, peer through her cell window while she was sitting on a pail, urinating.

Actually, he didn't really believe in the reality of these extreme possibilities (most probably they were merely taking down her deposition and then would let her go). But fantasy cannot be controlled: over and over again he imagined her sitting in her cell, watched by a strange man, interrogators pulling off her clothes. One thing puzzled him: these images did not arouse a single spark of jealousy!

You must be mine to die upon the rack if I want you, Keats's cry rings through the ages. Why should Jaromil be jealous? The redheaded girl now belonged to him more than ever: her fate was his creation; it was his eye watching her as she urinated into the pail; it was his hand touching her when a guard treated her roughly; she was his victim, his creation; she was his, his, totally his own!

Jaromil was no longer jealous; that night, he slept the deep sleep of a real man.

Part 6:
The Middle-Aged Man

1

The first part of our story embraced fifteen years of Jaromil's life, whereas the fifth part, although equally long, covered barely one year. In this book time thus flows in a tempo opposite that of real life: the tempo slows down as the years go by.

This is because we are examining Jaromil's story from an observatory which we erected at the point of his demise. For us, his childhood is in the far distance where months and years melt imperceptibly into each other. As he and his mother emerge from these misty horizons and approach nearer and nearer to our observatory, everything gradually becomes as distinct as a highly realistic painting showing every vein on every leaf.

Just as your life is determined by the kind of profession and marriage you have chosen, so our novel is limited by our observatory perspective: Jaromil and his mother are in full view, while we glimpse other figures only when they appear in the presence of these two protagonists. We have chosen this approach as you have chosen your fate, and our choice is equally unalterable.

Still, every person regrets that he cannot live other lives. You, too, would like to live out all your unrealized potentials, all your possible lives. (Alas, unattainable Xavier!) Our book is like you. It, too, yearns to be all the other novels it could have been.

That is why we are constantly dreaming about erecting other observatories. How about putting one up in the middle of the artist's life, or perhaps in the life of the janitor's son or that of the redheaded girl? After all, what do we really know about these people? We hardly know more than does foolish Jaromil, and he knows precious little about anyone.

What kind of novel would it be if we followed the career of the janitor's son, and Jaromil would appear only once or twice in the course of brief episodes about a poet and former schoolmate? Or we could follow the artist's story and learn at last what he really thought of his beloved Maman, whose belly he had used like a piece of canvas.

Man cannot jump out of his life, but perhaps a novel has more freedom. Suppose we hurriedly and secretly dismantled our observatory and transported it elsewhere, at least for a little while? Perhaps we could carry it a long, long way, beyond Jaromil's death! Perhaps all the way here, to the present, where there is almost nobody (his mother, too, died a few years ago) who still remembers Jaromil.

2

Good heavens! Imagine constructing an observatory that close! And perhaps looking in on all the poets who once sat with Jaromil on the stage of the policemen's hall! Where are the poems they recited then? Nobody remembers them anymore, and the authors themselves would deny ever having written them. For they are ashamed, everyone is ashamed...

What actually remains of that distant time? Today, people regard those days as an era of political trials, persecutions, forbidden books, and legalized murder. But we who remember must bear witness: it was not only an epoch of terror, but also an epoch of lyricism, ruled hand in hand by the hangman and the poet.

The wall behind which people were imprisoned was made of verse. There was dancing in front of it. No, not a danse macabre! A dance of innocence. Innocence with a bloody smile.

You say it was a period of shabby lyricism? Not quite! The novelist, who wrote about this period with the blind eyes of a conformist, produced mendacious, stillborn works. But the poet, who merged with his epoch just as blindly, often left behind beautiful verse. As we mentioned earlier, through the magic of poetry all statements become the truth, provided they are backed by the power of emotion. And the poets certainly felt so deeply that their emotions smoldered and blazed. The smoke of their fiery feelings spread like a rainbow over the sky, a beautiful rainbow spanning prison walls . . .

But no, let's not erect our observatory in the present. We are not concerned with describing the past, with catching its image in more and more mirrors. We did not choose that epoch because we were interested in it for its own sake, but because it seemed to offer an excellent trap for snaring Rimbaud and Lermontov, lyricism and youth. For what is a novel if not a trap for catching a hero? To hell with pictures of the time! We are interested in a young poet!

That young man, whom we have called Jaromil, must therefore never stray completely out of our sight. Yes, let us leave our novel for a little while, let us carry our observatory to the end of Jaromil's life and set it down in the mind of an entirely different character made of entirely different stuff. But let's not set it down any further than some three years after Jaromil's death, at which point Jaromil had not yet been forgotten completely. Let's fashion a chapter that would stand in about the same relationship to the rest of the story as does a small guesthouse to a country manor:

The guesthouse is on another part of the estate. It is a self-sufficient structure independent of the main house, it may have been sublet, and the inhabitants of the manor can get along perfectly well without it. Yet, on a summer day, kitchen smells and people's voices drift from the manor through the open windows of the guesthouse . . .

3

Let's pretend that the role of the guesthouse is played by a gentleman's flat: a foyer with a clothes closet built into the wall, a bathroom with a spotlessly clean tub, a small kitchen full of dirty dishes, and one big room serving as a combination living room and bedroom. It contains a wide couch, a large mirror, bookshelves all around the walls, several framed pictures (reproductions of antique paintings and sculpture), a coffee table between a pair of armchairs, and a window looking out on roofs and chimneys.

It was a late afternoon in the spring. The owner of the flat had just returned home. He opened his valise, pulled out a pair of wrinkled overalls, and hung them up in the closet. Then he went inside and opened the window wide; cool fresh air wafted into the room; the man went into the bathroom, turned on the hot water faucet over the tub, started to undress and examined his body with satisfaction; he is in his forties, but since the time he'd begun doing physical labor he has been feeling in excellent shape; his brain seemed lighter and his arms and legs stronger.

He stretched out in the bathtub and put a wooden board across the top of the tub to serve as a makeshift table. Several books lay on the board in front of him (that odd interest in Greek and Roman authors!); he gratefully soaked in the heat of the water, absorbed in his book.

Suddenly the doorbell rang. One short ring, two long rings, then after a pause another short one.

He hated to be disturbed by uninvited visitors, and for this reason he had arranged a set of signals with his friends and mistresses. But whose signal was this?

Perhaps he was getting old and his memory was slipping, he thought ruefully.

"Just a moment!" he shouted, got out of the tub, dried himself in a leisurely manner, put on his bathrobe, and opened the door.

4

A girl in a heavy winter overcoat was standing outside. He recognized her at once, and was struck speechless.

"They let me go," she said.

"When?"

"This morning. I was waiting for you to get home from work."

He helped her out of her coat—thick, brown, shabby—and hung it on a hanger. He realized she had on the same clothes she had been wearing the last time she had visited him, the same dress and the same winter coat. A winter day of three years ago seemed to throw a chill over the spring afternoon.

The girl too was surprised to find the room unchanged, while so much had happened in her life in the meantime. "Everything here is still the same," she said.

"Yes, that's true."

He motioned toward her favorite armchair. As soon as she was comfortably seated he started bombarding her with questions. Are you hungry? Are you sure I can't fix you a sandwich? Where are you going from here? Are you planning to go home?

She told him that she really should go home, that she had already gone as far as the railroad station, but had decided to come back and see him first.

He was still in his bathrobe. "Excuse me," he said. "Let me put on some clothes." He went into the foyer and shut the door behind him. Before he started to get dressed he lifted the phone and dialed a number; when a woman's voice answered, he explained that something had come up and that he would not be able to see her that night.

He was under no obligation to the girl sitting in his room; all the same, he didn't want her to overhear his conversation, and he spoke in a low voice. While he was talking, he kept looking at the shabby brown coat on the hanger. It filled the air with nostalgic music.

5

It had been three years since he had last seen her, and about five years since they had met. He had known much more attractive women, but this girl possessed several rare qualities. When he had met her she had been about seventeen years old, amusingly direct and outspoken, and erotically gifted. She was eager to make him happy; she understood within fifteen minutes that any talk of love was taboo, and without his having to explain anything obediently came to visit him only when he explicitly asked her to do so (it was hardly once a month).

The man did not hide his predilection for lesbian women; once, in the abandon of physical love, the girl had whispered in his ear how she once seduced a strange woman at a bathing resort, and described how they had made love to each other. The man was titillated by the story, and after realizing its improbable nature was moved by the warmth of the girl's desire to please him. Not all the girl's amorous exploits were imaginary. She introduced him to some of her girl friends, and she inspired and organized a number of pleasant, erotic entertainments.

She understood that her middle-aged lover not only did not insist on fidelity, but felt safer if his mistress had more serious involvements elsewhere. With innocent indiscretion she therefore treated him to accounts of her current and past love affairs, which he found interesting and amusing.

Now she was sitting in the armchair (the man had in the meantime put on a pair of slacks and a sweater). She said, "As I was leaving the prison, I saw horses."

6

"Horses? What horses?"

She explained that in the morning, as she was stepping through the prison gate, some people on horseback were just riding by. They were sitting high in the saddle as if they had grown out of the animals to form one huge superhuman monster. The girl had felt tiny and insignificant. Far above her head she heard snorting and laughter, and had squeezed herself fearfully against the prison wall.

"Where did you go from there?"

She had gone to the trolley stop. The sun was getting quite warm, and she felt uncomfortable in her heavy coat. She was embarrassed by the stares of passersby, afraid that the trolley would be crowded, and that everybody would gape at her. Fortunately, nobody was at the trolley station except one old lady. That was a blessing, to find only one old lady there.

"And you made up your mind to come and see me first?"

Duty demanded that she first go home to visit her parents. She had already gone to the railroad station, and was standing in line at the ticket window, but when her turn came she ran away. The idea of going home depressed her. She was hungry and bought a salami sandwich. She sat in the park and waited until four o'clock, when she knew he would be coming home from work.

"I am glad you came here first. It was nice of you to come," he said.

"You remember," he added after a pause, "you still

remember what you said? That you never wanted to see me again in your life?"

"That's not true," said the girl.

"Yes, it is," he smiled.

"No, it isn't!"

7

It was true, of course. When she came to see him that day, three years before, he had opened the liquor cabinet and was about to pour some brandy. The girl shook her head. "No, not for me. I'll never drink anything in your house again."

He was surprised. The girl went on, "I am not coming to see you anymore. The only reason I am here today is to tell you that."

He continued to show surprise. She told him that she really loved the young man she had told him about, and that she had decided not to deceive him any longer. She came to ask her middle-aged friend to sympathize with her situation and she hoped he would not be angry.

Even though he enjoyed a colorful erotic life, the middle-aged man was basically of an idyllic temperament and appreciated a certain calm and orderliness in his adventures. True, the girl was but a modest little star twinkling in his amorous constellations, but even a single star suddenly torn out of its proper place in the heavens can cause unwelcome discord in the celestial harmony.

Furthermore, he felt misunderstood and was hurt. Had he not been genuinely pleased that the girl had a young man who loved her? Had he not asked her to tell him everything about her young man, had he not advised her how to win his love? He had been so amused by the young swain, in fact, that he had even saved the poems the fellow had been writing to the girl. He found them distasteful, but he was interested in them, just as he was interested in the world springing up around him, which he observed from the warm comfort of his bathtub.

He was willing to watch over the two young lovers with all the cynical kindness he could muster, and the girl's sudden decision struck him as sheer ingratitude. He found it difficult to control himself sufficiently to conceal his irritation from the girl. Seeing the frown on his face, she talked on and on to justify her decision; over and over again, she declared that she sincerely loved her young man and was determined to be absolutely honest with him.

And now here she was three years later, sitting in the same armchair and wearing the same clothes, telling him that she had never said anything of the kind!

8

She was not lying. She belonged among those rare souls who do not distinguish between what is and what should be, and who mistake their ethical wishes for reality. Of course, she remembered perfectly well what she had said to her middle-aged friend; but when she realized that she should not have said it, she denied her recollection the right to real existence.

Of course she remembered: that was the afternoon when she had stayed with her middle-aged companion a bit longer than she had intended, and had been late for her date with the young man. The youth had been mortally insulted and she realized that only an excuse of equally mortal gravity could mollify him. She therefore had invented the story that she had spent the afternoon with a brother who was about to flee the country. Naturally, she couldn't have guessed that her young lover would urge her to denounce her brother to the police!

And so the very next day, as soon as she was finished at work, she ran to her middle-aged friend to ask for advice; he was kind and friendly; he suggested she stick to her lie and try to convince the young man that after a dramatic scene her brother had sworn to forget the idea of emigration. He told her in detail how to describe this fictitious scene to the young man. He also proposed that she make the fellow feel he was indirectly the family's savior, since without his decisive influence her brother would have gone ahead with his foolish plan, and no doubt would have been apprehended at the border or even shot by the frontier guards.

"How did your conversation with the young fellow come out, anyway?" he asked her now.

"I never saw him again. They arrested me just as I was coming back from seeing you. They were waiting for me in front of my house."

"So you never had a chance to talk to him again?"

"No."

"But surely they must have told you what happened to him..."

"No..."

"You really don't know?" the middle-aged man asked in surprise.

"I don't know anything," the girl replied, shrugging her shoulders as if to imply that she didn't care either.

"He died," the man said. "He died shortly after they took you away."

9

The girl hadn't known that. From far, far away she heard the pathetic words of the young man who had wanted to place love and death on the same scales.

"Did he kill himself?" she asked in a soft voice that was suddenly ready to forgive.

The man smiled. "Oh, no, nothing like that. He just got sick and died. His mother moved away. You wouldn't find a trace of them in the old villa any longer. But there is a big black monument in the cemetery. It's like the monument of a great writer. *Here lies a poet* . . . That's what his mother had them inscribe on the stone. Under his name they engraved that epitaph you once showed me, about wanting to die by fire."

They fell silent. The girl was reflecting on the fact that the young man hadn't killed himself but had died a perfectly ordinary death. Even his death turned its back on her. No, returning from prison she had never wanted to see him again, but she hadn't reckoned with the possibility that he was no longer alive. If he didn't exist, then the cause of her three-year imprisonment no longer existed, and everything became a nightmare, nonsense, unreality.

"How about some supper?" he asked. "Give me a hand."

10

They went into the kitchen, sliced some bread, made ham and salami sandwiches, opened a can of sardines, found a bottle of wine.

That was the ritual they had always followed. It was a soothing feeling for the girl, to know that this stereotyped bit of life was always awaiting her, unchanged, undisturbed, that she could still readily enter into it. At this moment, it seemed to her the most beautiful bit of life she had ever known.

The most beautiful? Why?

It was a piece of life that was completely safe. This man was kind to her and never demanded anything; there was nothing she had to feel guilty or obligated about; she was always safe with him; it was the kind of safety people feel when they are momentarily out of the reach of their own fate; she was as safe as a figure in a play, when the curtain falls after the first act and there is an intermission; the other characters, too, put down their masks and become ordinary people carrying on casual conversation.

The middle-aged man had felt himself outside the drama of his own life for a long time; at the start of the war he had escaped to England with his young wife, fought against the Germans as an airman, and lost his wife in an air raid on London. On his return, he had decided to remain in military service, and at just about the same time that Jaromil decided to study political science, the man's superiors concluded that he had been too closely connected with capitalist England and that he was not politically reliable enough to serve in the people's armed forces. And so he found himself working in a factory, his back turned on History and its dramatic shows, on his own fate. He concentrated entirely on himself, on his responsibility-free amusements and his books.

Three years before the girl had come to say goodbye, because he had offered her a mere interlude whereas the young man was offering her a lifetime. And now here she was munching a ham sandwich, sipping wine, happy that her middle-aged friend was volunteering her this intermission, slowly enveloping her in blissful peace.

She relaxed, and felt like talking.

11

Only crumbs were left on the empty plates, the bottle was half gone, and she discussed her experiences in prison, about fellow prisoners and guards, casually and without pathos. As was her custom, she elaborated on details which seemed interesting to her, connecting them in an illogical but pleasant stream of narrative.

And yet there was something odd about the way she

talked this time. Usually her conversation was naively roundabout but ultimately aimed toward the heart of the matter, whereas this time her words kept circling around the core as if intending to hide it.

But what core? The man understood at last. He asked, "And what about your brother?"

"I don't know..."

"Did they let him go?"

"No..."

Only now did he realize why the girl had run away from the ticket window and why she was so afraid of going home. She was not only an innocent victim, she was also guilty of bringing disaster to her brother and to her whole family. He could imagine the means which had been used by interrogators to force a confession from her, and how in her attempts to elude her tormentors she entwined herself in a web of new and ever more damaging suspicions. How could she explain to her family that it was not she who had denounced her brother but some mysterious young man who was not even alive any longer?

The girl was silent, and her middle-aged friend was overcome by a wave of sympathy. "Don't go home today. Wait. You've got a lot of time for that. You have to think everything over carefully. If you feel like it, you can stay here with me."

He put his hand on her cheek. He didn't caress her, he simply pressed his hand softly, tenderly against her skin.

The gesture was so loving that the girl's eyes filled with tears.

12

Since the death of his wife, whom he had loved very much, he didn't care for female tears. He was as terrified of them as he was of the danger that women would make him actively participate in the drama of their lives. He regarded tears as tentacles endeavoring to ensnare him and drag him from his idyllic state of non-fate, and he shrank from them in abhorrence.

That's why he was taken aback when he felt the dampness of tears on his palm. But he was even more startled to find that on this occasion he was completely helpless against their heartrending power. This time he knew they were not tears of love directed at him, that they were neither deception nor extortion nor show. There they were, pure and simple, streaming from the girl's eyes in the same natural way that sorrow or joy invisibly emanates from a person's body. He had no shield against their innocence, and he was touched to the depths of his soul.

It occurred to him that during his entire period of acquaintance with the girl they had never hurt one another. They had always been considerate of each other, had given each other brief periods of pleasure. And they were content. There was no need for reproach. He derived special satisfaction from the knowledge that at the time of the girl's arrest he had done everything humanly possible to rescue her.

He lifted her out of the armchair, wiped her tear-stained face with his fingers, and tenderly embraced her.

13

Somewhere in the wings, in a story we left three years back, death has been impatiently waiting. Now, its skeletal figure is throwing a long, long shadow, which falls across the scene of the middle-aged man and his young companion and chills the cozy flat with sudden darkness.

The man is holding her tenderly but she is huddled motionless in his arms.

What does this huddling mean?

She is giving herself to him. She has put herself in his arms and wants to stay there.

But by huddling she is not opening out to him! She has given herself, but she remains closed, locked. Her shoulders are hunched together to conceal her chest, and her head does not turn toward his but is resting on his breast. She is peering into the darkness of his sweater. She has given herself to him securely sealed, to be preserved in his embrace as in a vault of steel.

14

He lifted her bowed, wet face and began kissing her. He was stimulated by sympathy rather than sensuality, but situations of this kind often set in motion an automatic train of reactions difficult to escape. He tried to pry her mouth open with his tongue, but was unsuccessful; her lips remained closed and refused to respond.

Oddly enough, the more he failed to elicit a response from her, the stronger became the wave of sympathy that engulfed him, for he was becoming aware that the girl in his arms had had her soul torn out of her body, and that the wound of this bloody amputation had not yet healed.

He felt her poor skinny body, the wave of sympathy reinforced by falling darkness erased all sharp contours and deprived both their bodies of definiteness and materiality. At the same time, he felt in his own flesh that he was capable of loving her physically!

This was quite unexpected. He felt sensuous without sensuality, he was excited with excitement! Perhaps it was only sheer kindness, which through some mysterious transubstantiation had turned to physical arousal.

This excitement was so sudden and incomprehensible that it flooded him with passion. He caressed her body eagerly and tried to unbutton her dress.

She struggled to free herself.

"No, no! Please don't! I don't want to!"

15

Because mere words didn't seem capable of stopping him, she pulled herself free of his embrace and backed away toward a corner of the room.

"What is it? What's the matter with you?" he asked.

She pressed herself silently against the wall.

He went up to her and stroked her cheek. "Now, now. You're not afraid of me, are you? Tell me, what's the matter? What happened to you?"

She stood in the corner, silent, unable to find words. Before her eyes she saw once more the horses passing the prison gate, tall, vigorous animals mated to their riders to form single proud bodies. She was so far beneath them, so pitiful compared to their animal perfection, that she longed to merge with any nearby object, with the trunk of a tree or with a wall, to hide in their lifelessness.

"What's the matter with you?" he repeated.

"I shouldn't have come here. I wish you were old. Very, very old. An old lady. Or an old man."

16

He silently caressed her face and then asked her to help him make the bed (the room had already turned dark). They lay side by side on the wide couch and he talked to her in a soft, soothing voice, in a way he had not talked to anyone in years.

The longing for physical love had completely vanished, but he was filled with a tender sympathy so deep and intense that it could not be denied. He lit a lamp and gazed at the girl.

She was lying on her back, tense, awkward, her eyes fixed on the ceiling. What had happened to her? What had they done to her? Beaten her? Terrorized her? Tortured her?

He did not know. The girl was silent and he gently stroked her hair, her forehead, her cheek.

He caressed her for a long time, until it seemed to him that the terror in her eyes was easing.

He caressed her for a long time, until she closed her eyes.

17

The window of the flat was open and the cool air of a spring night was streaming in. The room was again dark and the middle-aged man was lying motionless next to the girl. He listened to her breathing, her troubled tossing and turning, and when he thought she had fallen asleep he lightly caressed her arm, happy that he was able to provide her a first night of rest in the new era of her mournful freedom.

The guesthouse to which we compared this part of the novel also has an open window and through this window we still hear the sounds of the novel which we left some time ago. Do you hear the distant sound of Death, impatiently stamping its feet? Let it wait, we are still here in the flat, in another novel, in another story.

Another story? No, not really. In the lives of the middle-aged man and the girl, the interlude we have been describing was only a pause in the story, not the story itself. Their encounter will hardly entwine them in an adventure. It was only a brief hiatus which the man granted the girl before the travail that awaited her.

In our novel, too, this section was only a quiet interlude in which an anonymous man unexpectedly lights a lamp of kindness. Let us gaze at it for a few seconds more, that quiet lamp, that kindly light, before it vanishes from our sight . . .

Part 7:
The Poet Dies

1

Only a real poet knows how lonely it is inside the mirrored house of poetry. The distant sounds of gunfire are heard through the window, and the heart aches with yearning for the wide world; Lermontov is buttoning up his military tunic; Byron is putting a revolver in the drawer of his night table; in his verse, Wolker is marching hand-in-hand with the multitudes; Halas is hurling rhymed curses; Mayakovsky is stepping on the throat of his own song; a glorious battle is raging in the mirrors.

Caution, I beseech you! If a poet makes a false move and steps outside his mirrored domain he will perish, for he is a poor marksman. If he fires a gun, he will kill himself.

Alas, do you hear them coming? A horse is galloping up a winding Caucasian mountain road, with pistol-packing Lermontov in the saddle. More hoofbeats, the creaking of a carriage: it is Pushkin, pistol in hand, riding to a duel.

What is this we hear now? It is a trolley car, a slow, rickety Prague trolley. It is conveying Jaromil from one suburb to another; he is wearing a dark suit, a necktie, a winter coat and a hat.

2

What poet never dreamed of his death? What poet never painted it in his imagination? *Must I die? Then let it be by fire.* Do you think it was only an accidental play of imagination that induced Jaromil to think of a fiery death? Not at all. Death is a message; it talks; the act of dying has its own semantics and it is not unimportant how a man dies, and in which element.

Jan Masaryk ended his life in nineteen-forty-eight with a fall into the courtyard of a Prague palace, after having seen his fate shattered against the hard keel of destiny. Three years later, the poet Konstantin Biebl—hounded by people he had considered his comrades—jumped from a fifth floor to a pavement of the same city. Like Icarus, the element he was crushed by was earth, his death symbolizing the tragic conflict between space and mass, dream and awakening.

Jan Hus and Giordano Bruno could not have died by the sword nor by the hangman's rope, but only at the stake. Their lives were thus converted into signal lights, beacons, torches that shine far into the ages, for the body is temporal and thought is eternal and the shimmering essence of flame is an image of thought.

On the other hand, Ophelia is unthinkable in flames, and had to die a death by water, for the watery depths are closely related to human depths. Water is the element that kills those who have drowned in their own selves, in their love, in their emotions, in their madness, in their reflections and maelstroms. Folk songs tell of the drowning of girls whose lovers fail to return from the war; Harriet Shelley drowned herself; Paul Celan met his death in the Seine.

3

He got off the trolley car and walked toward the dark-haired girl's villa, once the witness to his cowardly flight.

He was thinking of Xavier:

In the beginning there was only Jaromil.

Then Jaromil created Xavier, his double, his second existence, dream-like and adventurous.

And now the moment had come to eliminate the conflict between dream and reality, between poetry and life, between action and thought. To end the split between Xavier and Jaromil both had to merge into a single being. The man of fantasy must become the man of action, the adventure of dreams the adventure of life.

He was approaching the villa and felt twinges of his old lack of self-confidence. His nervousness was increased by a sore throat (Maman had not wanted to let him go to the party that evening because of his cold).

When he reached the door he hesitated. He had to remind himself of all his recent achievements in order to pluck up his courage. He thought of the redheaded girl, of her interrogation, he thought of the police and of the train of events he had set in motion by dint of sheer strength and willpower...

"I am Xavier, I am Xavier," he kept telling himself, and rang the bell.

4

The people gathered inside were young actors, actresses, painters, and students of Prague art schools: the owner of the villa was in evidence, and he had made all the rooms in the house available for the party. The film-girl introduced Jaromil to several people, handed him a goblet, urged him to help himself to his favorite wine, and left him.

Jaromil was wearing a dark suit, white shirt, and tie, and he felt painfully stiff and stuffy; everybody else was dressed casually, and quite a few of the men wore sweaters and slacks. He fidgeted in his chair and finally took off his jacket, threw it over the back of a chair, loosened his tie, and opened the front of his shirt. That made him feel somewhat better.

The guests were all surpassing one another in trying to call attention to themselves. The young actors behaved as if they were on the stage, talking loudly and unnaturally; everybody tried to impress the others with wit or originality. Jaromil, too, after having drunk several glasses of wine, tried to raise his head above the surface of the party. Several times he succeeded in throwing out a phrase that seemed to him wittily sarcastic and that caught people's attention for a few seconds.

5

Noisy dance music was pulsing through the wall. A few days previously, the government had assigned the third room on the second floor to a new family of tenants. The pair of rooms left to Maman and Jaromil were like a small nest of quiet surrounded on all sides by noise.

Maman heard the music; she was alone and she thought about the filmmaker. The very first time she saw her, she sensed the danger inherent in an affair between the beautiful girl and Jaromil. She tried to make friends with her, to secure a strategic position in the impending battle for her son. And now she realized with shame that all this maneuvering was in vain. It didn't even occur to the girl to invite Maman to her party! They had simply shoved her aside.

The cinematographer once confided to Maman that she worked in the police film club only because she came from a wealthy family and needed political protection to enable her to continue with her studies. And Maman understood that the scheming girl characteristically turned everything to her own benefit. She had used Maman as a mere stepping-stone to get to her son.

6

The popularity contest continued: somebody played the piano, several couples were dancing, loud conversation and laughter resounded from small groups. Everybody tried to impress everyone else with witty bon mots; to leap, if only for an instant, above the heads of the crowd.

Martynov was there, too: tall, handsome, somewhat operatic with his elegant uniform and large dagger, surrounded by women. O, how that man infuriated Lermontov! God was unjust to give a beautiful face to a fool and short legs to Lermontov. But if the poet lacked long legs, he had a brilliantly sarcastic wit that lifted him high over people's heads!

He approached Martynov's admiring circle and awaited his opportunity. Then he made a rude joke and watched the consternation on people's faces.

7

At last (she had been gone for a long time) she appeared in the room. "Are you enjoying yourself?" she asked, looking at him with her large brown eyes.

It seemed to Jaromil that the magic moment was returning, the magic evening when he had sat in her room and they had had eyes only for each other.

"No, I am not," he said, and looked her straight in the face.

"Are you bored?"

"I am here because of you, and you always seem to

be somewhere else. Why did you invite me, if you can't spend any time with me?"

"But there are so many interesting people here!"

"All of them are a mere excuse for me to be near you. They are but steps for me to climb to attain you!"

He felt self-confident and pleased with his eloquence.

"There are an awful lot of steps here today!" she laughed.

"Perhaps in place of a stairway you could show me some secret passage that would let me reach you more quickly."

She continued to smile. "We will try," she said, and took him by the hand and led him out of the room. She guided him up the stairs to the door of her own room, and Jaromil's heart began to pound.

It pounded needlessly. The room was jammed with other men and women.

8

The lights had long been turned off in the adjoining rooms. It was the middle of the night. Maman was waiting for Jaromil and she thought of her defeat, but then she told herself that after all she had only lost one battle and would keep on fighting. Yes, she would continue to fight for him; nobody could take him from her, nobody could push her aside. She was determined to follow him forever. She was seated in an armchair, but it seemed to her that she was following Jaromil, that she was going out into the long, long night after him, and for him.

9

The girl's room was filled with talk and smoke, through which one of the guests (a man about thirty years old) had long been attentively watching Jaromil.

"I think I've heard about you," he said to him at last.

"About me?" retorted Jaromil, flattered.

The man asked whether Jaromil was the same fellow who had been visiting a certain painter ever since childhood.

Jaromil was glad that a mutual acquaintance thus tied him more firmly to this society and he avidly nodded his head.

The man said, "But you haven't been to see him for a long time."

"That's true."

"And why not?"

Jaromil didn't know what to say and shrugged his shoulders.

"I know why you didn't. You thought it would stand in the way of your career."

"My career?" Jaromil forced a laugh.

"You're publishing poems, you're appearing in public, our hostess made a film about you to further her political reputation. But your friend the painter is not allowed to show his work. I'm sure you know they've accused him of being an enemy of the people."

Jaromil was silent.

"Well, did you know that or not?"

"It seems to me I've heard something about it."

"His paintings are supposed to be decadent bourgeois swill."

Jaromil was silent.

"You have any idea what your friend the painter is doing now?"

Jaromil shrugged.

"They threw him out of his teaching job, and he's working as a construction laborer. Because he didn't want to recant his beliefs. He paints at night, in artificial light. But all the same, he's painting beautiful pictures. Not like your poems, which are disgusting shit."

10

Another rude joke, and still another, until the handsome Martynov was insulted at last. He warned Lermontov before the entire company.

What? Was the poet to give up his right to make any remark he pleased? Was he to ask forgiveness for using his wit? Never!

Lermontov's friends remonstrated with him. There was no point in risking a duel over a lot of nonsense. It was better to smooth things over. Your life, Lermontov, is worth more than some will-of-the-wisp called honor.

What? Something more precious than honor?

Yes, Lermontov. Your life, your work.

No, there is nothing beyond honor!

Honor is only the hunger of your vanity, Lermontov. Honor is only a fleeting looking-glass reflection, glimpsed by an insignificant audience that will vanish by morning!

But Lermontov *was* young and each second he lived was as immense as eternity. The handful of ladies and gentlemen watching him were the eyes of humanity. Either he would stride in front of them with the firm steps of a man, or he did not deserve to live!

11

He felt the mud of humiliation seeping down his face and he knew that with such a shame-smeared face he could not stay there another minute. In vain they tried to calm him, in vain they tried to soothe him.

"It's no use," he said, "there are conflicts which simply cannot be reconciled." He rose to his feet tense with excitement and turned to the stranger. "Personally, I am very sorry that the painter is an ordinary laborer and that he doesn't have the proper light. But objectively speaking it doesn't make a particle of difference whether he is painting by candlelight or whether he's not painting at all. The whole world of his pictures has been dead for years. Real life is elsewhere! Somewhere else entirely! And that's the reason why I no longer see the painter. No use arguing with him about problems that don't exist. I wish him the best. I have nothing against the dead. May the earth cover them gently. And I say the same to you." He pointed at the man. "May the earth cover you gently. You're dead and don't even know it."

The man, too, rose to his feet, and suggested, "It might be interesting to try a contest between a poet and a corpse."

Jaromil's blood rushed to his head. "By all means, let's try it," he said, and swung his fist at the man. His adversary, however, caught Jaromil's arm, turned him around with a sharp jerk, then grabbed him by the collar with one hand and by the seat of his pants with the other.

"Where shall I deposit comrade poet?" he asked.

The young guests who a moment earlier had still been trying to pacify the two antagonists could not resist laughing. The man marched through the room carrying Jaromil high in his outstretched arms, Jaromil thrashing in the air like some desperate, gentle fish. The man reached the balcony door, opened it, set Jaromil on the threshold and aimed a sharp kick.

12

A shot rang out, Lermontov clutched his chest, and Jaromil dropped to the icy concrete floor of the balcony.

O land of the Czechs! O land where the glory of a pistol shot turns into the joke of a kick in the pants!

But is it right to ridicule Jaromil for being a parody of Lermontov? Is it right to ridicule our artist for imitating André Breton, even to the point of wearing a leather coat and keeping an Alsatian dog? Was André Breton not himself an imitation of something noble he wished to emulate? Is not parody the eternal lot of man?

In any case, there is nothing to stop us from changing the situation with a few strokes of the pen:

13

A shot rings out, Jaromil clutches his chest, and Lermontov drops to the icy concrete of the balcony.

He is wearing the gala uniform of a Czarist officer and rises to his feet. He is catastrophically alone. He cannot turn to literary historiography for a soothing balm that would lend his thrashing grandiose significance. There is no pistol to put a merciful end to his unmanly humiliation. There is only derisive laughter coming through the window, the sound of which dishonors him forever.

He leans over the railing and looks down. Alas, the

balcony is not high enough for him to be sure of killing himself if he jumped. It is bitter cold, his ears are burning, his feet are cold, he shifts from one leg to the other and is at a complete loss about what to do. He is terrified by the thought that the door might suddenly open to reveal grinning faces. He is caught. He is trapped in a farce.

Lermontov is not afraid of death, but he is afraid of ridicule. He longs to jump from the balcony, but he dares not, for he knows that while suicide is tragic, unsuccessful suicide is ridiculous.

(Just a moment! What a peculiar sentence! After all, whether suicide succeeds or not it is still the same act, resulting from the same motives and requiring the same courage! Then what distinguishes the tragic from the ridiculous? The mere accident of success? What distinguishes pettiness from greatness, anyway? Tell us, Lermontov! Only the stage prop? Pistol or kick in the pants? Only the scenery trundled out on the stage by History?)

Enough. It is Jaromil who is out on the balcony, in a white shirt and loosened necktie, shivering with cold.

14

All revolutionaries love flames. Percy Shelley, too, dreamed of a fiery death. His fictional lovers expired together at the stake.

Shelley projected himself and his wife into this fantasy. Nevertheless, he died by drowning. His friends, as if wishing to correct this semantic error of fate, made a large funeral pyre on the shore and delivered his fish-gnawed body to the flames.

Is death trying to mock Jaromil, too, sending him frost rather than fire?

For Jaromil was yearning to die. The thought of suicide attracted him like a nightingale's song. He knew he had a bad cold, he knew he was courting serious illness, but he was determined not to return to the room. He could not bear further mortification. He knew that only the embrace of death could solace him, an embrace to which he would give himself body and soul and in which he would achieve greatness. He knew that only death could revenge him, and turn into murderers those who had mocked him.

It occurred to him to lie down outside the door and let the frozen concrete bake him from below, to speed up the work of death. He sat down. The concrete was so cold that after a few minutes his bottom was numb. He wanted to lie down but hadn't the courage to press his back against the icy floor, and so stood up again.

The cold completely enveloped him, it was inside his shoes, under his trousers and shorts, it stuck its hand under his shirt. His teeth were chattering, his throat hurt, he could not swallow, he kept sneezing. He felt an urge to urinate. With numb, clumsy fingers he opened his fly and urinated into the yard below. He saw how the hand holding his penis was trembling.

15

He stamped his painful feet on the concrete floor, but nothing in the world could induce him to open the door on his tormentors. And what about them? Why didn't they come out to get him? Were they so drunk? Or so cruel? How long had he been out in the cold, anyway?

The lights in the room suddenly dimmed.

Jaromil stepped to the window and saw that only a small lamp with a pink shade was left burning, next to the couch. He kept staring in, and at last made out two naked bodies locked in embrace.

Shaking, his teeth chattering, he continued to stare through the window. The half-drawn curtain prevented him from seeing clearly whether the woman's body covered by the man was that of the filmmaker. Everything seemed to indicate that it was she, and her hair was dark and long.

But who was the man? Jaromil knew who it was! He had already witnessed the whole scene before! Winter! Mountains! Snow-covered plain, and in the window a woman and Xavier! But today Jaromil and Xavier were supposed to merge into a single being! How could Xavier betray him this way? How on earth could Xavier make love to Jaromil's girl before his very eyes?

16

Now the room turned completely dark. Nothing could be seen or heard. His mind was empty, too: no anger, no sorrow, no humiliation. Only terrible cold.

He couldn't endure it any longer, he opened the glass door and went inside. He didn't want to see anything and looked neither left nor right. Quickly, he crossed the room.

A light was burning in the hall. He ran down the stairs and opened the door to the room where he had left his jacket. It was dark, but a faint glow from the hall lit up the outlines of several sleepers, who were breathing heavily. He continued to shiver as he groped over the chairs for his jacket. But he couldn't find it. He sneezed. One of the sleepers turned over, muttering a curse.

He went out into the hall, took his overcoat off the hanger, put it on over his shirt, and hurried from the house.

17

The procession has already started. Up front, the horse is pulling the cart with the coffin. Jiří Wolker's mother is walking behind the cart. A corner of a white cushion is sticking out from under the black lid. It sticks out like a reproach that the final resting place of her boy (he was twenty-four years old) was badly made up. She feels an enormous urge to rearrange the cushion under his head.

The coffin is standing in the center of the church, surrounded by wreaths. Grandma is still recovering from a stroke, and has to lift her eyelid with a finger. She is examining the coffin, she is examining the wreaths. One of them has a ribbon with the name Martynov. "Throw it out," she orders. Her old eye, under its paralyzed lid, watches faithfully over Lermontov's last journey. He was twenty-six years old.

18

Jaromil (not quite twenty years old) is lying in his room. He has a high fever. The doctor has diagnosed pneumonia.

The sounds of a noisy quarrel vibrate through the wall, but the two rooms occupied by the widow and her son constitute an island of quiet. Maman does not hear the din from the tenants next door. Her mind is fully occupied with medicines, hot tea, cold compresses. Once before, when he was small, she had watched over him continuously for many days to snatch him, red and hot, from the land of the dead. Now she was determined to watch over him again, passionately and faithfully.

Jaromil sleeps, raves in delirium, wakes and raves anew; flames of fever lick his body.

Flames? Is he to be transmuted into fire, after all?

19

A man is standing in front of Maman. He wants to talk to Jaromil. Maman refuses. The man mentions the name of the redheaded girl. "Your son provided information about her brother. Now they are both under arrest. I must talk to him."

They are confronting each other in Maman's room, but for Maman this room has now become but an extension of her son's. She is guarding it like an armed angel guarding the gate of paradise. The visitor's voice is harsh and makes her angry. She opens the door and points to Jaromil's bed. "Very well then, there he is, talk to him."

The man sees the flushed, delirious face. Maman says with quiet determination, "I don't know what you are talking about, but I can assure you that my son knew what he was doing. Everything he's ever done has been in the interests of the working class."

As she pronounces these words, so often used by Jaromil but heretofore alien to her, she feels a sense of enormous power. Those words link her to her son more closely than ever. They are now wedded in one soul, one mind. She and her son form a single universe composed of the same matter.

20

Xavier was holding a briefcase, which contained a Czech notebook and a biology textbook.

"Where are you going?"

Xavier smiled and pointed toward the window. The window was open. Outside, the sun was shining and from afar came the sounds of the city, promising adventure.

"You promised to take me with you..."

"That was long ago," said Xavier.

"You want to betray me?"

"Yes. I will betray you."

Jaromil felt breathless with anger. He felt an enormous hatred for Xavier. Until recently he still believed he and Xavier were but two aspects of a single being, but now he realized Xavier was an entirely different person and his archenemy!

Xavier caressed his face. "You are lovely, darling, you are so beautiful..."

"Why do you treat me like a woman? Have you gone mad?"

But Xavier would not be put off. "You are very beautiful, but I must betray you."

Xavier turned toward the open window.

"I am not a woman! Don't you understand? I am not a woman!" Jaromil kept shouting after him.

21

The fever has let up a bit and Jaromil is looking around the room. The walls are bare; the framed photograph of the man in the officer's uniform is gone.

"Where is Daddy?"

"Daddy is gone," Maman says gently.

"How come? Who took him off the wall?"

"I did, darling. I don't want him to look down on us. I don't want anyone to come between us. There is no point in lying to each other any longer. There is something you should know. Your father never wanted you to be born. He didn't want you to live. You understand? He urged me to make sure that you wouldn't be born."

Jaromil was exhausted from fever and had no strength to ask questions or to argue.

"My beautiful boy," said Maman, her voice trembling.

Jaromil realized that the woman speaking to him now has always loved him, never eluded him, never given him reason for fear or for jealousy.

"I am not beautiful, Mother. You're the one who is beautiful! You look so young!"

Maman heard her son's words and felt like weeping with happiness. "You really find me beautiful? But you look so much like me! You never wanted to hear that. But you do look like me and I'm glad." She stroked his hair, which was yellow and silky. She kissed it. "My darling! You have the hair of an angel!"

Jaromil felt enormously tired. He had no strength to search for any other woman. They were all so far away, and the road to them was so endlessly long. "Actually, I never really liked any woman," he said, "except you. You're the most beautiful of all."

Maman wept and kissed him. "You remember the spa where we had such a wonderful time together?"

"Yes, Mother. I always loved you best of all."

Maman saw the world through a large tear of happiness. Everything around her dissolved; everything leapt out of the shackles of form, everything danced and rejoiced.

"Really, my dearest?"

"Yes," said Jaromil. He was pressing Maman's hand in his hot palm and he was tired, enormously tired.

22

Already, the mound of earth is rising over Wolker's coffin and, already, Mrs. Wolker is on her way back from the cemetery. Already, the stone is pressing down on Rimbaud's coffin, but his mother, so the story goes, had them open the family crypt. Do you see her, that severe old lady in the black dress? She is examining the dark, damp vault, making sure the coffin is in the right place and properly closed. Yes, everything is in order. Arthur is there, he is not running away. Arthur will never run away again. Everything is in order.

23

Was it to be water after all? Not fire?

He opened his eyes and saw leaning over him a face with gently receding chin and fine yellow hair. That face was so close to him that it seemed he was bending over a still pond watching his own likeness.

No. No flames. He will die by water.

He watched his own face in the water. Suddenly, he

saw great fear pass over that face. That was the last thing he ever saw.

Completed in June, 1969.